Praise for Maya Banks' *Colters' Woman*

"Colters' Woman grabbed me from page one and refused to let go until I read the last word...When a book still affects me hours after reading it, I can't help but Joyfully Recommend it and I fully recommend Colters' Woman by Maya Banks!"

~ *Talia Ricci, Joyfully Reviewed*

"Maya Banks delivers what just might be the best book I have ever read. Colter's Woman has everything you could ever want in a book...I can't say enough good things to say about this book. The writing is first class, the characters are real, and the passion is stellar."

~ *Tara Renee Two Lips Reviews*

"Oh, how satisfying it is to read a good book. The sex in this one is just completely off the charts. The Colter men are three of the sexiest studs I've read about in a long time. It's hard enough for an author to create a convincing relationship between two lead characters and virtually impossible to establish meaningful relationships between three heroes and a single heroine but in COLTERS' WOMAN Ms. Banks does it with ease."

~ *Ariel Summer, Road to Romance*

Colters' Woman

Maya Banks

A Samhain Publishing, Ltd. publication.

Samhain Publishing, Ltd.
2932 Ross Clark Circle, #384
Dothan, AL 36301
www.samhainpublishing.com

Editing by Jessica Bimberg
Cover by Anne Cain

First Samhain Publishing, Ltd. electronic publication: October 2006
First Samhain Publishing, Ltd. print publication: January 2007

Dedication

To Amy—for not thinking I'd completely lost my marbles. Well, you probably think, but at least you didn't SAY ;)

To TJ—for being thrilled for me even when I took my sweet time in being thrilled for myself.

To Jess—for loving this book as much as I do and for being patient with all my quirks.

Chapter One

Adam Colter drew his coat tighter around him and tugged his Stetson lower as he stepped out into the snow. He started down the winding driveway to collect the mail, his face numb from the biting wind.

Winter had set in, and already he was restless. The lodge was quiet, housing just him and his two brothers until next hunting season when clients filled the bunkhouses. For ten years, he had lived for the fall when he could guide hunters into the mountains. Now he felt edgy. Unsatisfied.

He yanked open the mailbox and reached inside for the pile of envelopes. He turned back to the house, thumbing through the junk mail when a flash of color caught his eyes. He blinked, bringing the object into focus. There, huddled in the ditch, half covered with snow, was a person.

Dropping the mail, he rushed over to the still form and knelt in the snow. Afraid of what he would find, he grasped a small shoulder and flipped the person over. To his shock, it was a woman. A beautiful woman.

He felt for a pulse, holding his breath until he felt the faint tremor in her neck. He brushed snow from her face and smoothed her blonde hair from her forehead. How had she gotten here?

Swinging her slight form into his arms, he stood up and strode rapidly back up the drive. He stared worriedly into her pale face and felt his groin tighten. A sharp tingle snaked up his spine, and he was besieged by unfamiliar emotions. Anger, possessiveness, concern, and pure unadulterated lust.

His cock swelled in his jeans, and his grip around her tightened. He was assailed by the nagging thought that she could be the one. He'd never reacted this strongly to a woman, and certainly not to one he knew nothing about, but he also knew no matter *his* reaction, his brothers might not be in agreement.

At any rate, he couldn't leave her to freeze to death. He couldn't concern himself with what his brothers thought until he made sure she didn't die on him.

As he shouldered his way inside, Ethan looked up from the couch where he was reading. He dropped the book when he saw the woman in Adam's arms.

"What the hell's going on?" he demanded, standing up.

"I found her out in the ditch," Adam murmured, examining his brother closely for his reaction.

Ethan closed the distance between them and looked down at the fragile looking woman. "Is she alive?"

"What's going on?" Ryan asked as he entered the living room. His expression was guarded, a look that had become second nature since his discharge from the military. For the first time in a long while, Adam felt a surge of hope. He'd give anything to be able to draw Ryan out from the private hell he endured. If she was the one…

Adam turned his attention back to the woman in his arms. "I need to get her warmed up. Go draw a hot bath while I get her out of her wet clothes," he directed Ryan.

Ethan raised a brow. "You going to strip her in here?"

Adam shrugged. "I doubt modesty is an issue when you're this close to freezing to death."

Ethan's eyes darkened, and he moved closer to the woman. He studied her then reached out his hand to touch her cheek. "She's beautiful," he said huskily.

When he looked back up at Adam, his eyes shone with a multitude of emotions. Desire, tenderness and possessiveness. Adam felt a surge of triumph. Ethan felt it too.

"Am I missing something here?" Ryan asked as he returned to the living room.

"Is the water drawn?" Adam asked.

Ryan nodded and Adam strode past him. "Ethan will explain," he said briskly.

Adam walked into his bedroom and gently laid her on his bed. She didn't even have a coat on. He frowned as he began to peel her wet sweater off. She was soaked through.

As he pulled the sweater over her head, he sucked in his breath. The skimpy bra she wore didn't do much to cover her breasts. The second thing he noticed was a large bruise that marred her porcelain skin. It covered an area the size of his hand. And he had large hands.

Had she been in some kind of accident? Is that why she was lying in the ditch?

He set to work pulling the damp jeans from her legs. As he rolled the material down her legs, his eyes were drawn to the dark curls clearly outlined against her underwear. So, she wasn't a natural blonde.

Suffering only a tiny moment of guilt, he peeled the scrap of silk down her legs, then unhooked her bra, leaving her completely naked beneath his gaze. He didn't think it possible that he could get any harder.

9

Every nerve ending in his body was on full alert. All it would take was one touch and he'd explode.

He cursed vehemently and worked to keep his raging hormones in balance. She was unconscious and injured, and all he could think about was plunging his cock so deep within her that he'd become a permanent part of her.

With shaking hands, he examined her limbs for any sign of a break. Her skin was cold, but she showed no sign of frostbite. The bath shouldn't do her any harm.

With great care, he picked her naked body up and walked out of the bedroom and into the huge bathroom he shared with his brothers. It was the size of a bedroom, with two showers and a huge Jacuzzi tub. The counter that lined one side of the wall had four sinks. A testament to their knowledge that one day one woman would share their lives.

The tub was full, and he leaned over to ease her into the warm water. She let out a small moan but didn't open her eyes. He held her so she wouldn't slip down further.

He turned when he heard the door open. Ryan stood there, his eyes hooded.

"Ethan says she's the one."

Adam nodded, not knowing what else to say. He knew Ryan would have to make up his own mind.

Ryan's gaze swept over the woman but he didn't move forward. "I'll wait until you're through. I wouldn't want her to awaken with both of us here. It might scare her."

"I won't be long," Adam said, trying to interpret the shadows in Ryan's eyes. "Do me a favor and put her clothes in the dryer."

Ryan shrugged and backed from the bathroom, closing the door quietly behind him.

Adam returned his attention to his charge just in time to see her eyes flutter open. Soft brown eyes stared at him in shock and confusion. Then fear.

The first thing Holly became aware of was delicious warmth. After being cold for so long, she was certain she'd died and gone to heaven. Or maybe it was hell judging by the temperature.

Then she opened her eyes and quickly decided it had to be heaven because the devil couldn't possibly look as good as the man bending over her.

After staring at him for a moment, she realized she was naked. In a tub. With a gorgeous stranger looking at her, completely unabashed by her nudity. Maybe instead of drooling she ought to be afraid.

"I'm not going to hurt you," the man said in a soothing tone as he backed a few inches away from the tub. "I found you in the snow."

She crossed her arms over her chest and drew up her knees, trying to cover as much of her body as possible. "Where am I?" she asked, hating how shaky her voice sounded.

"Three Brothers Hunting Lodge," he replied. "Are you hurting anywhere?"

She clutched her chest tighter and shook her head. "Where are my clothes?"

"In the dryer. I'll give you a shirt to put on until they finish."

Despite the warmth of the water, chill bumps raced over her body, her nipples tightening against her arms. The man was positively sinful. His dark hair was cut short, and he had shoulders that would barely fit through a doorway. He was built bigger than a linebacker.

He stood, giving her a good look at his long legs encased in tight jeans. She nearly groaned aloud when she saw scuffed cowboy boots sticking out from under his pant legs. She'd always been a sucker for a man in cowboy boots.

She gasped as he bent over and plucked her from the water. Before she could protest, he wrapped a huge towel around her and strode from the bathroom. She stifled her reprimand as he deposited her on a king-size bed. She gathered the ends of the towel and held them tightly around her.

He turned his back to her momentarily and disappeared into the closet. Seconds later, he returned with a flannel shirt and a pair of sweats.

"They're much too big for you, but they'll do until your clothes are dry."

He held them out to her, his gaze caressing her face. She should be afraid. She was in a strange man's house. Naked as the day she was born. And yet she didn't feel threatened by him.

She almost laughed at the absurdity. Most men terrified her. And with good reason. So why wasn't she screaming the house down? Why was she laying there staring at him like she'd love nothing more than to strip him down to those cowboy boots? She should be making a mad dash out the door.

Instead, she curled her fingers around the shirt he offered, flushing madly when his hand touched hers briefly. Fire lit his eyes and burned a trail down her flesh as his gaze raked up and down her body.

"I'll leave you to dress," he said. "When you're done, come on out to the living room and warm up by the fire."

"T-thank you," she stammered.

As soon as he left the room, she scrambled up, shedding the towel and yanking on the shirt. It hung to her knees, the sleeves dwarfing her arms. She rolled up each one so her hands were free.

She sat on the edge of the bed and pulled on the sweats. When she stood, they fell to her ankles. Hiking them back up, she pulled at the drawstring, trying to make the monstrous pants stay up. They promptly fell back down, and she growled in irritation.

Well, he'd seen her in a lot less. At least the shirt covered most of her. Hopefully her clothing would be dry soon.

She snuck a glance in the mirror over the dresser and winced at her appearance. Her hair was a mess, and the dye job was awful. It certainly hadn't achieved the desired effect of altering her appearance.

Straightening her shirt, she pulled it as far down her legs as she could and hesitantly walked out of the bedroom door. She moved down the hallway, looking left and right. At the end, she stopped and stared in embarrassment into the living room.

Three men, not just one, stared at back at her. Three gorgeous, hulking men. And here she stood in nothing more than a shirt. She started to retreat, but the man who had bathed her crossed the room and caught her elbow.

"Don't be afraid. I'm Adam, by the way." He led her further into the living room despite her reluctance. "These two are my brothers, Ryan and Ethan."

She eyed them nervously and hung back, hoping Adam's body would shield her from view. "You didn't say anything about brothers."

"I told you the name of the ranch," he said in amusement.

He reached behind him and squeezed her hand in his. "Don't worry, baby. No one's going to hurt you."

She shivered. Not from fear, but from the sex appeal in his voice. How could a complete stranger make her feel so safe? She licked her lips. "I'm Holly," she said in just above a whisper.

One of the two brothers rose from the couch and walked over to her, reaching behind Adam and gently pulling her forward. "Come over by the fire and get warm." His husky voice filtered over her like fine chocolate.

Oh Lord, she must be dreaming. "Which one are you?" she asked, hesitating for a moment.

"I'm Ethan." He smiled broadly at her. He tugged slightly on her hand, and she allowed him to lead her closer to the fire.

Ethan was as large as Adam. The only difference between them was their eyes. Both had dark hair. Almost black. But Adam had green eyes and Ethan's were a warm brown, while Ryan sported dark blue eyes.

Ryan was slightly smaller in build than his brothers and his hair was a lighter brown, but where his brothers' hair was short, Ryan's hung below his ears, just brushing the tops of his shoulders. He had a wild, haunted look, the kind of man a woman instinctively wanted to try to tame. He looked to be the youngest, but Holly wasn't certain. They were all pretty close in age, though Adam had to be the oldest.

Ethan coaxed her into an armchair next to the fire, and she drew her legs underneath her. She stretched her hands to the fire, letting the warmth seep into her body.

She was nervous as a cat in a dog kennel. All of them were staring at her. She could feel them. Had they all seen her naked? Was that why they were looking at her with such intensity?

Adam walked over to stand by the fire. "What happened to you, Holly? Why were you lying in the ditch? You weren't even dressed for the weather."

She tensed, unsure of how to answer. Her mind raced to come up with a plausible excuse. "My car broke down further down the mountain. I got out to find help. I must have fallen. I don't really remember."

Most of it was the truth. Actually, all of it was, but she wasn't going to go into any more detail than she had to.

"Are you sure you're all right?" Ryan spoke up for the first time. He looked closely at her as if trying to peel her secrets right out of her head. He was quieter than the other two and more serious looking by far.

"I'm fine. Really." She looked up at Adam. "Will my clothes be dry soon? I should be going."

Ryan surged to his feet. Ethan tensed, and Adam's expression darkened.

"I don't think you should be going anywhere in this weather," Adam said firmly.

Ethan nodded. "There's no reason you can't stay here until you're feeling better. Ryan and I will go look for your car and tow it here if we need to."

Uncertainty made her hesitate. Logically, she should get the hell out while the getting was good, but she felt safe here, and she was tired of running.

She looked down at her hands and tried to control the shaking. She was so damn tired, and she couldn't remember the last time she'd eaten.

Adam knelt beside the chair and cupped her chin in his large hand. "You don't have to go anywhere, baby. You can stay right here. We'll take care of you."

If she'd thought she couldn't become more aroused, she'd been dead wrong. Though he voiced the offer in gentle tones, she didn't miss the command. He wanted her to stay.

"I...I don't know." She closed her eyes, a wave of dizziness swamping her. She struggled to open them again, but the room swirled around her. Then it went dark.

Chapter Two

With a muffled curse, Adam caught Holly's head as it fell forward. He quickly pulled her from the chair and cradled her in his arms. She was clearly exhausted and probably hungry to boot if her thinness was any indication.

"I'll put her in my room," he said as he walked toward the hall.

"Ryan and I'll go look for her car," Ethan said.

Adam placed her on the bed and pulled back the covers. She moaned softly, an expression of pain crossing her face, but she didn't open her eyes.

A pulse beat in his temple and he gritted his teeth. She was running from something. Or someone. She was skittish as a newborn colt, and she had so many secrets in her eyes it was hard to tell the color at times.

The bruise on her ribs bothered him. It could be from a fall, but he doubted it. It didn't look recent. He fingered a strand of her hair, noticing the unevenness of the color. He'd bet money she was a brunette. The same color as the curls between her legs.

With tenderness he hadn't displayed in a long time, he tucked the covers around her neck and walked quietly out. He needed a cold shower to calm his raging hard-on, but he opted to walk out into the cold and wait for Ethan and Ryan to return.

A half hour later, they drove up in the Land Rover. Adam walked to meet them. "What did you find?"

"Nothing," Ethan replied.

Adam raised a brow. So the angel had lied. Was she not thinking clearly or had she honestly not thought they would find out?

"How is she?" Ryan asked.

"Sleeping," Adam replied. "She needs to eat."

Ethan looked troubled. A feeling Adam could relate to. That they had found their woman was nothing short of amazing. But it appeared she came with trouble.

Ryan shifted uncomfortably. "I never thought we'd find her. And now that we have, all I can think about is what if she doesn't want to stay? I felt it too. I know she's the one. Pop always said we'd know, but I thought it was bullshit until now."

"I know," Ethan said quietly. "I felt it too."

"She's hiding something," Adam said. "She has a bruise the size of my fist on her ribcage, and I don't like to imagine how it got there. And she's not a natural blonde. She did a poor job dying it. A sign she was probably in a hurry."

"You think someone's after her?" Ethan demanded, his face darkening.

Ryan clenched his fists. "Who could want to hurt such a little thing?"

"I don't know, but one thing's for damn certain. We can't let her leave no matter what we have to do," Adam said grimly.

"Who's going to approach her first?" Ryan asked.

Adam paused. "I will," he finally said. "It's the way it's done. It's my responsibility. You two will help by making her feel as comfortable as possible. We're going to have to ease into this or I'm afraid she might bolt."

"Go easy with her, Adam," Ethan warned.

Adam glared at him. "What's that supposed to mean?"

Ethan didn't back down. "You know exactly what I mean. You dominate. It's your nature. You're going to have to curb that with her. I don't think she's going to offer her trust on a silver platter."

Though Ethan's words irritated him, Adam knew he was right. He was the authority figure in his personal and professional life, and he was used to getting his way. In his mind, Holly was theirs whether she accepted it right now or not.

"I'll keep that in mind," he said dryly. "Now if we're done here, I'm going to go check on her. Why don't you and Ryan see about supper?"

Adam slipped back inside the bedroom to see Holly still sleeping soundly. After kicking off his boots, he pulled the covers back and gingerly settled down beside her. To his surprise, she let out a sigh of satisfaction and snuggled against him.

Her breasts rubbed erotically against his chest, and his cock swelled against her thighs. As she moved against him, her shirt rode up over her hips, exposing her luscious ass. Unable to help it, he smoothed his hand over her naked hip, pulling the shirt higher to her waist.

Her dark curls beckoned him, and he slipped his fingers to the soft folds of her pussy. She moaned as he dipped one finger to her clit and began a slow circular motion. She was hot and wet, and he was ready to burst from just touching her.

Using his fingers, he separated her pussy lips further and slipped his thumb down over her button. His middle finger drifted downward, teasing her entrance as his thumb continued stroking her.

Her breathing picked up, and she moved restlessly against him. He plunged his finger into her, closing his eyes and imagining it was his dick. She was tight. So damn tight.

He bent his head and nuzzled his lips inside the collar of her shirt until he found one taut nipple. When he latched onto it, she cried out. He worked his thumb faster as he sucked at her breast. Then she tightened beneath him and clamped her legs shut against his hand as she wailed her release.

He captured her cry in his mouth as he fastened his lips over hers. Slowly, he pulled his hand from her quivering pussy. He could smell her musky scent on his hand, and he ached to taste her. Ached to bury his head between her legs and love her like she'd never been loved.

Her eyes fluttered open, drowsy, drugged looking, her lips swollen from his kisses.

"Tell me I'm not dreaming," she whispered.

"You're not dreaming."

Her eyes widened, and she let out a startled shriek. She scooted away from him yanking the covers over her body. "What the hell's going on?" she demanded, her voice still husky with passion.

He watched the confusion register in her eyes as she fought against her enjoyment of what happened and her natural instinct to fight it.

"I made you come," he said simply.

"I—you..." She trailed off, her mouth opening and closing in rapid succession.

He put his hand behind her neck and pulled her to him. "In case you're wondering," he said as he kissed her long and hard, "I plan to do it again. Soon."

She jerked away and gaped at him. "But—"

"You want me," he said matter-of-factly. "And I want you more than I've ever wanted another woman. I'm going to take care of you."

Holly stared at him in shock. Her heart was beating double time. Not only had she experienced the most mind-blowing orgasm of her life—okay, the only orgasm of her life, and if this was normal, she had no idea how a woman survived it—but his declaration cut straight to her heart.

She couldn't believe him. It was her naiveté that had gotten her in this situation to begin with. Her yearning to be loved and cherished. The mere thought of how stupid she'd been made her want to puke.

His expression softened. "Who hurt you, baby? Who put that fear in your eyes?"

She swallowed nervously. This guy was too perceptive by far. How on earth could she be lying almost naked next to a guy she hadn't known for more than a day? She closed her eyes. This wasn't happening. It was all a dream. A wonderful dream, mind you, but a dream all the same. Any minute now, she'd wake up and be back in the horror that was her life.

"Let me go get your clothes for you," Adam said, throwing his legs over the side of the bed. "You need to eat something."

A few seconds later, he returned with her jeans and sweater. He dangled her underwear on the end of his finger and she hastily snatched them away from him.

"I'll be in the kitchen. Come on out when you're done."

When he'd left, she scrambled out of bed and quickly pulled on her underwear. Her pussy still throbbed from the explosive orgasm. Her fingers lingered near her crotch, and she slipped her hand underneath the silk of her panties.

She flinched when her finger made contact with her swollen clit. God, the man was lethal. Reluctantly, she pulled her hand away and reached for her jeans.

When she was dressed, she walked to the door and stood hesitantly with her hand on the knob. How could she face him after what happened? Her cheeks burned with embarrassment. He was going to think she was a complete slut.

Drawing in a deep breath, she opened the door and slipped down the hall toward the kitchen. The smells emanating from the stove made her mouth water. It had been too long since her last good meal.

The three brothers looked up as she slid onto a barstool. She looked down self-consciously, hoping Adam hadn't seen fit to fill his brothers in on what happened.

Ryan moved closer and rubbed a hand over her shoulder. "Are you okay?"

She shivered, horrified by her reaction to him. Surely she was still on edge from the orgasm she'd experienced just minutes ago. She was losing her mind. Slut didn't even begin to describe her. She was lusting after three men.

"I'm fine," she mumbled, flinching away from his touch.

Ethan put a plate in front of her. "I'll dish it up in just a sec. You hungry?"

Her stomach growled in response. "Starving," she admitted.

"How long's it been since you ate?" Adam asked, his expression pensive.

"Don't remember," she said vaguely.

He exchanged glances with his two brothers, and she hoped she hadn't raised their suspicions even more. She needed to disappear as quickly as possible before anyone figured out where she was. Or who she was.

A few minutes later, Ethan heaped bacon, eggs and a slab of ham on her plate. Her hands shook slightly as she cut into the food with her fork.

Adam stood back, his arms crossed over his chest. He watched while she shoveled food into her mouth as quickly as she could. "Slow down, baby. You're going to make yourself sick."

She flushed and set her fork down on the plate. Ethan plunked down a glass of orange juice next to her, and she smiled slightly at him before drinking down half the contents.

A loud knock sounded on the door, and Adam frowned. "Who the hell could that be?" He swiveled around as Ryan and Ethan both started forward.

"Hold up," he ordered. "We don't know who's out there."

They all turned around to where Holly was sitting, only she was gone. Adam swore. She'd run scared the minute she heard the knock.

"I'll go find her," Ethan said, his tone suggesting he'd take care of her and for Adam and Ryan to take care of the outside threat.

To their surprise, the door opened and Lacey McMillan stuck her head in. "You in there?" she called out. She stopped when her gaze rested on Ryan and Adam.

Adam relaxed. Lacey was the county sheriff, and she paid a call from time to time to see how things were in the high country. Tall, lanky and redheaded. All the things Holly wasn't. At one time, Adam had thought Lacey might be the one, but his brothers hadn't shared his attraction.

23

She removed her Stetson as she walked further into the cabin. She threw Adam a saucy grin. "Aren't you glad to see me?"

Ryan scowled and sat back down at the bar.

"What brings you out?" Adam asked, folding his arms and affecting what he knew to be an intimidating stance. Normally he wouldn't mind shooting the shit with Lacey, even doing a little light flirting, but that was in the past. Now he just wanted her to be gone as soon as possible.

Lacey slid onto a barstool beside Ryan, hitching her long legs up to balance on the lower rung of the stool.

"Where's the third stooge?" she asked, looking around for Ethan.

"Around," Adam said.

She arched a brow but didn't comment further on his being so close-mouthed.

"I'm up here to find out if y'all have seen a young woman. Early twenties. Brunette. Short, maybe five two. We're dealing with a possible abduction, though she may have escaped. We found an abandoned car at the base of the mountain, and we're checking out the area. Maybe you saw something?"

Adam shook his head then fixed his gaze on Ryan. "You and Ethan see anything when you were out?"

"Nope."

He turned his attention back to Lacey. "You think she's still in the area?"

Lacey shrugged. "Dunno. Could be, though if she's on her own, I don't imagine she'll last long in the backcountry. City girl from what I gathered. Got a bulletin from the Denver PD and the Feds wanting our department to be on the lookout. Seemed to think she might be headed this way."

"Do you need trackers?" Adam asked, knowing if he didn't offer, it would seem odd. He and his brothers had tracked missing persons before for the sheriff's department. Last summer, they had found a little girl who had wandered off from her parents' campsite.

Lacey shook her head. "Nah. Like I said, I'm just checking out the possibility anyone saw something. We don't even know who the car belongs to. Teddy's running the plates as we speak. Could be she never came this way."

Adam itched to ask more questions. Who did Holly belong to and who supposedly kidnapped her? But he knew it would arouse Lacey's suspicions, because if nothing else, the Colter brothers kept to themselves and didn't borrow trouble from anyone.

"Well, let us know if we can help," he said dismissively.

Lacey chuckled then rose from the barstool. "There was a time when you were more welcoming," she said softly as she brushed by him, letting her full breasts rasp across his folded arms.

He stepped back, only anxious for her to be gone so he could question Holly.

"I guess I'll see you around," Lacey said, a resigned expression on her face. She replaced her hat then walked to the door. "Let me know if you see anything, okay?"

"Will do," Adam said.

When she shut the door, Adam let out his breath.

Ryan glanced up, his expression brooding.

"She was looking for Holly," Adam said, a frown twisting his brows.

He turned and strode for the bedroom, Ryan following close behind. An invisible hand squeezed his chest when he saw

Holly huddled on the bed, her knees hugged to her chest. Ethan sat beside her, rubbing a soothing hand up and down her back, but she barely registered his presence.

Adam cursed under his breath and knelt down on the floor in front of the bed. He reached a hand for hers and pried it away from her legs.

"Baby, listen to me. You're safe here. That was just our sheriff."

Holly's eyes widened in alarm, and she shivered in fear.

"No police," she croaked.

"No police," he agreed.

"Promise me," she said, her voice coming out in a pathetic squeak.

"You can trust us," Ethan said quietly. "We won't allow anyone to hurt you."

She relaxed a tiny bit, leaning more into Ethan's caress.

Adam still held her hand in his, and he brushed his fingers over her upturned palm, trying to infuse his calm into her. "Listen to me, baby. We need to ask you some questions."

She let out a panicked moan. "No, no questions. Please, let me go. I need to leave."

Ethan's hand stilled on her back, and beside Adam, Ryan stiffened. Adam knew he had to handle this just right. He couldn't chance her running. They couldn't keep her safe if she ran.

He exchanged looks with his brothers. They were all united in this cause. They were not going to let her go. And they sure as hell weren't going to let anyone hurt her.

He stood then sat down on the bed beside her. "Honey, you can trust us. We aren't going to hurt you. We aren't going to let anyone else hurt you. But we need to know what's going on. What happened to you."

Panic flared in her eyes. Fear spread out like a forest fire over her face. "Y-y-you don't understand," she stammered out. "No one can help. No one can stop h-h-him." She said *him* like she spoke of the devil himself.

"Who, baby? Who are you talking about?" Adam whispered.

She shook her head, her agitation increasing with each second. On the other side of her, Ethan shook his head, a warning to Adam that he was pushing too far. She looked about ready to shatter.

"Why don't you get some rest?" Adam said, though he wanted very badly to have all the answers to his questions.

Ethan gently pulled her to him then lifted her up off the comforter. He stood beside the bed while Adam and Ryan turned back the covers. Then Ethan laid her down and pulled the sheets over her. "We'll be right outside if you need us," Ethan said, bending down to kiss her forehead.

Her eyes were closed before they even left the room.

The brothers assembled in the kitchen, all of them wearing grim expressions.

"What did Lacey want?" Ethan asked.

Adam quickly filled Ethan in on all Lacey had to say.

"So someone kidnapped her?" Ethan asked incredulously. "That doesn't make any sense. Wouldn't she be more than willing to spill the story and go to the police?"

"I agree it makes no sense," Adam replied. "Which is why we aren't going to tell anyone about Holly. At least not until we have the full story from her. She's scared to death of someone. A man. The son of a bitch has hurt her."

"She's attracted to us," Ethan said. "All three of us. It confuses her, but her reaction to us is there."

Adam nodded, satisfaction filling every inch of his body. After so long of waiting, they finally had the woman they would spend the rest of their lives with.

Chapter Three

She dreamed of them. They came to her on the heels of a nightmare. A sweet balm to her battered senses. They replaced images of the devil and hell. Their hands soothed away the hurt. Adam, Ethan and Ryan, their touch gentle, yet demanding, their lips worshipping her body.

Holly awoke dripping with sweat, need and a healthy dose of embarrassment. Maybe she wasn't any better than a whore. Maybe Mason was right.

She shivered as a chill settled over her damp skin. She looked at the window to see darkness beyond. How long had she slept? Her gaze settled on the bedside clock. Four-thirty. In the morning? It must be.

Chances were the brothers weren't even awake. It would be a perfect opportunity for her to steal away. She endangered them by staying here. Mason would find her, and he would kill anyone in his way. And the idea of her three saviors being harmed because of her hurt in a way she couldn't explain.

She slid her legs from the covers, careful not to make a sound when her feet hit the floor. Her shoes, a simple pair of sneakers, lay by the door, her socks stuffed inside.

She quickly pulled on her socks then laced up her shoes. She had no coat to wear over her thin sweater so she retrieved the flannel shirt she had worn yesterday. It would have to do.

With extreme care, she opened the bedroom door and peered out into the hallway. The other bedroom doors were slightly ajar, much to her chagrin. She'd have to sneak past them the best she could.

She tiptoed down the hall and breathed a sigh of relief when she reached the living room. That is until she saw Adam lying on the couch. He must have slept there last night since she'd taken over his room.

A low fire burned in the fireplace, and she longed to go stand in front of it, anything to infuse as much warmth as she could before she stepped into the cold.

Taking in a deep breath, she took small measured steps toward the door. If she could just reach the door. She glanced over at Adam who didn't stir. She reached out a hand for the door and held her breath as she turned the handle.

She opened it a crack and slipped out before a rush of cold air could blow in. She eased the door shut behind her and breathed a sigh of relief. She'd made it.

The icy cold air made quick work of her inadequate clothing and infused an uncomfortable chill into her body. The Land Rover stood parked in the drive, and for a moment she contemplated taking it, but she wouldn't steal from the men who had been nothing but kind to her.

She'd walk until she found another means of transportation.

"Going somewhere, doll?"

She whirled in the direction of the voice to see Ethan and Ryan standing a few feet away, their arms loaded with firewood.

Her jaw worked up and down, and she struggled to say something, to respond. But nothing would come out. So she did the only thing she could think of. She ran.

Behind her, a set of curses rang out as she sped as quickly as she could across the snow. She had no idea where she was going. She only knew she had to get away.

She hadn't gotten far when arms plucked her off her feet. She met with a hard chest and found herself staring up into Ethan's face.

"Damn it, don't look at me like that," he ground out. "I'm not going to hurt you. I'd kill anyone who hurt you."

She looked at him in complete bewilderment at the possessiveness in his tone. "Let me go," she begged. "I can't stay here."

"And where would you go?" Ryan demanded beside them. "You wouldn't survive an hour out here."

She knew he had a point, but she couldn't stay *here*. She didn't understand the attraction she felt for the brothers, why she shivered if one of them so much as looked at her. One she could understand, but all three of them? What kind of freak did that make her?

"Give me your coat," Ethan said to Ryan. "She's freezing already."

A moment later, she was bathed in warmth as Ryan's body heat bled into her. His coat smelled like him, felt like him, as if he held her instead of Ethan.

"I can't stay here," she whispered, dangerously close to tears.

Ethan stared down at her for a long moment. Then to her complete surprise, he bent his lips to hers and caught her in a long, intense kiss.

He caught her gasp of shock and swallowed it up as his tongue danced over hers. She forgot all resistance as she melted like hot butter into his chest.

Jesus, Mary and Joseph. He was every bit as lethal as Adam. And she shouldn't be reacting this way to him. Not after what she had done with Adam.

Hot tears flooded her eyes, and she let out a moan of distress.

"You're scaring her, Ethan," Ryan growled beside them.

"I'm a whore," she whispered. "Just like he said."

Ethan went rigid, his arms like bands of steel around her body. "Who called you a whore?" he asked, his voice deadly quiet.

She struggled in his arms until he was forced to put her down, but he still kept a firm grip around her wrist.

"Does it matter? He was obviously right," she said in a tortured voice. "All any of you have to do is look at me and I go up in flames. What kind of woman am I?" she demanded.

"Our woman," Ryan answered. "That's the kind it makes you."

Her mouth rounded in shock at his announcement. She looked back and forth between the two men, looking for an avenue of escape.

"Come on, doll," Ethan said gently. "Let's get you back to the house. You're freezing. Adam's not going to be happy about you running."

She tensed and Ryan spit out another curse. "Quit scaring her, Ethan."

"We'd never hurt you, Holly. You're going to find out very quickly, that we'd do anything to save you hurt," Ethan said, as he bent to swing her back into his arms.

She lay still in his arms as he strode back to the house. Her mind fought to comprehend the bizarre conversation she'd just had with the brothers.

Ryan opened the door, and Ethan walked into the house with Holly still in his arms. Adam stood a few feet away, his arms crossed over his chest, his expression formidable.

Despite Ethan's assurances, she began to tremble in his arms. She turned her face into his chest, trying to hide from Adam's scrutiny. His power terrified her. Mason was nothing next to this man, and yet he'd done so much to hurt her. Adam could do much more.

Ethan's arms tightened around her. "Don't be scared, doll," he whispered in her ear. He walked her over to the fire and set her down. She quickly arranged herself behind him so he stood as a barrier between her and Adam.

To her surprise, Adam laughed. "So is this going to be the way it is? You hide behind Ethan every time you do something to piss me off?"

She frowned and stuck her head out from behind Ethan. Adam was smiling, and Ryan looked at her with quiet intensity. For a moment, she saw something in Ryan's eyes she recognized, could relate to. Torment.

"I-I don't understand," she began lamely. "I don't understand any of this."

Adam looked at her standing behind Ethan, clutching fiercely at his shirt. She looked lost and forlorn and very afraid. He was glad she at least trusted Ethan, even if she had no idea she did. She was clearly assigning Ethan the role of protector. From him.

Ethan warned him with his eyes not to push. Hell, he could figure that much out without Ethan's warnings. Holly looked like a frightened fawn. Ready to bolt with the least provocation.

He sighed and sat down on the couch. "Come here, baby."

She clutched at Ethan's hand and chewed nervously at her lip.

What had made her so afraid? Who had hurt her so badly that she couldn't trust him or his brothers?

Ethan's arm went around her, squeezing her reassuringly even as he guided her forward. Ethan cupped her chin and forced her to look up at him. "No one will hurt you, doll. I swear it. No one will *ever* hurt you again."

She relaxed a bit at his vow then turned her nervous gaze at Adam. "Are you angry?" she asked softly.

He held out a hand to her and felt an insane sense of victory when she trustingly curled her hand into his. He pulled her into his arms and smoothed her hair from her eyes. "I'm not angry, baby. Not at you. Never at you. I'm angry at the son of a bitch who hurt you, who put that fear I see into your eyes."

He tugged her down further into his arms then kissed her, gently, lightly, feather soft across her mouth. For a moment, she melted into his arms, and she fit so damn perfect, like she'd always belonged there. Then she tensed and yanked away from him, torment and self-loathing burning brightly in her eyes.

With an inarticulate cry, she ran past him and down the hall to the bedroom.

Adam started after her, surprised by her reaction. Ethan's hand on his arm stopped him.

"You're going to have to explain," Ethan said. "Now."

"What the hell are you talking about?"

Ethan sighed and dragged a hand through his hair. "She thinks she's a whore."

"*What?*"

"Come on, Adam, you know she has to be confused. She's attracted to the three of us. Some bastard has told her she's a whore and now she believes him. She doesn't *understand* herself or us. You have to explain it to her."

"You're right," Adam said with a deep sigh. "I'll talk to her."

Adam walked down the hall to the bedroom, his brothers following a short distance behind. He knocked softly, not wanting to alarm her by barging in. "Holly, honey, it's me, Adam."

"Go away." Her voice, muffled by sobs, filtered through the door.

He opened the door, flinching when he saw her huddled on the bed, her eyes red-rimmed. She'd discarded Ryan's coat on the floor. He stepped around it and walked over to sit on the bed next to her. He pulled her into his arms. She didn't fight him much to his delight.

"Tell me why you're crying," he said softly.

"What would you say if I told you not two minutes before I kissed you in the living room, I was outside kissing Ethan?" she said, her lip trembling.

He smiled and smoothed his hand over her hair. "That makes me very happy, actually."

Startled eyes flew to his face. "Happy? I'm acting like a slut and that makes you happy?"

He looked sternly at her. "I won't tolerate you talking about yourself that way. If you say anything like that again, I'll turn you over my knee and spank your pretty ass."

Her mouth fell open.

"There are some things you should know," he said. "Starting with the fact that you belong to us. All of us."

He expected to see fear at his statement. Instead, he saw surprise. Ethan and Ryan, who had been standing in the doorway, moved closer to the bed. Ethan sat down behind Holly and slipped his hands over her shoulders, rubbing soothingly.

Holly looked uneasily between the brothers as Adam allowed time for his declaration to sink in. She wet her lips nervously and turned troubled eyes back to him.

"Does that mean you're not going to let me leave?"

He chuckled. "If you're asking if you're a prisoner, the answer is no. If you're asking if we're going to open the door and let you waltz out of our lives, the answer is no."

He moved in closer, cupping her chin in his hand. Her breathing sped up. Beside her, Ryan curled his hand around hers. All three brothers were touching her, soothing her.

"You belong to us, Holly," Adam whispered. "I can feel your want, your need. It's as strong as our need for you. You're frightened, but you want us."

"So you want a sex slave?" she asked in a strangled voice.

His eyes narrowed. She was afraid. Not just of him and his brothers but of herself and the unknown man who had done so much damage to her both physically and mentally.

"If you think this is only about sex, you're wrong," Adam said in a low voice. "We're talking about forever. You would be our wife, our mate."

"W-what?" she squeaked. "B-but...you can't all marry the same woman!"

"Can't we?" Ethan asked behind her.

"It's not legal!"

"You're thinking with your mind," Adam chided. "There's no law that says you can't live with three men. In our hearts, you would be bound to all three of us. Wife to each one of us. Cherished by all of us."

She shook her head in denial, in confusion.

"It's that way in our family," Ryan said quietly. "If you're wondering if it's genetic then no, it isn't. We have a choice, and we're choosing you. Our fathers chose our mother, our grandfathers chose our grandmother. But we aren't bound by an invisible compulsion to lead that kind of life. It's something we decided when we were old enough to do so. We always knew there would be but one woman for the three of us. And so we've waited."

Adam watched Holly's reaction to Ryan's sincere explanation. A sheen of tears rimmed her eyes, and her hands shook in her lap.

"I can't," she whispered.

"But you want us," Ethan persisted.

She nodded a little shamefully.

"Then why can't you?" Adam prompted, wanting to hear the demons she fought.

"Because I'm already married," she choked out.

Chapter Four

Cold fingers of dread gripped Adam's chest. Already married? He looked up to see the same dread mirrored on his brothers' faces. He glanced down at her finger, unbelieving that he would have missed a ring. But none shone there.

Ethan's hands had stilled on her shoulders. Ryan's grip on her hand had loosened. His own hand had dropped from her chin. Could it be the one woman meant for them was forbidden?

No, he wouldn't accept that. Couldn't.

"Who is he?" Adam growled possessively.

Her hand fluttered to her throat, a defensive gesture. Panic flared across her face, quickly running out of control.

"He's the man you're running from," Ryan said, his face stony.

"He's the man who put the fear in your eyes," Adam added, tilting her chin up once more.

She closed her eyes and nodded.

Relief poured over Adam. Ethan's hands once again smoothed over Holly's shoulders. This was something they could deal with. She would simply divorce the bastard.

"You're not going back to him," Adam said simply. "You'll never go back to him."

"You don't understand," she whispered. "He'll never let me go." Tears sparkled in her cinnamon eyes.

"He doesn't have a choice," Ethan muttered.

"He'll hurt you, just like..."

Her voice trailed off but Adam understood what she had left unsaid. *He'll hurt you, just like he hurt me.* He had never dealt with such rage as what built within him. It swirled like an out of control storm.

She cleared her throat and continued on. "He's a very powerful man. He'll kill you. All three of you. Murder means nothing to him. I can't let him do that."

"And you think you going back to him is the answer?" Ryan asked incredulously.

She shook her head. "No, I'll never go back to him. Not willingly. But I also can't stay here. If he doesn't know I'm here, if I'm somewhere else, he can't very well hurt any of you."

A smile tugged at the corners of Adam's mouth. The little spitfire was trying to protect them. He felt a surge of pride. Their mate was proving very worthy indeed.

"I realize you've only known us a short time, baby, but you're going to have to learn to trust your husbands," Adam said.

Her eyes flew open even wider. "But you're not my husbands! Weren't you listening? I'm already married."

"A mere technicality," he said calmly. "One we intend to rectify as soon as possible."

She made a sound of frustration. "Did you hear anything I said?"

He smiled. "We heard everything, but your concern is unfounded. We can take care of ourselves, but more than that, we can take care of you."

Her hand fell, a helpless gesture that stated she was at a complete loss as to what to do or say. They were pressing too hard, something they couldn't afford to do if they didn't want to lose her.

"Come into the kitchen. Let us fix you some breakfast," Adam said, changing the topic to something neutral. Safe.

He saw the relief in her eyes. She nodded.

"I'll be there in a minute," she said, her voice husky.

Adam got up and motioned for his brothers to follow him. A few seconds later, Holly was alone in the big bedroom, her senses reeling from what she had just experienced.

They wanted her. All of them. And damn it, she wanted them too. She desperately wanted to see where this whole bizarre episode would take them. But there were several problems with doing that.

One, Mason would find her if she stayed here. She knew that just as well as she knew he would step on anyone who got in his way.

Two, her longing to be cherished, protected, was what got her into her present mess, and here she was falling under the spell of three gorgeous cowboys. She had to quit looking to others for her happiness.

Their wife. She shook her head, still unable to comprehend what they had proposed. As progressive as today's society was, she didn't think it was so forward-thinking as to excuse one woman living with three men.

But then, why should she care what anyone else thought? She sure hadn't when she had run from Mason Bardwell's home in the dead of the night. On their wedding night at that.

She closed her eyes and rubbed her forehead. She needed aspirin and maybe a good stiff drink. Nothing made sense to her, and it hurt to try and sort through the myriad of emotions swimming around in her head.

"Holly," Ryan said from the door.

She looked up to see the youngest brother leaning against the doorframe, studying her quietly.

"It's time for breakfast."

She nodded, not trusting herself to speak. Not trusting that she wouldn't throw herself across the room into his arms.

As if reading her mind, he ambled over to the bed and extended his hand down to her.

Slowly, she reached out and took his hand, liking the warmth that spread up her arm at an alarming rate.

He pulled her to stand beside him. His gaze slid over her, heating a path where it fell.

"You haven't kissed me," he murmured.

Her eyes widened in surprise. She hadn't expected him to say anything of the sort.

"You've kissed Ethan and Adam, but not me. If I was a jealous man, I might take exception to that."

Her mouth fell open. What to say to that?

"What do you say we remedy that?" he asked huskily.

He bent down, his mouth hovering a mere inch above hers. Sweet Jesus, how could she possibly resist? His hand slid over her jaw, to the back of her neck. His fingers plunged into her hair and pulled her to meet his mouth.

She sighed against his lips and let herself melt into his chest. The kiss was slow, hot, and thorough. Not as demanding as Adam's, not as gentle as Ethan's. Hot. It was the only word she could come up with to describe it.

Her nipples hardened against his chest, her breasts swelling and plumping in desire. An ache built in earnest between her legs, and she felt a sudden wetness. She clenched her legs together, trying to ease the burn, but it only grew stronger.

His big hands traveled down her back and settled on her ass, cupping and squeezing, pushing her against his groin. His cock, hard, *big*, bulging in his jeans, thrust into the cradle of her pelvis.

"Can you feel how much I want you?" he whispered.

He didn't wait for an answer. Instead, he resumed devouring her lips, raining a trail of heated kisses over her jawline and down to her neck.

She threw back her head and moaned when his teeth nipped the delicate curve of her shoulder. One hand still cupping her ass, his other hand slid around to her belly, then underneath her sweater, upwards until he cupped her breast.

Her breath caught in her throat when he thumbed her nipple. Exquisite currents of pleasure radiated in all directions from her breasts. Her pussy pulsed in response. Her clit tightened, ached, strained.

She moved restlessly in his arms, so close to something wonderful. Then he shoved her shirt up and lowered his head. She clenched her teeth together in anticipation. Hot breath blew over her nipple, puckering it, tightening it unbearably. But still he didn't suck it into his mouth.

"Please," she gasped out.

"Please what? Tell me what you want, Holly."

"Your mouth. Please. I want your mouth there."

"Here?" he asked, kissing the soft underswell of her breast. "Or here?" He kissed the area above her nipple.

Losing patience with his teasing, she shoved her hand into his hair and pulled his head to her nipple.

He chuckled. "Oh, you mean here." He sucked her nipple into his mouth and her body exploded in pleasure.

"Oh my God!"

She held him tightly against her, demanding his mouth not leave her breast. Currents of fire streaked down her belly and into her pelvis. Wetness gushed from her pussy. How could she be so close to coming when he'd only sucked her nipples?

"I hate to interrupt, but breakfast is getting cold," Adam said lazily from the door.

Heat rushed to Holly's cheeks, and she yanked away from Ryan. She pulled at her sweater, trying to restore a semblance of modesty to her appearance.

But Ryan wouldn't let her get away that easily. He pulled her to his large frame and kissed her, hard. "Pay him no attention. He's pissed because he wants very much to be on the other side of you."

"True," Adam said with a shrug. "Soon enough. She'll be ours."

"Want breakfast?" Ryan asked as he motioned to the door.

"You go first," she said nervously. The idea of passing by Adam was enough to make her knees turn to jelly. She much preferred the protection Ryan's body offered as a buffer between her and Adam.

Ryan's eyes glittered with unspent need as he tucked her hand into his. He pulled her along with him as he walked by Adam. She was almost out of the bedroom when Adam snaked an arm out and caught her.

To her dismay, Ryan let her hand fall from his and ambled on toward the kitchen. She found herself hauled up against Adam's rock hard chest and staring into his green eyes.

"You have no reason to be afraid of me," he said seriously. "There's no reason to hide behind Ethan and Ryan every time I say something to you. I'm very glad you feel safe with my brothers, but they have no need to protect you from me."

She bit her lip nervously. "It's just that you're so..."

"So...what?" he prompted.

"So big," she blurted out.

He arched an eyebrow. "And Ethan and Ryan aren't?"

She flushed. "No, yes, I mean yes, they're big but I don't think they'd hurt me."

His lips tightened. "And you think I would?"

"Not intentionally," she said lamely. "M-Mason is nothing compared to you and yet..." She broke off, not wanting to blurt out what all Mason had done. "If he could do so much, what then could you do?"

"Is that the bastard's name?" Adam demanded.

She pressed her lips together, refusing to say any more.

Adam sighed and dragged a hand through his hair. "Come here, baby." He pulled her over to the bed and sat down, settling her on his lap. "I don't know what all this Mason bastard has done to you, though I fully intend to find out, but it's obvious he's destroyed any trust you might've had within you. I can accept that. What I can't accept is the fear in your eyes every time I look at you."

Her heart thudded painfully. Adam looked earnest. Hard, but earnest. She felt silly over the fear that nagged her when he was focused on her, but she knew without a doubt, she would never be the same after meeting this man. And maybe that was what she was most afraid of.

"I have been very honest with you," he continued on. "I want you. More than any other woman. Ever. I won't be satisfied until you're in my bed. In our bed. Bound to us. Pregnant with our children. Belonging to us heart and soul forever. I can't put it any straighter than that. I won't let you go without a fight, that's for damn sure, but I sure as hell won't ever hurt you, and I'll move heaven and earth to make sure no one else docs cither."

She felt his speech to the very depths of her soul. How could she not? No one had ever spoken so honestly with her or with such conviction.

"Give us a chance, Holly. It's all I ask."

Not examining the voice inside her that warned her to run far, far away, she slowly nodded.

A slow, triumphant smile spread across his face. "Now, let's go eat that breakfast."

Chapter Five

Holly sat at the bar between Adam and Ryan as Ethan served up plates of ham and eggs. She glanced between them often, gauging their mood, their reaction to her, but they seemed unruffled.

It was as if they made such proclamations every day. She shook her head and speared another piece of egg with her fork. How could such a relationship work? Jealousy would be inevitable. And things would be much more difficult for her than for any of them. They only had one "spouse" to contend with, she had three.

Three men to please, put up with, all different. The mere idea of the complexities involved in the situation made her head ache even harder.

Ethan was obviously the easiest going of the three brothers. She relaxed around him. It was a natural reaction. Even if she didn't know Adam was the oldest, it was as clear as if it was written across his forehead. And even though he had gone to great lengths to make her feel at ease, she knew he could be dangerous when crossed. He exuded power and authority, wore it like a mantle draped around him.

Her gaze flitted sideways to Ryan. He was an enigma. The only one she didn't have an idea formed about already. He was quiet and serious, but more than that, she saw pain in his eyes.

Like her, he'd seen the darker side of life. She'd bet her last dollar on it.

"Are you all right?" Ethan asked.

She looked up to see him frowning at her.

"Just a headache," she replied.

He walked to one of the cabinets and retrieved a bottle of ibuprofen, shook out several pills and handed them to her. Just one more example of them taking care of her. It warmed her to her toes and scared the hell out of her all at the same time.

"What's on your mind, baby?" Adam asked.

Was she that easy to read? Could they already see inside her mind and soul? Her fingers tensed on her fork for a moment as she contemplated denying that anything was on her mind, but Adam's honesty compelled her to be equally honest.

"The dynamics of the whole relationship you all propose... It's rather mind-boggling," she admitted.

She didn't miss the triumphant smiles passed between the brothers. Surely to them, this was a sign they were making headway. And maybe they were, as insane as she was to even contemplate it.

"Anything in particular you want to talk about?" Adam prompted.

She sighed and set down her fork. "This has all pretty much blown me away. I don't even know where to begin. I keep expecting to be told this is one huge joke at my expense."

Ryan put a hand on her knee. "This is no joke. Now tell us what's on your mind."

She took in a deep breath, told herself she was completely nuts and then proceeded to tell them precisely what concerns she had.

"The thing is, you guys only have one person to concern yourselves with, relationship wise. I have three. Three overbearing, overprotective, rather large men. I don't see how it's remotely possible that I could please all of you all of the time."

Cocky, self-assured grins adorned the three men's faces.

"I don't think any of us expect perfection," Ethan said. "Though," he added with an up and down sweep of her, "I'm not arguing with what we've been given."

"We've discussed this many times," Adam said in a serious tone. "We know it won't always be easy. It wasn't always easy for our mother and fathers, but if we all work at it, there's no reason we can't live in harmony."

"I guess I just don't understand the concept," Holly said. "I can't wrap my brain around it."

Ryan reclaimed her attention by turning her back around to face him. "Then think of it this way. Three men completely devoted to your happiness. Three men worshipping your body with theirs. Three men who would love you with complete abandon. Three men who would protect you and cherish you always."

She stared at him open-mouthed. "Well, when you put it that way," she muttered.

"Damn, Ryan, why didn't you speak up earlier?" Ethan said in amusement.

"The first order of business is to go into town and buy you some clothes and whatever else you need," Adam said, changing the subject.

"But I don't need anything," she protested. Well, that wasn't entirely true, but she didn't want them buying her a bunch of stuff.

"Ryan, you care to repeat that part about three men devoted to her happiness, worshipping her, etc.?" Ethan spoke up. "Because I'm pretty sure making sure our woman is clothed and provided for falls under that heading."

Holly blushed.

"Ethan, you and Ryan want to drive her into town? I need to check out the horses and get the hay out. It's supposed to snow again tonight." He turned to Holly. "There's a western store in town. It isn't much but you'll be able to get boots, jeans and some shirts. And a coat. You need a decent coat. Next week, we'll drive into the city to do the heavy shopping for you."

"Thank you," she said softly. She couldn't manage much more around the huge knot in her throat. She felt dangerously close to tears and fought to contain them.

Adam leaned forward and brushed his mouth across hers. He was surprisingly gentle. For the first time, she reached a hand out to touch him, running her fingertips across his cheek, feeling the slight stubble along his jaw.

When he drew away, his eyes were burning with passion, and she felt heady with the knowledge she had affected him so.

"Well if we're going into town, we need to go now. We don't want to be late getting back if it's going to snow," Ryan announced, standing up from his seat at the bar.

"Is it...is it safe for me to go into town?" she asked. The idea that someone might see her and report back to Mason struck fear into her heart, no matter the brothers' vow to protect her.

"We'll make sure you're not seen," Ethan said. "Riley's Western Store is on the edge of town. We'll park you in a corner of the store and do your shopping for you, let you try on stuff if you need to, and we'll keep a sharp eye for anything unusual going on."

"Okay," she said, expelling a long breath. "Let's do it then."

♥ ♥ ♥

The drive into town was long and quiet as they traveled down the mountain. Holly sat up front while Ethan drove and Ryan sat in the back of the Land Rover. During the course of the trip, Ethan reached over and twined his fingers with hers.

She drew comfort from the small gesture and readily laced her fingers in his.

Mid-morning, they drove into the small town of Clyde. Adam had been right. There wasn't much beyond a small grocery store, a feed mill, a few cafes and the western store, but there was a quaint main street and the businesses were clean and well-kept.

Ethan pulled up at the western store, and he and Ryan surveyed the area before opening their doors. Ryan opened her door and gestured for her to get out. Once she was out, Ethan and Ryan flanked her and they headed into the store.

They led her to the area beside the one small dressing room and had her sit.

"Now tell us what sizes you need, and we'll bring you some stuff to look at," Ryan directed.

She laughed. "There's no one else in here. I think I can look myself if that's okay."

Ethan glanced around once more. "Okay, I'll go stand by the door. Ryan, you keep an eye on Holly while she shops."

Holly walked over to the racks in the center of the store and began thumbing through the shirts. She found a few long sleeve flannel shirts in her size and removed them from the rack. She wasn't sure how much she should spend so she only took a few and moved onto the jeans.

As she was searching for her size in the pants, Ryan walked up behind her with several more shirts over his arm. At her self-conscious glance, he shoved the shirts toward her, his expression brooking no argument.

"Take them up to the counter for me, will you?" she asked. "I'm fairly certain they'll fit."

"Want me to pick you out a pair of boots while I'm up there?" he asked.

She smiled. "I'd like that. Thanks."

She walked closer to the window overlooking the street and picked out a few pairs of jeans in dark blue and one each in black and khaki. As she turned to follow Ryan to the checkout, her eyes stopped on a familiar black vehicle pulling down the street.

Frozen to the spot, she watched in horror as Mason Bardwell climbed out of the flashy BMW, his gaze flitting up and down the street.

Her stomach knotted, rolled, tightening until she knew she would vomit. She glanced around in panic, looking for a place to hide. Somewhere he couldn't see her.

Ethan frowned as the BMW pulled into a parking spot across the street. Unusual vehicle for this part of the world. If it wasn't four-wheel drive, the locals had no use for it.

He glanced back to where Ryan was looking at boots and then at the racks where Holly was. Only she wasn't there. He scanned the store, looking to see where she moved, but she wasn't anywhere to be seen.

"Ryan," he barked.

Ryan turned around, his eyes searching for Holly as well. His features hardened when he saw no sign of her either.

They fanned out, darting between the clothes racks. Ryan walked to the back toward the fitting room, and Ethan scoured the front by the window.

He found her huddled behind a clearance rack, only her feet sticking out from under the clothes. When he parted the hangers, she flinched, as if afraid of who had come.

"What's wrong, doll? Who's scared you so bad?"

"He's here. Outside. He's come for me. He knows I'm here," she said with a low moan.

She rocked back and forth, abject terror in her eyes. She hugged her knees tightly to her chest, a protective measure. Ethan wanted to march into the street and kill the bastard on the spot.

"I'll kill him."

For a moment, Ethan thought he had spoken his thoughts aloud, but then he realized Ryan had walked up behind them.

"No!" she protested. "Please, take me home. He can't see me. Please!"

"We won't let him hurt you, doll," Ethan soothed. He turned to Ryan. "Pull the Rover around back. I'll take her out that way."

He turned his attention back to Holly and gently picked her up. Cradling her to his chest, he strode toward the rear of the store, careful to keep her hidden from view.

He stopped at the counter for the briefest of moments when he caught the storeowner's curious stare.

"Riley, I need a favor," Ethan murmured. "There's a mean son of a bitch outside, and he's looking for this woman. If he asks you, you haven't seen her."

Riley's gaze hardened, and he fingered the shotgun he kept behind the counter. "Don't worry, Ethan."

Ethan nodded then hurried out the back. Ryan was there, holding the door open. "You drive," he ordered as he climbed into the back, still holding Holly.

A few seconds later, they pulled onto the main street. Holly lay in the seat, her head on Ethan's lap. He stared at the BMW on their way past, committing the license plate to memory. Not that it was hard. California plates. Personalized. MASON. Arrogant bastard to boot.

He stroked Holly's hair, his rage building as he felt her tremble beneath his touch. When they were out of town, he pulled her up beside him.

She clung to him, her face buried in his chest. She felt better than he had ever imagined a woman could feel. That the woman who would complete them all was finally with them was incomprehensible. And he sure as hell wasn't going to let some abusive bastard take her away from them.

"How is she?" Ryan asked from the front seat as he sped up the mountain, taking the switchbacks as fast as he dared.

"Good question. How are you, doll?" he asked, smoothing her hair from her face.

"I'm okay," she said in a shaky voice. "He didn't see me, did he?"

"No, doll, he didn't. I promise. You're safe."

He continued to caress her, running his hand up and down her back. "We're almost home."

He nuzzled the top of her head, pressing kisses to her hair. Gradually she ceased shaking, but she held him tightly, a fact he wasn't complaining about. Whether she wanted to admit it or not, she trusted him. She trusted all three of them. It was a start.

Chapter Six

Adam was furious when Ethan and Ryan arrived with a visibly shaken Holly. He scooped her up in his arms and hugged her tightly against his chest. His eyes flashed over her head, demanding to know what happened from his brothers.

"Her h—the bastard was in town," Ethan spat.

"Did he hurt you, baby?" Adam demanded.

She shook her head against his chest.

He looked up to his brothers for confirmation.

"He didn't see her," Ryan said. "At least we don't think. He was parked on the street. Holly saw him from the store window."

"Fuck."

This certainly complicated things. He exchanged glances with his brothers. All silently agreed. Something would have to be done about the bastard. They couldn't allow Holly to be terrorized any longer.

Adam pulled Holly away from him slightly and framed her face in his hands. "Listen to me, baby. We won't let him hurt you, I swear it."

She stared at him for a long moment then slowly nodded.

He let out a growl of satisfaction. "Go run some bathwater, Ryan."

Ryan left for the bathroom, leaving Adam and Ethan in the room with Holly. Adam ran a hand down her cheek, down the curve of her slender neck and down to the neckline of her shirt.

"Let us take care of you," he murmured. "First a bath..." He let his voice trail off suggesting there was more to come.

She shivered in his arms. But she didn't look at all worried about the idea of more to come.

"Adam, there's something...there's something you should know."

He lifted his brow at her nervous statement. He looked over at Ethan who shrugged.

She pushed away from him, and he allowed her space. She stood up and moved several feet from both him and Ethan.

"I feel so stupid saying this," she began. She wrung her hands in front of her, her agitation increasing.

"Holly," Ethan said. "Whatever it is, just tell us. It can't be so bad, no matter what you may think."

She took a deep breath and looked between them. "I thought you should know, I mean I don't even know how this whole thing works. Between us, I mean. About sex."

She broke off, her cheeks pink with a blush.

Adam waited patiently for her to come around to her point. The fact she was entertaining thoughts of sex was promising, but she wasn't sure how it would work between them. He smiled. She was delightfully innocent.

"It's just that I've never done this before," she said awkwardly. "I mean sex in general."

Not that innocent surely! His head jerked in surprise, and he looked at Ethan to see the same surprise blazoned on his face.

"Say that again?" Ethan said.

Her blush deepened.

"But you're married," Adam began.

"I left him on our wedding night," she mumbled.

A slow smile spread across Ethan's face, and the same sense of satisfaction took hold of Adam. She was going to be more than just theirs. She would *only* belong to them. They would be her first. And her last.

"Maybe you should explain, baby," he said gently. They needed to know all they could about her. The more they knew, the better chance they had of keeping her. And letting her go wasn't an option.

"Water's ready," Ryan called from the door.

"We'll let you talk in the tub," Adam said. He stood and closed the distance between him and Holly. She stepped back slightly when his hand slid under her shirt.

"Trust me, baby. I won't hurt you. We need to get you out of your clothes."

She licked her lips then captured her bottom lip between her teeth and nibbled furiously. She was, in a word, adorable.

Holly glanced between the three men in front of her and nearly hyperventilated. She wanted them, but she wasn't sure she wanted to be naked in front of them. The mere idea had her wanting to hurl.

Adam's hand slid underneath her shirt, his fingers brushing the underside of her breast. The thin material of her bra did nothing to muffle his touch. She felt the scorching blaze of his heat to her very depths.

Feather light, his fingers brushed across her skin, around to her back and to the clasp of her bra. With a flick of his hand, the clasp broke free.

Another hand slipped underneath her shirt, shoving it upward. She gave a startled gasp as she realized Ethan had joined Adam.

Ethan pushed her shirt to her neck then Adam gently tugged it over her head. She self-consciously covered her chest with her arms.

"Don't," Ryan said huskily. "You're beautiful."

She looked up to see him staring at her from across the room, his eyes burning into hers.

Slowly she let her hands fall away until she stood in front of them in only her jeans.

"Jesus," Ethan breathed.

Adam undid the fly on her jeans then slid the zipper down.

"If you don't hurry, the water is going to get cold," Ryan drawled.

"We can't have that," Adam said in a voice that sent spasms from her belly to her pussy. Her muscles clenched in red hot need.

He began to peel her jeans down her body until she stood in only her panties. Ready for the agony to end, she hooked her thumbs in the waistband and quickly shimmied out of her underwear.

"You're perfect," Adam said.

She found herself lifted into his arms, and he carried her into the bathroom. He lowered her into the huge tub of foamy suds, and she moaned in pleasure as the warm water lapped over her body.

"We'll give you some time to relax," Adam said as he stood back up. He dropped a kiss on top of her head. "I'll be back to wash your hair and dry you off in a few minutes."

She watched as they filed out of the bathroom, and she sunk lower into the suds, closing her eyes. Would they want to have sex with her now that she had told them she was a virgin? She was nervous about the whole idea. Not only had she never done it, but she had three men wanting to make love to her. And she had no idea how they planned to go about it. But damned if the idea of it didn't have her toes curled.

"This changes things a bit," Adam said as he faced his two brothers in the bedroom.

"What are you talking about?" Ryan demanded.

"Holly's a virgin," Ethan said.

Ryan lifted a brow but said nothing more. He merely pinned Adam with a questioning stare.

"What?" Adam asked, sensing there was a lot on his youngest brother's mind.

Ryan sighed and shoved his hands into the pockets of his jeans.

"How do we know she won't change her mind? How do we know she didn't have cold feet and take off from her husband?"

Ethan started to protest but Adam silenced him with a look. He could see the uncertainty in Ryan's eyes, knew of anyone, Ryan would be the most distrustful.

A twinge of pain squeezed his chest. Would he ever know what Ryan had endured in Iraq? Sadness weighed heavy on his mind. God knows he and Ethan had tried to get Ryan to open up, but ever since his return a year ago, he hadn't uttered a word about the time he spent in captivity.

"Ryan, she needs us. I'm not saying it'll be easy. Hell, she's married. She's scared to death, and she's confused over what she's feeling for us. All we can do is protect her and show her how very good it can be with us."

He turned to Ethan. "She trusts you. She's already established a bond with you. I think you should be her first."

"She's not a piece of meat to decide over," Ryan said in disgust.

He turned and walked out of the bedroom before Adam could respond.

Ethan chuckled softly. "He's right, you know. You don't have to control everything, Adam. No need to orchestrate the entire act of sex. I think we can handle it on our own."

Adam didn't respond. That wasn't what he meant, but maybe they were right. He was trying too damn hard. He rubbed a hand through his hair and massaged the back of his neck.

"I'll be out in the barn," Adam said. "You can see to Holly."

Truth was he needed some fresh air. Needed to think.

The water had grown tepid, and Holly wasn't going to wait on the men any longer. Hell, it wasn't as if she couldn't handle herself anyway. Yet, she sat docilely in the tub like an obedient stooge.

She stood up, water running down her body. She reached for a towel that hung on the rack beside the tub and began drying off.

"Let me."

The towel slipped from her fingers as Ethan took it and began rubbing her back.

"I can do it," she said, more sharply than she intended.

She reached for the towel, not liking the fact she stood naked before him.

He probed her with his stare for a second then let her have the towel back.

"I'll be in the living room if you want to join me," he said as he walked out of the bathroom.

She took her time, her mind a mass of confusion. She was seriously deluding herself if she thought it would be as easy as setting up a new life here with the three brothers. She knew nothing about them, had no idea what she would do here, and there was the little matter of her marriage to a vile, sadistic monster.

Oh, he hadn't shown himself for the asshole he was until their wedding night. She'd been starry-eyed and all agog that he had chosen her to be his wife. She'd quickly learned that behind his charming exterior lurked a controlling, abusive man.

Would things have been different if she hadn't witnessed him killing a man in cold blood on the day of their wedding? Probably not, after all, he'd had no difficulty raising a hand to her. No regret, no emotion had crossed his face as she'd laid there crying.

She shuddered and shook her head to rid herself of the memory. Never again would she put herself in such a position. If she remained here, it would be because she wanted to, not because Adam dictated it.

If she remained here. Was she contemplating? Really?

"You're out of your mind," she muttered to her reflection in the mirror.

You want them as much as they want you. Maybe more.

Her nipples puckered as she imagined them making love to her. She felt an unbearable tightening in her groin. It spread throughout her pelvis, and her clit pulsed in reaction.

She may be a virgin, but she wasn't an idiot. She was as horny as a priest in the Playboy Mansion.

Rolling her eyes heavenward, she dressed and slipped out of the bathroom. She meandered down the hall and, for the first time since her arrival, took stock of her surroundings.

The cabin exuded masculinity. All the rooms were sparsely decorated in earth tones. The living room was dominated by the stone fireplace, and the glow spread warmth over the rustic wood floors. It was, she imagined, just as a cabin may have looked a hundred years ago.

Ethan sat at a desk several feet from the fireplace. He was concentrating on a computer screen and occasionally tapping on the keyboard. Did they have internet access here in the middle of nowhere?

She looked around for the others, but the house was silent. Taking a deep breath, she crossed the room until she stood behind Ethan.

"Ethan?" she asked, damning how quivery her voice came out.

He swiveled around in his chair and looked inquisitively at her.

"Can I ask you some questions?"

"Of course," he replied.

He stood up and tucked her hand in his then pulled her over to the couch.

"Let's get comfortable."

She sank down beside him, careful to keep a safe distance from him. One touch from him and she was likely to throw herself into his arms and beg him to make love to her.

She stared at him for a long time then gathered her courage around her. "Is this for real?"

His gaze softened, and he sat back as if realizing she needed the space.

"This must be difficult for you."

She nodded. She swallowed back what she wanted to say then hesitated. Holding back her emotions wasn't natural for her, as problematic as it may be. Something told her she could be honest with Ethan.

"It's difficult, but not in the way you'd think."

She promptly blushed and looked away as she spoke.

He didn't prompt her to say more, he merely waited.

"I don't understand," she began again, trying to formulate her thoughts. "How can you all want me? I mean I can understand wanting me, wanting to have sex that is, but Adam said... He made it sound like you wanted me to *stay*."

Ethan nodded.

"But how? You don't know me. How can it be any more than lust at this point?"

He smiled and reached over, curling his strong fingers over her palm. He picked up her hand then turned it over until her palm faced up. Bending his head, he pressed his lips to her skin.

She shivered in reaction, a chill racing straight up her arm.

"Lust? Oh yeah," he said, lowering her hand. "But it's more than that."

Her hand fell to the couch, but she wanted to press it back to his mouth. The curl of urgency between her thighs had her shifting to alleviate the discomfort.

"If you're asking me if we're in love with you," he began, "well, I can't speak for my brothers, but I don't think it's that simple. As you said, we don't really know you. But we recognize you. Does that make sense?"

She shook her head wordlessly.

"Put it this way. I recognize you as the woman I *will* fall in love with. Maybe I've already started down the path. I won't know until we've had more time to explore each other." He flashed a wicked grin at her. "And explore, I plan to do."

For some reason, his simple honesty comforted her more than a declaration of undying love and devotion. She'd gotten those from Mason, and they certainly hadn't done her any good.

"What do *you* want?" he asked softly.

"I want never to have gotten married," she blurted out, allowing her regret to pour out of her soul.

Tears stung her eyelids and she looked away.

"Ahh, doll."

He scooted forward and pulled her against his chest. He tilted her chin up until she looked him in the eye.

"You don't have to stay married to the bastard."

Sadness swelled in her chest. "I don't think he'll let me go. I know...I know too much," she said.

He arched his brow.

"What do you know, doll?"

She closed her eyes. She needed to release the heavy burden she'd been carrying for the last two weeks.

"I saw him kill someone," she whispered. "On our wedding day."

Ethan's grip tightened around her.

"Hell."

She pushed away from him, gritting her teeth to keep the tears at bay.

"You see, that's why I can't stay here. He'll find me. He'll kill you. It's nothing to him."

Ethan released his breath then looked over her shoulder.

"You hear everything?" he asked.

She swiveled around until she saw Ryan leaning against the wall behind her.

Ryan nodded, his eyes glittering dangerously.

"Did you email Cal?" Ryan asked.

She looked back at Ethan in confusion.

Ethan nodded. "Yeah."

"Who's Cal?" she asked.

"He's a lawyer," Ryan said.

Her eyes widened. She looked between the brothers, checking their expressions for something, some clue as to their intentions.

"He's a good friend of ours. He practices law in Denver. I emailed him about your situation. Asked him how best to proceed with terminating your marriage."

She stood up in agitation, shrugging off Ethan's hand.

"You can't tell him where I am!"

"No one's going to tell him where you are, doll."

"Don't you want to be rid of him?" Ryan asked.

She looked up to see him studying her, probing her as if measuring her reaction. Her eyes narrowed. Did he think she wanted to stay married to Mason?

"After what you heard, how can you doubt that?" she asked, staring back at him just as intently.

They squared off, neither backing down as they burned holes through each other with their eyes.

He relaxed his stance then crooked his finger at her.

"Come here."

It pissed her off that she found herself crossing the room to stand in front of him.

He pulled her roughly into his arms and melded his lips to hers.

She moaned low in her throat. God, he felt so damn good. She threaded her arms around his neck, and in that moment, she didn't give a damn what he thought about her. She wanted to rip his clothes off.

He sucked her bottom lip between his teeth and nipped erotically. He wasn't gentle, his touch was demanding. He slid his hands underneath her shirt, upward until he cupped her breasts in his palms.

She flinched when his thumbs flicked her nipples. She arched closer to him, wanting more.

Her breath came in ragged spurts as his mouth left hers. He burned a trail down her neck then sank his teeth in the curve of her shoulder.

She cried out, her legs collapsing beneath her.

Something caught her. Not something. Someone. She found herself rocked against two hard chests. One in front. One in back.

Gentle kisses rained where before Ryan's teeth had seared her skin. She leaned back, wanting more of Ethan's touch.

Ryan shoved her shirt upward, baring her breasts. He bent and sucked one nipple into his mouth. God, he was hot. No preamble with him. No teasing. He went for it. Hard and fast.

"Do you want it?" Ryan murmured.

Did she want it? If she didn't get it, she was going to kill someone.

"If you don't want this, now is the time to say so," Ethan said as he rocked her ass against his rock hard erection.

"No, don't stop. Please."

"Never let it be said I could refuse a lady," Ethan said, his voice thick with desire.

Ryan pulled the shirt the rest of the way from her body and tossed it on the floor. He hooked his finger in the waistband of her jeans and pulled her hard against him.

He devoured her mouth with his as he fumbled with the zipper. In a few seconds, he was shoving her pants impatiently down her hips.

"You've got too many clothes on," she protested.

Ryan's eyes flashed. "In the bedroom. Now."

She slipped past him and walked on shaky legs down the hallway toward Adam's bedroom. She was clad in only her panties, but for some reason, she couldn't bring herself to be the one to divest herself of that last barrier.

She turned around as Ryan and Ethan walked through the door. Ryan yanked his shirt from his jeans while Ethan slowly unbuttoned his.

Her eyes were drawn to Ryan's groin as he unbuttoned his jeans. He let his pants drop then pulled his cock from his underwear.

He was magnificent.

"Come here," he said, as he fisted his cock in his hand.

She knew what he wanted, didn't need further instructions. She went to him and knelt on the floor in front of him.

He grasped the back of her head and guided his cock into her mouth. He let out a harsh groan as he slid into her throat.

He smelled musky and wild, tasted exotic.

"Goddamn," he muttered.

She didn't wait for him to set the pace. She was eager to explore him on her own. She made light sucking noises as she took him deeper into her mouth.

He was big and hard. She couldn't take him all, but damned if she wasn't going to try.

Ryan's hips rocked forward and he thrust with more urgency.

"You feel so damn good," he said.

Ethan's hand tangled in her hair, and she felt her head pulled away from Ryan only for Ethan's cock to replace Ryan's.

She opened her mouth obediently to accept his larger circumference, and he slid rapidly back and forth.

"Oh, fuck yeah," Ethan said in a tortured whisper.

She felt the light seep of fluid in the back of her throat. Tangy, slightly salty. She swallowed, expecting more, but he pulled away from her.

Ryan lifted her to her feet and walked her backwards to the bed. The backs of her knees pressed against the mattress, and he laid her back until her legs dangled from the bed.

He leaned over and pressed his lips to her belly just above the band of her underwear. Then he began pulling them down her legs, his lips burning a trail in the same direction.

When she was free from the panties, he tossed them over his shoulder and nudged her knees apart. He knelt between her legs and ran a finger over the soft folds of her pussy.

She jerked in reaction. God, she was wet. Her clit hummed, waiting for him to touch her there.

He spread her wider then teased her entrance with one finger, two fingers. Then he bent his head and flicked his tongue over her clit.

She nearly shot off the bed. Ethan gently pushed her back down. The mattress sank under his weight as he sat down beside her and began rolling the tips of her breasts between his fingers.

Ryan swirled his tongue around her tight button then lapped downward to her opening.

Ethan's mouth closed over her nipple. Then her other. She closed her eyes and opened her mouth in a silent scream.

Ryan slipped a finger inside her, then two. He slid them back and forth as he sucked her clit into his mouth.

Her entire body tightened, jerked, then the world exploded around her. She lost the battle to remain silent, and she cried out as her orgasm racked her body.

She felt a gush of wetness between her legs, but still Ryan continued tormenting her with his mouth. Ethan sucked one nipple and pinched the other with his hand. Unbelievably, she felt the slow crawl of her release build again. Not again. She couldn't.

Suddenly Ryan pulled away, and she felt her legs spread unbelievably wide. Ethan moved his lips to capture hers in a breathless kiss.

"Relax, doll," he whispered.

And she knew what was coming. Craved it, wanted it more than anything.

Ryan's cock nudged her entrance then in one firm push, he slid into her body.

Her eyes flew open at the myriad of sensations accosting her. Pain, incredible pleasure, longing, want, need. She needed badly.

He remained still for a moment as her body adjusted to his invasion. He was big. He wasn't all the way in. Could he fit?

"I can't hold on anymore," Ryan said through tightly compressed teeth.

He pulled back then surged forward, more powerfully than before. She gripped Ethan's head, yanking him down to her mouth. He held her tightly as Ryan began thrusting between her legs.

She'd never felt anything like this before. Ryan leaned forward and jerked his hips powerfully.

"Oh!" she exclaimed as he seated himself fully within her. She could feel his balls nestled against her ass.

"Am I hurting you?" Ryan gritted out.

"God no, don't stop," she pleaded.

Her words seemed to shove him right over the edge. He began tunneling into her, his hands gripping her hips.

In her haze, she registered another presence. Adam. The bed dipped again.

"It would appear I'm missing all the fun." His deep voice washed over her, nearly sending her over the edge.

Adam put a hand behind her neck and pulled her head up far enough that he could slide his cock into her mouth.

She closed her eyes and sucked him deep within, in matching rhythm to Ryan's thrusts.

Adam gripped her head tightly and thrust hard, not allowing her to control the tempo. He paused to let her catch her breath then began stroking to the back of her throat.

Ethan's mouth closed over her nipple once more, his teeth grazing the sensitive tip. Then he sucked it into his mouth, and she nearly lost all sense of time and place.

She couldn't think, she could only react. She could feel Ryan's urgency mount, and he shook the entire bed with the force of his thrusts. Then he tightened between her legs, and she felt the hot jets of his release.

She whimpered in protest. She wasn't ready yet. She was close, so close. She didn't want Ryan to stop.

Adam slid all the way out of her mouth and paused a moment. Then he curled his hands into her hair and thrust all the way into her mouth, his cock sliding down her throat. His balls rested on her chin, and he kept her still, allowing himself to fill her mouth completely.

Ryan pulled out, and she felt the loss keenly. Adam withdrew and began pumping in and out of her mouth. He was close to his release, she could tell. He'd tightened, swelled, become even harder in her mouth.

Precum filled the back of her mouth, and she swallowed quickly as he thrust faster.

The bed dipped and her legs wobbled and fell as Ryan left her. Before she could utter any sound of regret, her legs were spread wide once more.

Ethan slid into her. She moaned around Adam's cock. Ethan felt so different yet every bit as good as Ryan had felt.

Ethan began a slow in and out motion, gentle, deep.

She gagged slightly as Adam's hand gripped her neck tighter and he surged forward again.

"Oh God, baby, I'm coming, get ready."

The wet sounds of her sucking filled the room as he fisted his cock in his other hand and forced himself deeper.

Hot liquid filled her mouth, jetted against the back of her throat and spilled down her chin. She swallowed as fast as she could but it kept coming. He thrust one more time and held it deep, holding her against him as he finished in the back of her throat.

Slowly he let her head down until she was flat against the mattress again. She opened her eyes to see him staring down at her, desire and approval in his eyes.

He lowered his hand to caress her breasts, feathering his fingers across her taut nipples.

Ryan took the position vacated by Ethan, and he turned her head toward him. He was already hard again. He slid his cock into her mouth and groaned. He was surprisingly gentle, much more so than when he'd fucked her.

Ethan stroked between her legs, the soft smacking noise of flesh meeting flesh filling the air. He pressed a thumb to her clit as he thrust deeper, and she began to squirm restlessly as her orgasm built, fanned out of control.

Ryan's cock in her mouth, Adam's hands on her breasts, Ethan deep within her pussy, it was all too much. She'd held on as long as she could.

As Ryan filled her mouth with his cum, Ethan sank deeply inside her and poured himself into her. She bucked wildly beneath them, spasms rocking her body.

Ethan slipped from her and leaned heavily on her belly, his breath coming in ragged bursts. Ryan eased his cock from her mouth then gathered her in his arms.

She closed her eyes and sucked in deep mouthfuls of air, trying desperately to calm her raging senses. She shook from head to toe from the force of her orgasm. In short, she felt like jelly.

She felt her legs lifted then separated. A hard cock slid into her, and she moaned. "I can't," she whispered. She couldn't take another orgasm like she'd just experienced. It would kill her.

Adam chuckled, the sound husky and erotic to her ears. It was the laugh of a predator. One who knew he had his prey right where he wanted.

"Oh yes, baby. You can. Just lay back and feel."

She was impossibly sore, and yet as he pushed into her, lapped her legs over his shoulders, she felt her body react.

"That's it, baby."

Ryan and Ethan ran their hands soothingly over her body, feathering over her soft belly, her ribcage, then to her breasts. Both dark heads dipped and sucked at her nipples, lavishing them with attention.

Her body shuddered as Adam drove powerfully into her. He was so hard, so big.

He withdrew and she opened her eyes.

"Turn over," he commanded.

Ethan and Ryan helped her turn over, their hands warm and comforting.

"Up on your knees," Adam said.

She shook in reaction. Was he going to take her from behind? This was by far the more erotic of her fantasies. The thing she'd wanted to try most. It was the one position guaranteed to turn her on.

He gripped her hips in his strong hands and with his thumbs spread her buttocks until she felt cool air wash over her ass and pussy.

He ran a finger over the seam of her ass, pausing at her back entrance.

She flinched and tightened reflexively. Surely he wasn't going to...

He chuckled again as if reading her thoughts.

"Not yet, baby. But soon. Very soon."

Chills dotted her entire body at the idea of him fucking her ass. Would it feel as good as she imagined? Or would it be one of those things better left in fantasy and not in reality?

She didn't know, but she wanted to find out.

He positioned himself behind her then surged forward, nearly rocking her off her knees.

She screamed as a wave of pleasure, so sharp, raced over her. He was so deep. Deeper than she imagined he could go. He rocked forward, setting an insane pace, driving her forward. The slap of his thighs against her ass ricocheted through the room, the sound incredibly erotic to her ears.

Ethan knelt on the bed and positioned himself in front of her. His cock stood erect mere centimeters from her mouth. She opened her mouth obediently and he thrust inside.

Ryan's lips slid across her back making her shiver. His hands curled around to tweak and pinch at her nipples.

"You like this?" he murmured.

She nodded, unable to speak around Ethan's cock shoving impatiently into her mouth.

"Imagine how it will be when you are taking all three of us," he continued, his voice raspy with lust. "Would you like that? Adam in your ass, me in your pussy, Ethan in your mouth."

She shuddered and bucked in reaction to his provocative words.

Adam thrust harder in response, making her cry out.

"I think I want to fuck you again," Ryan whispered. "Would you like that?"

She let Ethan's cock slide out of her mouth long enough to shout yes before Ethan reclaimed her lips.

Adam withdrew, but he hadn't come yet. Ryan took his place and slid his hard cock into her quivering pussy.

"Oh yeah, you feel so damn good," Ryan said with a groan.

He fucked in and out, his fingers digging into her hips as Ethan continued his assault on her mouth. Never had she felt so powerful, so desirable and so in control of her own destiny. She reveled in it, giving as good as she was getting.

Ryan stopped all too soon, but Adam was there to take his place. They began taking turns, driving her up the peak to her release only to stop before she catapulted over the top.

Three, four, five thrusts, then another would take his place.

She sucked Ethan's cock with all the intensity of her raging desire. She wanted to come damn it. She needed to come.

"I'm coming, doll," Ethan said hoarsely.

He shot into her throat, thrusting forcefully. She swallowed as she bucked back into the cock impaled in her pussy.

Finally she felt Adam tighten against her ass. She raised up on her hands as high as she could and pushed back against him. He gripped her shoulders with his hands, pulling her back as hard as he could.

He shot cum into her pussy until she felt it run down the inside of her thigh, but still she hadn't found her release.

He pulled out and Ryan quickly grabbed her hips and plunged into her. The fire in her pussy burned out of control. It ballooned into her pelvis, into her stomach, tightened her legs until she feared she would collapse.

He fucked her harder, knowing what she needed.

She closed her eyes and screamed as his hard thighs slammed against her ass. He reached underneath and pressed his fingers to her clit.

Black spots filled her vision. The world blurred around her. Her pussy felt as though it exploded as her orgasm finally burned over her.

Behind her, Ryan cried out. He thrust forward and convulsed against her.

She collapsed forward, no longer able to bear her weight with her hands. Ryan came with her, his big body covering hers, his cock still buried deeply within her.

She couldn't catch her breath fast enough. She panted as the aftershocks rocked her limp body. Then she simply blacked out.

Chapter Seven

Holly opened her eyes and blinked to adjust to the darkness. Her body was cocooned in warmth, and she let out a drowsy yawn.

She was curled against Adam's chest, his arms wrapped around her. A bare back pressed into hers, and she glanced over her shoulder, trying to see if it was Ethan or Ryan.

Best she could make out, it was Ethan. She frowned. Where was Ryan?

"You're awake," Adam murmured.

She ducked her head shyly, glad he couldn't see her well in the darkness.

His arms tightened around her and he tucked her head under his chin.

"Are you all right?"

She nodded against his chest. She was better than all right. She'd never felt righter in her life.

She snuggled deeper into his chest, loving how safe she felt in his arms. She turned up her face so that her lips were in the direction of his ear.

"Where is Ryan?"

Adam stiffened slightly but continued to rub his hand up and down her back.

"He went to his room," he said quietly.

"Why?"

Adam leaned back on his pillow, taking her with him so her head was cushioned on his arm. He stared up at the ceiling.

"He doesn't sleep well. He has nightmares, and he doesn't want us to hear."

Holly frowned. She knew she'd seen torment in Ryan's eyes, but what could be so bad that even his sleep would be haunted?

"Ryan got back from Iraq a little less than a year ago. He was Special Forces, got captured behind enemy lines. He was a POW for several weeks before our men got in to rescue him. He hasn't been the same since."

"What happened?" she asked in horror, afraid to know what he might have endured.

Adam sighed. "I wish I knew. He won't talk about it."

"Will you two shut up so I can sleep?" Ethan complained, his voice muffled by his pillow.

She grinned and elbowed him in the side.

How natural it felt to be in bed with these two men, comfortable, easy, no awkwardness.

Ethan rolled over and slid his hand up over her breast.

"I'm glad to see we didn't kill you."

She smiled. "But what a way to go."

"Come snuggle me. Adam's gotten you the entire night," Ethan groused.

She giggled but curled into his arms and laid her head on his chest.

"Now shut up and go back to sleep," he muttered.

She closed her eyes, marveling at how truly happy she felt.

When Holly woke again, sunlight streamed through the window, nearly blinding her as she cracked her eyes open. She was alone in the bed, a fact she found disappointing.

A quick glance at the bedside clock told her why she was alone. It was nearly nine.

She stretched, testing the limits of her body. She felt sore, but unbelievably content. She swung her legs over the side of the bed, groaning a little when her muscles protested.

She started to grab the sheet to cover herself then laughed at the absurdity of that notion. Instead, she padded nude across the floor to the bathroom. The idea of a long, hot bath sounded like heaven.

She started the water running, and soon steam filled the large bathroom. When there were several inches of water in the bottom, she stepped in, sighing as the hot water lapped over her.

She leaned back in the tub and closed her eyes, allowing the water to rise around her. Images from the previous night filled her mind. Her body tingled, her thighs clenched, her nipples tightened in response.

It was the single most fantastic experience of her life. If she didn't remain with the brothers, what could she possibly look forward to in the sex department? It wasn't as if she'd find someone else to satisfy her as they had.

And there was the fact that she had no desire to leave. She was tired of running, tired of living in fear, but could she trust that she would be safe here? What if she brought Mason to their doorstep?

Her conversation with Ethan the day before wavered in her mind. The truth was, she could see herself falling in love with them too. Maybe she wasn't yet. Maybe she was on her way much like Ethan had said.

She sighed. She should be happy. Instead, she was filled with dread.

She shook her head, not wanting to get mired down in the muck of her reality. Reaching for the soap, she lathered her body and quickly rinsed. When she was done, she stepped from the water and wrapped a towel around her.

She went in search of her clothes, unsure of where Ryan and Ethan had put them after their shopping trip yesterday. Her stomach clenched. Had it only been yesterday that she had seen Mason in town?

Sweat broke out on her brow as sudden realization hit her. He was but a few miles away.

She sank onto the bed, her breath coming in painful wheezes. It was a full-scale panic attack.

"Holly? What's wrong?"

She looked up to see Ethan standing in the doorway, a look of concern marring his face.

He hurried over and knelt in front of her. He gently pried her hands apart and curled his fingers around hers.

"What is it, doll?"

"Mason's here," she croaked. "He'll find me."

He cupped her chin in his hand and forced her to look at him. "Get dressed and come into the living room. We'll tell you what we've come up with."

She stared at him, daring to hope that maybe they could keep her safe and that she wouldn't be the cause of their death.

He stood and kissed the top of her head. "Your clothes are in the top drawer."

He walked out, leaving her alone to dress.

She rummaged through the drawer and pulled out a shirt and a pair of jeans. To her surprise, she found a package of white cotton underwear and two bras in her size. Ryan must have picked them up at the western store when he was choosing her boots.

She hurriedly dressed and headed for the living room. She paused at the doorway enjoying the sight of the three men. Ryan was sprawled on the couch, beer in hand. Ethan sat at the computer, aimlessly clicking the mouse. Adam stood by the fire, his stance one of impatience.

Adam looked up and saw her, his eyes smoldering much like the flames in the hearth.

Her confidence deserted her. She had the insane urge to turn tail and run back into the bedroom where it was safe. She took one step back, crossing her arms protectively over her chest.

Adam frowned but didn't move. Ryan looked up from the couch and waggled one finger at her from around his beer bottle.

Ethan rose and crossed the room, holding out his hand to her.

"Come on over. We've got a lot to discuss," he said as he pulled her further into the living room.

She eased down onto the couch, inches from Ryan's outstretched feet. She sensed this was the point of no return. They wanted her to stay, and she would have to decide whether to listen to her heart or do everything in her power to keep them from harm.

The weight of the decision pressed down on her like a sandbag.

"It's time to talk," Adam said. He shoved his hands into his pockets and propped the heel of one boot on the hearth behind him.

She glanced at Ethan and Ryan, gauging their reaction. Ethan looked attentive. Ryan's eyes were guarded. No emotion shone on his face.

"We've talked to Cal Davis, a lawyer friend of ours in Denver. He can file the necessary papers for your divorce," Adam said.

Her heart sped up, thumping painfully in her chest. She opened her mouth to speak, but her mouth went dry.

To her surprise, Ryan swung around, planting his feet on the floor. He reached over and tucked her hand in his. The gesture comforted her.

She glanced at him, trying to get a read on his thoughts. Did he still think she didn't want to be free of her husband? After everything that had happened last night?

He stared back at her, not budging in the least. He was stubborn. Well, so was she. She glared defiantly at him, daring him to voice his doubts.

A reluctant smile tugged at his lips.

"Well, Holly," he said lazily. "What's it going to be? Asshole husband or take a chance on three men who'll do everything they can to take care of you?"

"It's not that simple," she said angrily.

Ryan tipped a finger under her chin and stared directly into her eyes. "Yes. It is."

She stood up, wrapping her arms around her waist. "I—I care a lot about you. All of you," she said, sweeping an arm out to encompass all three men. "Don't you see? I couldn't bear it if something happened to any of you because of me."

"Baby, listen to me," Adam said, turning her to face him. "If you believe nothing else of us, believe this. We will not let that bastard get to you."

"It's not me I'm worried about!"

She wanted to scream in frustration. Why couldn't they understand?

"We told you we'd take care of you," Ryan said calmly. "If something happened to us, we couldn't take care of you. Therefore, by making you the promise that we'll protect you, you can be damned sure no pencil-necked bastard is going to touch us."

"You do have a way with words," Ethan said.

The absolute conviction in Ryan's voice made her pause.

"The question is, do you have that kind of faith in us?" Ryan said, raising his brow questioningly at her.

He'd turned it back on her. If she persisted with her protests, she would be demonstrating a lack of faith in them. Damn it. What was she supposed to do?

Adam caught her waist and pulled her against his chest. "Answer one question. If there was no Mason. If you weren't married. Would you stay?"

She nodded before she thought better of her response.

"Then it's settled," Adam said, satisfaction glimmering in his eyes. "We'll tell Cal to proceed with the divorce action, and we'll come up with a plan to make sure the bastard doesn't come within a square mile of you."

She opened her mouth to protest but he shushed her with his finger.

"Trust us, baby."

She sighed. The thing was, she did trust them. It was insane. She'd only known them a few days, and yet she trusted them more than she'd ever trusted another living soul.

"Okay," she said quietly.

Adam bent his head and kissed her hungrily. His hand shoved into her hair and kneaded the back of her neck as his tongue delved into her mouth.

When he pulled away, she was breathless.

"Well, I must say, this is a surprise," a feminine voice drawled.

Holly whirled around to see a tall redhead in a cowboy hat and wearing a badge.

Adam swore. "Damn it, Lacey, don't you know how to knock?

Chapter Eight

Ryan grasped Holly's wrist and shoved her behind him. His face darkened into a thundercloud, and Adam stepped forward in an effort to defuse a potentially explosive situation. He knew Ryan didn't like Lacey at all, and if she posed a threat to Holly, Adam wasn't sure what Ryan would do.

"What the hell are you doing here, and what do you want?" Adam demanded.

Lacey raised a brow in surprise at his vehemence.

"The question is what is she doing here?" Lacey said with a nod in Holly's direction. "Unless I'm mistaken, she bears an uncanny resemblance to the woman on a missing person's report lying on my desk."

Fuck, fuck, fuck. Why did Lacey have to show up now of all times?

"Her husband claims she was abducted," Lacey continued. "What does the lady have to say about that?"

"I wasn't kidnapped," Holly said hotly.

Ryan shoved her back behind him and glared harder at Lacey.

"As you can see, she's perfectly fine," Ryan said icily. "I'm sure your services are required elsewhere. They aren't here."

Lacey flinched. "You never did like me." She shook her head. "But that's not the point. The point is I have a worried husband searching for his missing wife. Now if she's here of her own free will, that's her business, but I need her to come to the station with me and give me a statement. Away from any undue influence," she said looking pointedly at the three brothers.

"Over my dead body," Adam growled.

"She's not going anywhere near her bastard husband," Ethan spoke up.

Lacey sighed and moved her hand to rest on her hip, mere inches from her gun. "You guys aren't going to make this easy I see."

"I'll go," Holly said softly, moving in front of Ryan.

Adam's chest clenched at the blatant fear in her eyes.

"No, baby. You're not going."

She turned troubled eyes on him. "I won't cause you any trouble. I'll go."

"Fuck that," Ryan said. "Lacey can take your damn statement here."

"Look, I don't know what the hell is going on here, but I need to hear Mrs. Bardwell's version. One that isn't colored by three huge-ass men glowering over her shoulder. She'll need to come with me. Don't make me force the issue, Adam. You know I don't want to have to do that."

"What the fuck is your problem, Lacey?" Ethan interjected, surprising Adam with the anger in his voice.

"I'm doing my job," she said in an even voice. "You lied to me when I asked if you'd seen her. I have a very important man raising all sorts of hell in my town looking for his missing wife. His new wife I might add. Now I find her here. She looks frightened out of her mind, so you'll have to excuse me if I want to hear from her own mouth what the hell is going on."

"It's not *us* she's frightened of," Ryan pointed out.

"Fine, then she can come with me and explain," Lacey said.

Holly sucked in her breath, trying valiantly not to panic. She couldn't allow the brothers to get into trouble because they were protecting her. And it was time she stood up for herself. Adam had said his friend could handle her divorce. She would have to go with this Lacey person and explain as much as she dared. Otherwise all hell might break loose.

She moved toward the tall woman, determined not to be intimidated. Ryan caught at her arm and tried to drag her back.

She turned to him, trying to keep the fear from her eyes. "I have to do this," she said.

"We'll go with you," Ryan said.

She shook her head. "No, you can't. This is something *I* have to do."

Uncertainty flashed in Ryan's eyes, and for a brief moment, she could swear she saw fear. Then his expression hardened into an impenetrable mask.

"I'll come back," she said softly.

"I don't like it," Ethan broke in.

"Her husband goes nowhere near her," Adam bit out. "You hear me, Lacey? You get your damn statement, but you keep that bastard away from her. I'm charging you with her safety."

Holly shivered at the hardness in his voice. Lacey blanched but nodded.

Hand on her holster, Lacey dipped her head toward the door. "After you, ma'am."

Holly turned to look at the three brothers, a sudden surge of uncertainty gripping her. She didn't want to leave the safe haven she'd found here.

Before she could follow Lacey, Adam stepped forward and hauled her against him. His lips found hers, pressing hungrily against her as if infusing his strength into her.

Lacey cleared her throat by the door, and Holly turned to leave. She stepped into the cold and shivered. She hadn't thought to get her coat.

She trekked to the Jeep Cherokee, her boots crunching in the snow. Lacey gestured toward the passenger seat before stalking around to the driver's side.

Holly slid into the warm interior, grateful Lacey had left the engine running. She glanced out the window as Lacey backed out of the drive, a knot swelling in her throat as they drifted further away from the cabin.

"We can't just let her go!" Ethan said.

Ryan stood where Holly had left him, staring broodingly at the door.

Adam scrubbed a hand through his hair and wondered what the hell they had done. "I don't trust that bastard as far as I could throw him. I vote we ride into town and keep an eye on things. If she needs us, we'll be a lot more use than if we sit here on our fucking hands."

Ethan nodded his agreement.

Adam looked at Ryan who still hadn't moved. "You coming, bro?"

"She left," he said in a strained voice. "How do we know she'll want to come back?"

Even as the statement angered Adam, he knew Ryan was voicing his fears.

"She left to protect us," Ethan snarled. "It's our job to protect *her*."

"Let's go, we're wasting time," Adam said. He had no desire to mediate a fight between his younger siblings.

Holly and Lacey rode into town in silence. As Lacey pulled up to the small wooden building that housed the sheriff's department, Holly stiffened. Her heart began to thunder. Mason's BMW was parked a few feet away.

"You didn't say he would be here," she said, turning her furious gaze on Lacey.

Lacey shrugged. "He's your husband. Where else would he be? He's been worried sick about you."

"You know nothing about my husband," Holly spat.

Lacey sized her up in a quick glance. "Look, he says you were kidnapped. If you weren't, fine. Just come inside, sign a statement and you can be on your way."

Holly fumbled with the door, her hands shaking. She stepped onto the icy pavement and waited for Lacey to precede her into the station.

At the doorway, she wiped her sweaty palms down the legs of her jeans. She would find courage. She would. She could do this. Mason couldn't hurt her in front of a witness, and she wouldn't go with him, no matter what. This was her chance to be rid of him.

"Darling! There you are!"

She cringed as Mason's voice echoed across the room. Just as quickly she found herself yanked into his arms. She pulled away, putting as much distance as she could between them.

Mason turned to Lacey. "Thank you so much for returning my wife to me. If you don't mind, we'll be on our way. I want to make sure she hasn't been harmed in any way."

Holly gasped. "I'm not going anywhere with you."

Mason rounded on her, his back to Lacey. His eyes glittered dangerously. "I realize what an ordeal you've been through, my love. I'll take you far away from this shit hole."

Holly backed away, looking to Lacey for help.

Lacey cleared her throat. "Mr. Bardwell, your wife claims she wasn't abducted. She's here of her own free will and apparently has no wish to leave."

Mason whirled back around but Holly could see he donned his most charming smile. "I appreciate your concern for my wife, but this is a private matter best resolved between us. Perhaps we could have a moment of privacy."

"No!" Holly cried.

"I'm afraid that's impossible, Mr. Bardwell. Unless that is what Mrs. Bardwell wishes?"

She looked to Holly for confirmation.

Holly shook her head vehemently. "You said all I had to do was sign a statement. I won't go with him."

Mason reached out and grasped her arm in a bruising grip. His fingers dug painfully into her upper arm, and she gasped in pain. "I've arranged a flight out of Denver. We must be on our way soon if we're to catch it."

She stared over at Lacey who looked a little flustered. "Can we have a moment? Two minutes. If I'm not outside that door in two minutes, come in for me."

Lacey arched a brow in surprise but nodded. "I'll be outside." She pinned Mason with a hard stare. "Don't try anything stupid, Mr. Bardwell."

As soon as Lacey disappeared through the door, Holly wrenched her arm free and backed hastily away from Mason.

"Stay the hell away from me," she hissed. "I'm never going back with you."

"Maybe you don't remember what happens when you defy me," he said, his voice carrying a heavy warning.

She jerked her chin up, determined not to show him the horrible fear that ate at her. Instead, she took a huge gamble.

"I know what you did on our wedding day," she said quietly. "I saw you kill that man."

Mason's lips compressed in a fine white line. "Don't threaten me, Holly. I'll make you sorry you were ever born."

"Don't you threaten *me!*" she countered. "I am going to file for divorce, Mason, and you are going to give me that divorce or I swear to God, I'll go to the media, the police, the FBI, whoever I have to go to in order to tell the world what a sorry bastard you are."

Mason's eyes flared in surprise. "You little blackmailing bitch."

She clenched her teeth. "I am going to walk out of here, and I'm never going back with you. If you ever come near me again, if you ever so much as breathe my name, I'll make sure you rot in prison."

Surprise flickered in Mason's eyes. He'd underestimated her. She could read it in his expression. Well, that was fine. But she'd make damn sure he didn't do it again.

The door opened and Lacey walked back in. "Everything okay in here?" She eyed Holly as she spoke.

"I was just leaving," Mason said, anger coloring his voice. "Apparently a mistake has been made."

He stalked by Lacey and slammed the door behind him.

A buzzing started in Holly's ears, and she felt dangerously close to fainting.

"Here," Lacey said, shoving a chair at her. "Maybe you ought to sit down."

Holly sank into the chair, her hands curled into fists in her lap. She'd done it. She'd faced Mason and stood up to him. Now she just wanted to get back to Adam, Ethan and Ryan.

"Can I use your phone?" Holly asked hoarsely.

Lacey gestured toward the desk. "Be my guest."

Holly rose and walked over to the desk then realized she didn't even know the phone number to the cabin. Her cheeks flaming, she looked up at Lacey. "Do you know Adam's phone number?"

Lacey rattled off the number with a familiarity that bothered Holly.

She punched the numbers and waited anxiously as it rang. After ten rings, she gently replaced the receiver, her chest tightening in worry.

"You could try the cell phone," Lacey said dryly.

Heat raced across Holly's face again, but she picked up the phone and looked expectantly at Lacey. After punching in the series of numbers Lacey once again supplied, she raised the phone to her ear and waited.

The brothers were nearly to town when Adam's cell phone rang. Adam snatched it up and barked a hello.

"Adam?"

Holly's soft voice filtered over the line.

"Baby, are you all right?" he demanded.

"Can you...can you come get me?"

"Where are you?"

"I'm at the sheriff's office," she replied.

"We'll be there in five minutes," he promised. "Are you okay?"

"I'm fine," she said, her voice stronger than before.

"Hang tight, baby. We'll be right there."

He hung up and tossed the phone aside. He had a dozen questions he'd wanted to ask, but his priority was getting to Holly as fast as he could.

"What's going on?" Ethan demanded.

"She wants us to come get her at the sheriff's office," Adam replied.

He glanced at Ryan in his rearview mirror and saw relief flash across his brother's face.

They roared into town and down the street toward the sheriff's office. Adam frowned when a BMW nearly took off the front end of the Land Rover.

"Son of a bitch," Ethan swore. "That's her husband."

Adam slammed on the brakes, opening the door before the Land Rover came to a complete stop. Had the bastard taken her? Had Lacey let him walk out with her?

The brothers hit the pavement running.

Adam was first to the door and flung it open, scanning the interior for Holly. Tension left him when he saw her huddled behind a desk. She looked up and, with a small cry, launched herself across the room and into his arms.

She hit him square in the chest, and he caught her up in his arms.

"Thank God you're all right," he said in a low voice.

She clung to him tightly, her face buried in his neck.

"I did it," she whispered. "I told him I wanted a divorce."

Adam stroked her hair and kissed her temple, all the while satisfaction humming through his veins. Reluctantly, he set her down. Just as quickly, Ethan folded her up in his arms, holding on as tight to her as Adam had. Ethan kissed her lingeringly, his relief over her safety evident.

Across the room, Lacey's mouth fell open. Then her eyes widened in understanding. Adam knew the realization had hit her.

"It wasn't me," she said faintly. "It was never me. It was *them.*"

Adam didn't pretend to misunderstand. He ran a hand through his hair and walked a few steps closer to Lacey.

"I made a mistake," he said honestly. "You're a good woman, Lacey."

"Not good enough apparently," she said bitterly.

Adam sighed. He hadn't wanted this scene between them and especially not in front of Holly. Once he'd been attracted to Lacey, even thought his brothers might feel the same, but they hadn't. Ethan had reacted indifferently to her, and Ryan had instantly disliked her. He knew then it would never work between them, but it hadn't stopped him from spending time with her on occasion. She'd been good company and someone to have a beer with. But she wasn't the one destined to occupy a place in his heart. That was reserved for Holly.

He gazed at the hurt he saw in Lacey's eyes and wished he wasn't the cause of it.

"We should be going," Ryan said, speaking up for the first time. "It's supposed to snow."

"I need her to sign that statement," Lacey said flatly. "Then y'all can be on your way."

She rummaged around on her desk for a moment then flipped a piece of paper and a pen to the end. Holly approached and looked down at the blank paper.

"What should I say?" she asked softly.

"Whatever's on your mind," Laccy drawled. "I'm married but don't want to be. Or maybe, I'm fucking with the minds of four men." She shrugged. "Just make it quick. I've got work to do."

"That's enough, Lacey," Adam said, his voice harsher than he intended.

Holly scribbled three lines then signed her name with a flourish. She flicked the pen back across the desk at Lacey then turned away. She walked toward the door where Ryan and Ethan still stood, her intention clear. She was ready to go.

"Let me get your coat," Ryan said gruffly. "You forgot to bring it."

He ducked out of the office and was back within thirty seconds carrying Holly's coat. He helped her into it then wrapped his arm protectively around her.

"I'm taking her out to the Rover."

Adam nodded and watched as Ethan followed them outside. He turned back to Lacey, his lips pulled thin.

"I understand you're upset, but that's no reason to be a bitch to Holly."

Lacey's cheeks flamed at his reprimand.

"Why didn't you ever tell me they had to accept me too?" she demanded.

"Because they didn't," he said quietly.

"So I never had a chance."

Adam shook his head. "No."

Her fingers curled into fists at her sides. "Well then, there isn't much more to say is there? Have a nice life with your helpless little doll."

Adam's eyelids narrowed at her insult, but he refused to be baited into further argument. Holly waited for him to take her home. And that was all that mattered.

He turned and walked away.

Chapter Nine

Holly slid into the backseat with Ryan while Ethan got into the front. Despite the warmth of her coat, she shivered. Mostly in reaction to the last hour.

Beside her, Ryan shrugged out of his coat leaving him in a t-shirt that stretched tightly across his muscled chest and shoulders.

She wanted nothing more than to burrow into that chest, but she hesitated. She still wasn't sure where she stood with Ryan. He seemed to have a lot of mistrust regarding her. So she focused her attention out the window and waited for Adam to come out.

She would have to be a fool not to notice the sparks between Adam and Lacey, and that bothered her. Bothered her a lot. Had they been lovers? There was more than idle interest burning in the redhead's eyes. And then there was her comment about Ethan and Ryan which led Holly to believe Adam had wanted Lacey but his brothers hadn't.

She frowned and closed her eyes. She was tired and mentally exhausted, and she didn't like to dwell on the burning jealousy in her gut.

She barely registered the door opening and closing as Adam got in. He turned to look at her, but she didn't meet his gaze, wasn't sure she wanted to see what was there. She was feeling way too insecure to try and figure out what the hell was going on between him and Lacey.

They backed out of the small parking lot and headed out of town. And further from Mason.

She began to shake in earnest as the reality of what she had done hit her. She'd stood up to the bastard and won. Now maybe the awful fear that gnawed at her gut would go away.

A warm hand kneaded and massaged her neck. She glanced over to see Ryan staring at her. She searched his face for some sign of what he was thinking, but could find no clue.

"Come here," he said.

She flew into his arms and buried her face in his hard chest. Strong arms wrapped around her and a hand rubbed up and down her back.

"I'm proud of you," he whispered.

Tears streaked down her face as relief poured out of her system. So many weeks of constant fear had eaten away at her. Now she was free.

She snuggled deeper into Ryan's arms, curling herself as close into him as she could.

The next thing she knew the engine had stopped and cold air brushed over her as a door opened. Had she fallen asleep? All she really knew was that she had no desire to move from Ryan's arms. Reluctantly she picked her head up. They were back at the cabin.

She slid over as Adam opened the door for her then she climbed out of the Land Rover. She pulled her coat tighter around her and hurried for the front door, anxious to be inside where it was warm.

They all entered the house, stamping the snow off their feet inside the door.

"I'm hungry," she announced, realizing she hadn't eaten a thing since the day before.

"Go warm up in front of the fire, and I'll start on lunch," Ethan said, pushing her toward the living room.

Adam and Ryan followed her and Adam went to add more logs to the dying embers.

"So what happened in there?" Ryan asked.

Adam paused in his task and turned to look at Holly, obviously wanting to hear as well.

"Mason was there when we got to the sheriff's office," Holly began.

Adam swore. "Lacey must have known he was there all along."

"He tried to leave immediately, but I refused to go with him. I thought he was going to force the issue, but Lacey wouldn't let him. I asked Lacey to leave us alone for a few minutes."

"You did what?" Ryan demanded, his expression darkening.

"It was the only way," she said. "I told him that I knew what he'd done on our wedding day, that I'd seen him kill that man. Then I told him I wanted a divorce, and he was going to agree to that divorce or I'd make sure the whole world knew what he'd done."

"Fuck," Ryan said.

"Yeah, fuck is right," Adam said, rubbing the back of his neck.

She looked at them in surprise. "But I thought you wanted me to get a divorce."

"Baby, we do," Adam said, pulling her into his arms. "But we want you safe, and you've just told us that the bastard now knows you can put him away for life."

"It was the only way to get him to agree to the divorce," she said defensively.

Adam rubbed her shoulders soothingly. "Don't worry about it, baby. You'll get your divorce, but more importantly, you won't ever have to face that bastard again."

Ethan called to them from the doorway. "I threw together some sandwiches. Come eat."

Holly turned and walked toward the kitchen. Had she made a mistake by threatening Mason? She frowned, worry inserting itself back into her mind.

She sat down at the bar and Ethan shoved a plate in front of her. The brothers took their places, and they began to eat.

"What now?" she asked, unable to keep the question back any longer.

"What do you mean?" Adam asked.

She hesitated a moment, feeling unsure about the entire situation. "I mean us."

"We go to Denver to see Cal so he can fast-track your divorce. And then we get on with our lives. Together."

She looked down at her plate and fiddled with the sandwich. A thousand questions crowded her mind, and she didn't know where to start.

"Want to go riding after lunch?" Ryan interrupted.

She looked at him in relief. Fresh air and a break sounded very inviting. She nodded then caught herself.

"I assume you mean horseback riding? I haven't ridden in a long while."

Ryan shrugged. "I'll make sure you have a good mount."

"Don't go too far," Adam warned. "We're in for a storm."

"I don't need a babysitter," Ryan said darkly.

Holly shoved her plate aside, no longer hungry. Maybe getting out of the house for a while would help. She wanted to relax and not worry about looking over her shoulder for once.

Ryan pushed away from the table. "You ready?"

She nodded and stood up. "Let me go get something warmer on."

"I'll be in the barn. Head on out when you're done."

"They're a lot alike you know."

Adam turned his head to Ethan after watching Holly leave the room. "What do you mean?"

"Ryan and Holly," Ethan replied. "They both know pain. You can see it in their eyes."

Adam's lips tightened. He didn't like to think of either of them in pain, but he knew Ethan was right. Holly and his younger brother fought their demons. He just hoped they won.

"What do you suppose happened over there?" Adam muttered.

Ethan shook his head, sorrow washing into his eyes. "I wish to hell I knew. I wish he'd talk about it. Maybe then the poison would leave his system. I never wanted him to join the damn military anyway."

Adam nodded in agreement. But Ryan was stubborn, and once he'd made the decision, no one had been able to sway him. He'd left a cocky, arrogant young man and come back a brooding, tortured soul.

"Maybe she's what he needs," Ethan murmured. "Maybe she's what we all need."

"And maybe she needs us just as badly," Adam added.

Holly stepped into the snow, shivering as a wash of cold air blew over her. She crunched her way down the slight incline to the barn. Ahead of her the terrain sloped upward, a testament to the mountain they were nestled on. Snow-capped peaks jutted skyward on the horizon. Around her the world was ablaze with white.

Her breath came out in a cloud in front of her as she mounted the last few steps to the barn door. Then she slipped inside, enjoying the warmth that greeted her.

Eight stalls lined either side of the barn. In the back, there was a large open area where stacks of hay bails stood. Ryan stepped out of one of the stalls leading a horse by the reins.

He glanced in her direction. "I've got her saddled for you. Come hold the reins while I ready my mount then we'll head out."

Holly hurried forward and took the leather reins from Ryan.

Ryan motioned toward the back. "Take her over there and wait."

Holly moved to the back, her horse clopping obediently behind her. While she waited for Ryan, she smoothed her hands over the mare's neck. She was a beauty. Gentle looking. Her head bobbed appreciatively as Holly stroked her mane.

A few seconds later, Ryan walked up, leading his mount behind him. "You ready?"

Holly nodded. As Ryan moved ahead of her, she cast an appreciative glance over his body. Damn, the man filled out a pair of jeans like no one else. He looked exceedingly masculine in his lambskin-lined coat, cowboy hat and scuffed boots. And his ass. What could she say about a man who had an ass that begged to be touched, fondled and squeezed?

She squeezed her legs together and picked up her pace. She was a walking hormone. But who could blame her after the night she'd experienced? Her cheeks warmed to the point of discomfort when she thought of all they had done. She couldn't wait to do it again.

"Do you need help up?" Ryan asked, his voice close to her ear.

She jumped and looked around. Hell, she hadn't even realized they'd walked outside. Hard to notice the cold when her entire body was erupting in flames.

She flushed and turned her attention to the horse. She was short, and it was a long way up into the saddle.

She looked back at Ryan. He grinned and in one swift motion, he wrapped his large hands around her waist and hoisted her up as easily as a sack of potatoes.

"Misty's a good mount. She'll follow my lead, so don't worry about it. Just enjoy yourself," Ryan said.

She smiled down at him. His hand lingered on her leg then he squeezed it before he walked over to mount his horse.

They picked their way through the snow around to the front of the cabin and down the drive to the road. Holly glanced back at the cabin. It was fully ensconced on the mountain as if the brothers had carved their home right into the surface. Snow covered the roof, and smoke drifted lazily from the stone chimney. It looked like a scene straight from a Christmas card. And it was now her home.

Her chest tightened, and she had the absurd urge to grin like a kid in a candy store. Home.

Life was a strange chain of ironies. She'd learned that quickly enough. Only in the demise of her dreams had she actually found them.

But would it work out?

A shadow of doubt marred her jubilation. She'd thought Mason was the answer to her dreams. Wealthy, seemingly doting on her, protective. The stuff a girl's dreams were made of. Or nightmares.

Was she making the same mistake again? She sure hadn't given any more thought or care to this decision than she had the one to marry Mason, and it had landed her in a kettle of hot water.

She frowned. If there had never been a Mason, if she had never made such a monumental mistake, if she hadn't desperately needed a place to run and hide, would she have been drawn to the brothers and what they offered?

She fought to try and place herself in the frame of mind she'd been in before she'd ever met Mason, but found it impossible to match the woman she'd become to who she'd been.

Her head hurt. She was trying too hard to analyze her feelings. She knew what she thought she felt for the brothers, but what if she was wrong? What if her attraction to them was merely a measure of self-preservation? Gratitude for the safe haven they provided?

Fuck a duck.

It wasn't fair to them. They wanted a woman who could love all three of them, not a woman who couldn't think for herself, who was a weak mess, one who'd made one bad decision after another.

"If you frown any harder, you're going to screw up that pretty face of yours forever," Ryan said mildly.

She glanced up, guilty heat suffusing her cheeks. She hadn't even been paying attention to him, her horse or where they were going. And Ryan knew it.

"Sorry," she said in a low voice. "I was just thinking."

Ryan shrugged. "It's why I asked if you wanted to go out for a while. You looked like you could use a break."

He turned back around in his saddle and stared ahead, silence looming between them once more.

She sighed. He wasn't pushy. She liked that. But then none of the brothers had pushed her hard. Adam could be demanding. Any fool could see that, but he hadn't pressed her boundaries.

"It's beautiful here," she said, focusing her attention on Ryan.

He nodded. "No place on earth is more beautiful than the Rockies."

He loved it here. She could tell by the way his eyes scraped across the landscape. Some of the bleakness and torment he wore like a permanent tattoo disappeared, replaced by satisfaction.

"How did you all end up here?" she asked.

He shrugged again. "We grew up on a ranch. It was only natural that we'd want one of our own. And we like to hunt. So we decided to combine those factors and make our living at it."

She thought on that a moment. The cabin they lived in was large. Though they didn't take meals in the dining room, the room sported a table that could easily sit two dozen people. And there were several rooms she hadn't explored yet. An uneasy thought crept into her mind.

"So when it's hunting season, there'll be lots of hunters in the cabin?" she asked.

He studied her for a moment as if delving into her thoughts.

"Are you worried about what they'll think?" he asked, his tone slightly challenging.

"I don't know," she said honestly. "I mean I don't know how I'll be presented. How do you introduce me to other people?"

"As our woman," he said.

Her stomach turned over. On the one hand, it did funny things to her, the idea of three sexy as hell men claiming her as their woman, but on the other hand, it could be awkward as hell.

"You'll get used to it," he said.

She felt her cheek warming again as another thought struck her. One she hadn't considered, but in light of their very different relationship, she wasn't sure.

She cleared her throat, wondering how to present such an awkward question.

Ryan sighed. "Just say it, Holly. Whatever's on your mind. I don't bite."

She stared up at him, sure she was growing redder by the minute. "It's just that I wondered, that is I wasn't sure..." She took another steadying breath. "You won't want there to be others, right?"

His eyes darkened and a scowl twisted his features. "I'll kill any other man who touches you."

Her breath eased from her in relief.

Ryan scrubbed a hand over his chin. "Holly, just because we have a different situation, in that all three of us are fucking the same woman, it doesn't mean we're going to be sharing you with every man who crosses our path. You're ours. You belong to us, heart and soul, and if another man so much as looks at you, we'll rip off his dick and cram it down his throat."

She couldn't help it. She laughed. Then she sobered. "I hope you all aren't making a mistake," she said quietly.

He tipped up his Stetson to get a better look at her. "Are we making a mistake, Holly?"

She flinched under his frank appraisal. "I don't want you to be making a mistake," she whispered. "I don't want any of this to be a mistake."

"Maybe you're rushing things," he said. "There's no hurry. We've got all the time in the world."

She drew comfort from his words. And maybe she *had* felt rushed. As if she should immediately feel right with the situation she found herself—no, that she chose to be—in. Relationships took time, even if she had a habit of hurling herself into them. It sounded as though they were more than willing to grant her time, and for that she was grateful.

She was surprised to see they were nearing the cabin again. She hadn't even paid attention to their ride, so deep in her thoughts she'd been.

They rode around to the back and stopped outside the barn. Ryan slid from his horse then held up a hand to help her down. She landed inches from him, his body heat reaching out and enveloping her. He smelled so damn sexy. Just like a man should. Of wood, leather and a hint of wildness.

She placed her hand on his hard chest, unable to resist the temptation. His heat seared her palm. He growled low in his throat.

"Let's get the horses in before I fuck you right here in the snow," he said.

Goose bumps assaulted every inch of her body. Her nipples tightened and streaks of pleasure burned between her legs at his explicit words.

Her hands shaking, she followed him into the barn. She watched as he groomed the horses. She imagined it was her his hands roamed over instead of the horse. Sweat beaded on her brow. She wanted him. Right here. Right now. And if she could gain the courage, what was to stop her from taking what she wanted?

Chapter Ten

Holly's courage deserted her halfway to Ryan. As if sensing her approach, he turned around after locking the stall. He studied her for a moment.

"Did you want something?"

What a question. She swallowed. Then swallowed again.

"I want you," she said simply, it all coming out in a quick rush

He flashed her a sexy, arrogant grin.

"Then come get me," he said, spreading his arms out in a gesture or surrender.

She trembled with nervousness, but she walked slowly toward him. Her gaze focused on the bulge in his jeans, the bulge that had grown larger with her announcement. She knew precisely what she wanted to do with it. She wanted to taste it again. Like she had done before.

With shaking hands, she reached out for the button of his jeans. She heard his quick intake of breath when she worked it free. She pulled the zipper down until she could see the band of his underwear.

"Take it out," she whispered. "I want to see you pull it out."

Somehow the image of him pulling his cock out of his pants excited her wildly. She wanted that image to come to life.

"Get on your knees," he rasped.

She hastily complied, and he reached into his pants and pulled out his erection. She reached up, wanting to touch it. She curled her hands around it. It was inches from her lips, straining, hard as a rock.

She flicked her tongue out and delicately swirled it around the broad head. He flinched and groaned then moved forward, seeking more of her mouth.

She wrapped her hand around the base of his cock and guided him toward her lips. She let him rest on her lips for the merest of seconds before sucking him gently into her mouth.

"Ah damn, sweetheart. That's it. Take it all."

His hand tangled in her hair as he gripped the back of her neck. His hips surged forward as he thrust into her mouth.

She delighted in the contrast of soft, smooth skin and iron hardness. He tasted exotic, all male, like he smelled. Silky fluid spilled on her tongue as he surged to the back of her throat. She wanted more. She wanted to make him come. Make him as wild for her as she felt in his arms.

Soft sucking noises filled the barn. They sounded erotic to her ears and spurred her excitement. She drew him in then slid her mouth back down the length of him until the tip rested against her tongue.

"You're a temptress," he said hoarsely.

She smiled. She *felt* like a temptress. Gloried in it. She let his cock fall from her mouth and ran her tongue down the underside, following the thick vein down to his balls. She sucked one in her mouth, loving the way his entire body tightened. She lavished attention on the other, sucking and laving with her tongue.

"You have to stop," he choked out. "Or I'm gonna come."

She sat back on her heels and flashed him a wicked smile. "That's the point."

He hauled her up against him and slammed his mouth down over hers. Their tongues dueled. Their lips met in breathless gasps.

"Get your damn pants off," he demanded.

She wasted no time shucking first her boots and then her jeans. He reached down and ripped her underwear, the slight material tearing easily from her body. Before she could register what he was doing, he hoisted her up in his arms, spreading her legs around his waist.

In one hard plunge, he thrust deeply into her wetness. She cried out, the noise echoing over the barn. Her pussy convulsed around his cock, milking him, inviting him further.

He held her tightly with one arm and began yanking her coat off with the other. As soon as she was free, he wrapped both arms around her waist and began thrusting into her. She felt the denim of his jeans scratch at her ass as he worked his way further into her.

She wrapped her arms around his neck and threw her head back in abandon.

"You are so fucking beautiful," he said tightly.

Buried deeply within her, he moved her back until she was firmly against the wall of the barn. Then he began to fuck her in earnest.

He kissed and sucked his way over her shoulder to her neck, and when he reached the delicate skin just below her ear, he sank his teeth in.

Her hands fisted in his hair. She wasn't gentle. But neither was he. She yanked his head from her neck and fused their lips together. She was hungry. Hungry for him and she couldn't get enough.

He fucked harder and harder, her back slamming against the wall. She didn't care. She wanted him deeper.

His hands crept downward, over the globes of her ass until he cupped both in his palms. He spread her wider to meet his thrusts. She felt his fingers feather across the tight entrance to her ass, and she tightened.

"Relax," he whispered against her ear.

Before she could react, he thrust one finger inside. She bucked against him, the tight pinch of pain nearly sending her over the edge into a mind-blowing orgasm.

Then another finger joined the first. His cock was wedged tight in her pussy, his fingers pressing into her ass. It was more than she could stand. He pulled back, and then slammed into her at the same time he pushed his fingers further into her tight opening.

She exploded at the seams.

"Oh God, don't stop now!" she wailed.

He held her up, supporting her in his strong arms as he fucked long, hard strokes. Thank God, because she would have completely wilted. Her body went flying into a million directions as her orgasm consumed her. She saw bright flashes of color then she squeezed her eyes shut, no longer able to bear the sensations.

"Oh God, baby, I'm coming," he shouted hoarsely in her ear.

She slumped forward onto his chest, her arms wrapping weakly around him as he flooded into her pussy. His hips bucked underneath her ass, his zipper pressing into the soft flesh of her backside.

She rested her face in his neck, her breath coming in gasps. His arms wrapped around her, holding her close, his cock still buried deep inside her. They stood that way for several long moments until finally he pulled her face from his neck and kissed her gently.

"Can you stand?" he asked huskily as he lifted her slightly so that his cock fell free.

She nodded, though she was altogether unsure she could. He let her slide carefully down his body, holding onto her until he was sure she could support her weight.

He tucked his cock back into his pants and buttoned the fly back up. Then he reached for her, holding her against his chest. He rested his chin on top of her head, and they stood in silence.

As her body calmed, the chilly air blew across her exposed bottom half. She shivered in his arms and he pulled away. He hurried over to where her jeans lay in a heap on the ground and retrieved them.

She pulled them on then found herself just as quickly back in Ryan's arms. He bent his head and kissed her. Thoroughly, leisurely. Slower than his usual hot as hell pace.

She sighed against his lips and sagged against his chest. She was as weak as a kitten, but completely sated.

"Let's get you back to the house," Ryan said, his deep voice rumbling his chest against her cheek.

She rummaged for her boots and coat, pulled them on then followed Ryan out of the barn. They stepped into the kitchen, stamping the snow from their feet. She shrugged out of her coat, pulled her boots off again and padded into the living room.

It amazed her that already she sought out the presence of the others. Wanted to know where they were. Felt secure around them.

Adam was on the computer and Ethan was sprawled on the couch watching television. She walked over and crawled onto the couch with Ethan, her confidence bolstered by her act in the barn. Besides, she wanted a good cuddle after her romp with Ryan.

Ethan snaked his arm around her and nestled her against his chest. His brow arched as he took in her rumpled appearance.

"You and Ryan have a good time?"

She flushed and ducked her head, resting it on his shoulder.

He chuckled as he smoothed her hair from her cheek. She yawned and snuggled closer against his body.

Chapter Eleven

When Holly awoke, she found herself alone on the couch. She blinked sleepily and looked around the room to find it empty. Yawning broadly, she sat up and squinted at the clock. At least she hadn't slept the entire day away.

She got up and padded to the kitchen. A glance out the pane glass of the back door told her Adam was chopping wood. She guessed Ethan and Ryan were either tending the horses or doing other chores.

She sat down on one of the barstools and cupped her chin in her palms. What was she going to do here? What kind of contribution could she make? She knew from her talks with the men that they guided during hunting season, but she wasn't entirely sure what they did for the rest of the year.

A disgusted sigh escaped her. She mentally ticked off her qualities and stopped before she reached five. She wasn't a brainless twit, but even she had to admit, she hadn't done much in life on her own.

Poor little rich girl. She winced at the apt description then shook her head in denial. No, she wasn't that helpless creature any longer.

Her parents had both been killed in the same accident when she was still a teenager. A distant cousin had overseen her inheritance until she reached twenty-one at which point she'd been solidly on her own. Only it hadn't taken her long to seek the shelter of Mason's authority.

A wry smile twisted her lips. She'd been such an idiot. Thank God she'd waken up and taken steps to protect herself before it was too late. She had no doubt had she stayed with Mason, she'd probably be dead. Or worse. Completely under his thumb.

Here, she felt free. Free to be herself. Free of her stupid past. It was a chance to start over and finally do things right. Make the right choices.

"Don't screw this up, Holly," she muttered.

She glanced again at the clock then stood up. She had time for a shower before supper. When the men came in, she'd ask what she could do to help out around the cabin.

Holly walked into the bathroom and turned on the shower. She stepped away and slipped out of her pants then walked to the sink in just her shirt while she waited for the water to heat.

She glanced at her reflection in the mirror and winced at the god-awful color of her hair. When they went to Denver, she was going to make a stop at a salon so she could get them to repair the dye job.

Behind her, she saw steam start to rise from the shower. She began to unbutton her flannel shirt when the door opened. She looked up to see Ethan walk in.

He paused for a moment before moving behind her. He cupped her shoulders in his hands and bent to press a kiss to her neck.

She shivered, goose bumps rippling up her spine.

"Want company?" he murmured.

She smiled and turned around until she was cradled in his arms. "Are you offering to scrub my back?"

"I'm offering to do a lot more," he said wickedly.

"Then I'll meet you there."

She grinned and shrugged out of her shirt. Then she moved around him and slipped into the shower.

She barely had time to move under the hot spray before the shower door opened and a very naked, very aroused Ethan stepped in.

Her eyes devoured him. Water beaded in his hair and ran down his neck then trickled down the muscled wall of his chest to his tight abdomen. From there it disappeared into the thatch of hair surrounding his bulging erection.

He reached for her hands then pulled them high above her head, pressing her against the shower wall. The water coursed over them both as he bent his head to kiss her.

His hard body covered hers, rocked against her with the promise of what was to come.

She tried to pull one of her hands away. She wanted to touch him. But he kept them locked above her.

His cock nudged her soft belly as his mouth burned an erotic trail down the curve of her neck.

Then he let her go.

"Turn around," he commanded.

She turned her body until her back was nestled against his chest. He reached around her for the bar of soap and lathered it on his hands.

He started at her stomach, kneading and softly soaping. Then he worked his way up to her breasts, cupping them in his hands, rolling the nipples between his fingers.

She moaned and leaned further back into him.

His right hand smoothed back down her skin, down to her pelvis. He rubbed lightly then slid his hand between her legs.

117

With his left hand, he continued his attentions on her breasts, but his right hand burrowed further between her legs, sliding, teasing, spreading her folds.

She writhed against him, tension building in her body, stretching her impossibly.

Then his finger slid over her clit and her legs spasmed and threatened to fold on her.

Without warning, his hands left her, and she felt herself being pushed belly first against the wall of the shower as water continued to rain down on them.

The wall felt cool, the water felt hot, and her body trembled in anticipation as she felt him spread her legs.

Again, he raised her hands above her head and continued to nudge her legs apart with his thigh. She felt his cock brush against her ass then settle between her legs. With his knee, he propped her ass up enough to position himself at her pussy opening.

Then he plunged deeply inside her, rocking her against the tile wall.

Oh God, he was so deep. He felt so good. She closed her eyes and pressed her cheek against the shower.

"Keep your hands up," he choked out as he let his own hands fall from hers.

She obeyed, keeping them above her head, pressed firmly against the walls. He positioned his hands at her hips, lifting her higher, holding her in place as he plunged again and again.

It was hot. It was hard to breathe. She'd never felt such exquisite pleasure.

Her ass rested against his hard abdomen, his cock seated as deeply within her as he could go. Still she wanted more. He slowly withdrew, pushing forward, retreating before easing forward once more.

She bit her lip to keep from screaming out at the delicious agony. She felt poised to burst, and yet he wouldn't allow it with his deliberate movements. He could send her spiraling over the edge at any second and yet he delayed, opting to instead enjoy a slow, leisurely pace.

One hand gripped her hip, and the other stole around, slipping between her legs. He found her clit and began working it in a circular motion as he fucked back and forth behind her.

"Ethan!" she cried out.

"Easy, sweetheart, I've got you," he whispered. "Not yet. Not yet."

She wailed as he paused. She was so close. So damn close.

His hand left her pussy and moved up to her breasts. He lazily circled one nipple with his fingers, brushing them ever so softly across the puckered tip. She felt the twinge all the way to her core.

He moved to the other one, plumping her breast in his hand, thumbing the nipple, teasing her unmercifully.

"Please, Ethan," she gasped out. "Let me come!"

He laughed softly. "You want it hard, sweetheart?"

"Oh God, yes, fuck me please!"

He plucked her nipples until they stood erect, stiff peaks, straining for more. Then he wrapped both hands around her hips and rocked against her, plunging deep, hard.

"Yes, yes!" she cried. She was getting close.

She closed her eyes and threw back her head. Her hands slid down the walls as he fucked her harder. The water turned cool and she didn't care.

The slap of his hips against her ass filled the bathroom, the soft sucking noise made louder by the wetness of their bodies.

The buildup was nearly painful in its intensity. Fire raged in her groin and spread rapidly to her stomach and breasts. Every muscle in her body tightened and clenched.

"Let go, sweetheart, come with me," Ethan growled in her ear.

He thrust harder, in the throes of his own release. She felt the hot jet of semen burst from his cock, and she fell right over the cliff into oblivion.

His arm curled around her, under her breasts, holding her up and against him so she wouldn't fall. He was seated deeply within her, and her body shook with the force of her orgasm.

Her head lolled forward, sliding down the wet surface of the shower wall. She put out her hands to brace herself, her breath coming in heavy gasps.

They were going to kill her.

She felt him slide out of her, felt the warm rush of cum run down her legs. Then he lifted her, turned her around and held her close to his chest.

"I love you."

The words murmured against her hair made her stiffen in surprise. Had she heard him correctly?

She pulled her head away and looked up into his eyes. They burned with desire, but they gleamed with something else. Love.

Thick emotion knotted in her throat. Tears burned her eyelids and threatened to spill over the rims. She didn't know what to say, how to respond. But she knew he meant it.

"Let's get you cleaned up, doll," he said gently.

He washed her, tenderly covering every spot on her body. Then he shampooed her hair and rinsed it for her.

When he was finished, he turned the water off and stepped out of the shower, reaching his hand back for her. He wrapped a big fluffy towel around her then hugged her to him, holding her tightly for several long seconds.

She felt ridiculously giddy, and yet hesitant. She felt compelled to return the sentiment, tell him she loved him too, but the words stuck in her throat. She wasn't ready yet, wasn't sure exactly of the depth of her feelings, and more than anything, she wanted to get this *right*.

Chapter Twelve

Holly felt deliciously sore and drowsy as she left the bathroom with Ethan. Love. He *loved* her. It didn't seem possible even though he'd all but told her it would happen.

They joined the others in the kitchen where Adam was standing by the stove. Ryan sat on a barstool drinking a beer.

She walked over to Adam and wrapped her arms around him, resting her cheek on his back. He stiffened—in surprise?—for the briefest moment before turning around in her arms.

He smiled down at her and kissed the top of her head.

"You seem happy," he said.

Her cheeks grew warm and a ridiculous smile attacked her face.

"I am."

He tipped her chin up with his fingers then bent to kiss her. His lips moved possessively over hers. His tongue pressed inward, tasting her, laying claim to her mouth.

He slowly released her. "Have a seat. Supper will be ready in a few minutes."

She floated over to where Ryan and Ethan sat and took the stool between them.

As Adam puttered around the kitchen, laying out the plates and glasses, Holly decided to broach the subject of her usefulness.

"I was thinking," she began.

The men turned their attention to her.

"That is I was wondering what it is I could do to help out. I mean, if I'm not going to be a guest, that is, I'm going to stay."

She took a deep breath and cursed her insecurity.

"Holly," Ethan said, his tone slightly reprimanding. "We want you here. We want you to stay. This is your home. I realize it might take you a while to get used to things, but there is no need to dance around any subject, nor is there any need for you not to embrace your status here."

She smiled and ducked her head. "At any rate, I wondered what I could do to help."

"There's always something that needs to be done," Adam said with a shrug. "At present, we divide chores and responsibilities. We'd be glad to have the help."

"I can't cook," she blurted, embarrassed by the admission. She felt hopelessly inadequate. Her upbringing hadn't trained her to do much.

"No one said you had to cook," Ryan said calmly.

"I could learn," she added quickly.

Adam plunked down the platter of chicken fried steak on the bar and stared at her. "Holly, we don't want a domestic slave. You're here as our wife. Our mate. The mother of our children. We managed fine on our own. We can cook just fine. If you want to help out in other ways, I'm sure we can come up with something."

Her cheeks warmed with embarrassment. "I'm making a mess of things, aren't I?"

123

Adam sat down and passed the platter over to Ethan.

"You're uptight," Adam said gently. "We just want you to be happy. Relax. You don't have to do anything right now. Let's concentrate on freeing you from your current marriage so the bastard has no claim on you. Everything else will fall into place."

"When do we go to Denver?" she asked, grateful to change the subject.

"Day after tomorrow. I've arranged for Riley to come in and feed the horses while we're gone. We'll drive down, check into a hotel, then see Cal the next morning."

She nodded then cleared her throat. "I wonder if there would be time for me to hit a salon while we're there?" She twirled the ends of her hair nervously with her fingers. "I'd like to get the color fixed."

"We can do whatever you want," Adam said.

"I also need to stop by a bank. I need to start an account so I can have funds wired in. I don't trust Mason not to empty them."

"You don't have to worry about money," Ryan said darkly. "We're more than able to provide for you."

"It's not his money," she said. "I'm not taking money from him. I'm protecting mine."

"He seemed to be fairly wealthy," Ethan said.

She sighed. "He is. But if he can find a way into my trust fund, he'll empty it to spite me."

Adam raised his brow. "Trust fund?"

"From my parents," she explained. She shifted uncomfortably on her stool. "They were wealthy. They died when I was a teenager, and I came into my inheritance when I turned twenty-one."

"I see, and how old are you now?" Adam asked.

"Twenty-four."

"And when did you meet Mason?"

"Shortly after my parents died. He...well, he stepped in and took care of me."

Ryan muttered something unintelligible under his breath. Ethan and Adam exchanged knowing glances.

"What? What are you looking like that for?" she demanded.

"Just how much money are we talking about in your trust fund?" Adam asked.

She shrugged. "I don't really know."

"Take a guess," he said.

"Fifty? Sixty million?"

"Jesus," Ethan muttered.

"How sure are you of Mason's financial stability?" Adam asked quietly.

She opened her mouth but her reply stuttered and halted in her throat. Buzzing began in her head, and she felt incredibly, *incredibly* stupid. Her cheeks burned, and her throat constricted painfully.

Without another word, she got up and walked out of the kitchen.

"Holly!"

She heard Ethan call out to her, but she didn't stop. She wanted to bear her current humiliation alone, thank you very much.

She stopped at the front door long enough to yank her coat off the coat rack then she opened the door and stepped onto the front porch. Cold air assaulted her, and she hurriedly pulled on her coat.

She walked to the railing and leaned out, staring at the rising moon over the snow. She closed her eyes and breathed deeply in. She needed the cold to cool her hot face.

Stupid, stupid, stupid. She'd never even considered Mason had an ulterior motive for singling her out. He'd stepped in when her parents died and acted as her protector and confidante. He'd pressured her to marry him when she turned twenty-one. Now she knew why. But she hadn't wanted to marry right away. The only semblance of common sense she'd shown in the whole fiasco.

She propped her elbows on the porch railing and buried her face in her palms. He had only wanted her money.

It didn't hurt that he didn't love her, or that he had married her for other reasons. She knew he hadn't been capable of loving her when he'd struck her, when he'd killed another person in cold blood. But what stung was her utter naiveté.

Of course he wanted her money. It all made perfect sense now. His preoccupation with "protecting" her, his endless questions about how she was managing her money. All in the guise of wanting to make sure she was taken care of. Thank God she hadn't stayed around long enough to turn everything over to him as they had planned once they were married.

"Jesus, how stupid can I get?" she whispered. She'd been prepared to give him everything. He probably would've found a way to get rid of her inside of six months.

She heard the door open behind her, and she squeezed her eyes harder shut.

"Holly."

Adam walked to stand beside her. She opened one eye to see him rest his hands on the railing beside her.

"I'm a complete idiot," she choked out.

He sighed and gently pulled her into his arms. "You're not an idiot, baby. I'd say you're an amazing woman."

She shook her head in denial. "I'm pathetic. Pathetic!"

She clenched his coat lapels in her hands and buried her face in his chest. Then she laughed. It sounded harsh even to her.

Adam's strong arms wrapped around her and held her tightly against him.

A tear leaked down her cheek, quickly absorbed by Adam's shirt.

"I wanted to belong to someone," she whispered. "I wanted someone to care about me and not my money or who my parents were. I was so very lonely."

Adam rubbed a hand up and down her back. "You do belong to someone, baby. And we don't give a damn about your money."

For some reason, his declaration opened the floodgate of tears she'd been holding at bay.

She hadn't realized how truly lonely she'd been or how desperate she was for someone to love her. Desperate. That about summed her up in a nutshell. And now she'd latched onto the brothers. Maybe they weren't the same caliber as Mason but she hadn't given her commitment to them any more thought than she had given her marriage to Mason. And that scared the hell out of her.

They wanted forever. She wanted forever. But. There was always a but. If only she hadn't made so many bad decisions. Then she might be able to trust the decision to stay with Adam, Ethan and Ryan.

Adam continued to hold her, stroking her hair. The sound of a ringing cell phone jarred her senses. Adam cursed softly, and she felt him fumble for his pocket. She drew away to give him easier access, and he pulled his phone out to answer it.

"Adam here," he said shortly.

There was a long pause then he turned away. Holly stood shivering lightly. She wanted back into the warmth of his arms.

"All right, I'll be right there," he said as he turned back around.

He clicked the phone shut and shoved it back into his jacket. "I've got to run into town. Lacey needs my help."

A sharp pang twisted in Holly's chest. She was surprised at its ferocity.

"Come back inside where it's warm," he said. He took her arm and led her back in the door.

In the living room, Ryan and Ethan both looked up.

"I've got to run into town. Lacey's got a problem, and her deputies are out on calls."

"Do you need us to go with you?" Ethan asked.

Ryan snorted in disgust.

"No. At least I don't think so. Looks to be a runaway. If I need trackers, I'll call you. I'd rather you stay here and look after Holly."

Holly gritted her teeth. She didn't need looking after, damn it, and she sure as hell didn't want Adam off with a woman who very clearly wanted him.

Jealous? Oh, hell yeah, she was jealous. And it pissed her off. She hadn't thought she could feel more miserable than before, but she was wrong.

"There isn't anyone else she could call?" Holly asked.

Adam looked strangely at her for a moment. "We've helped track missing persons before for her."

Holly bit her lip to keep from saying anything further. There was nothing more unattractive than a shrew.

"I'll call if I'm going to be too late."

Adam bent and gave her a quick kiss then turned to the door. He put his Stetson on and walked outside.

Holly watched him go, hating the way it made her feel. She glanced at Ryan and Ethan and winced. It was obvious they could see right through her. She seemed to have a knack for humiliation lately.

Her shoulders sagged, and she turned to head down the hallway toward the bedrooms. She stopped in the middle. Hysterical laughter bubbled from her. Whose room would she take refuge in?

She opted for the bathroom instead. She ran cool water in the sink and splashed her face. When she raised her head up, she saw Ryan's reflection in the mirror. He stood in the doorway, leaning against the frame.

"Wanna play Monopoly with me and Ethan?"

She managed a shaky smile and nodded. At least he wasn't trying to dissect her emotions.

She waited a second then headed back to the living room. Ethan was setting up the Monopoly board on the coffee table, and Ryan was carrying in three mugs from the kitchen.

"Want some hot chocolate?" Ryan asked.

"Sounds yummy," she replied.

She took position on the couch while Ethan and Ryan both sat on the floor at either ends of the coffee table. She cupped the mug in her palms and sipped at the cocoa. Anything not to think of where Adam was and who he was with.

"I hate to see you so upset," Ethan said in a low voice.

She jerked her glance sideways, startled from her own thoughts. Her jealous thoughts.

She sighed and set her mug down. She rubbed tiredly at her temple. "I'm being unreasonable."

Ryan muttered something under his breath.

She turned to him, sensing an ally. "Why don't you like her?"

"She's a manipulative bitch."

Holly laughed. "Thanks. I needed that, I think. She doesn't seem to like me, that's for sure."

Ryan grunted. "She's pissed because she set her sights on Adam, and he never took the bait."

"Never?" she asked softly. "It seemed to me that you and Ethan were all that stood between Adam seeking a deeper relationship with her."

Ethan fixed Ryan with a hard stare.

"Is he sleeping with her?"

She meant the question to sound casual, but instead it came across as fearful.

Ethan swore. "Look, sweetheart, I don't know if he ever slept with her. I know that he isn't now. Not after you."

Somehow the idea that Adam *had* slept with Lacey didn't make her feel any better. It wasn't as though Holly had been here any length of time.

"We're not saints, Holly. We've had our share of women, but we're not faithless jerks. Adam wouldn't screw around with another woman. Not after committing himself to you."

Ryan nodded in agreement.

"Then why is he going to her?" Holly strained out.

"He can't stand the idea of not helping a woman in need," Ryan said. "He has a weakness for damsels in distress."

Holly felt the blood drain from her face. Was that what she was? God, she certainly fit the mold. Tears swam in her vision, and she blinked hard to keep them back. She didn't want to make an ass of herself. More than she already had.

Ethan threw one of the dice at Ryan, hitting him in the head. "You're not the brightest bulb are you?"

Holly got up. She wasn't going to bother keeping the pretense up any longer. She was far too upset to act like nothing was wrong.

"I'd like to go to bed," she said. "Is there a room I can use?" She hoped her meaning came across. She wanted a room to herself.

"Use Adam's," Ethan said. "He can take the couch when he comes in."

"Thanks," she mumbled as she headed toward the hall.

As soon as she was out of sight, she bolted toward Adam's bedroom. When she was inside, she locked the door and leaned against it.

The tears she'd tried so hard to hold back spilled down her cheeks. All the pent-up emotion from the last several years came roaring to the surface. The disappointment and the sense of betrayal, her humiliation over the horrible lack of judgment she'd demonstrated. It was enough to make her cringe.

She didn't bother undressing. She jerked back the covers and crawled underneath, pulling them tightly around her as she curled into a ball.

Chapter Thirteen

Adam stepped inside the cabin and hung his Stetson and his coat on the hook by the door. He glanced around but only saw the dying embers of the fire. Everyone else must have gone to bed already.

His groin tightened. Would he find Holly in bed with his brothers? He knew Ethan and Ryan had both fucked her separately, and the truth of the matter was, he looked forward to doing the same.

He walked quietly down the hall and frowned when he saw his door closed. None of them ever slept with a closed door. He tried the knob and found it locked. What the hell? Locked out of his own bedroom?

He spun around and walked a door down to Ethan's room to see if he was there. The door was ajar. Adam nudged it further open and peered inside. Ethan was asleep amidst rumpled sheets. Alone.

He walked over and shook Ethan's shoulder. Ethan came awake instantly.

"What the hell time is it?" Ethan demanded in a groggy voice.

"Three A.M."

Ethan sat up and rubbed his eyes. "Where the fuck you been?"

"Helping Lacey find the Turner boy. Where's Holly?"

"In your room," Ethan replied.

"Why's the door locked?"

Ethan reached over and flipped on the lamp beside the bed. He pinned Adam with a disgusted stare. "She's hurting, Adam."

Adam's heart lurched. He didn't like to think of Holly hurting. She'd been upset before he left, but he'd hoped Ethan and Ryan would have soothed any worries she had.

"Why didn't you and Ryan solve the problem?" Adam demanded.

"*You're* hurting her, Adam. Not us."

"Me? What the fuck did I do?"

Adam felt his anger rising. He wasn't into playing stupid mind games, and Ethan was fast pissing him off.

Ethan sighed and slid his legs over the side of the bed. "Look, Adam, she's having a rough time, and you running off at Lacey's calling isn't helping matters. She's insecure and who can blame her with what that fuckhead of a husband did to her?"

"She's upset because I went to help Lacey?"

"Maybe if you had explained the nature of your relationship with Lacey, Holly wouldn't feel as she does, but she knows something is between you two, and she knows Lacey doesn't like her one bit. Lacey's acted like a jealous bitch at every turn. Much like a woman scorned. Holly isn't stupid, Adam. Neither am I. Something went on between you two."

The muscles in Adam's face twitched, and he pressed his lips together. "What did or didn't happen between us isn't any of your business."

"That's where you're wrong," Ethan said evenly. "Dead wrong. It is very much my business. I love Holly. And I think you do too, Adam. I think Ryan probably does as well although he may have a hell of a time admitting it to himself. Anything you do that hurts Holly is my business. She's as much mine as she is yours and Ryan's. If this relationship is going to work, you're going to have to pull your head out of your ass."

Adam blew out his breath in one long sigh. "Christ. Nothing happened between me and Lacey tonight, Ethan. I wouldn't do that to Holly."

"I know," Ethan said quietly. "But she doesn't know that. Not yet. We haven't *earned* her trust. She's not going to offer that lightly after what she's gone through."

"And in the meantime, I'm locked out of my fucking bedroom."

Ethan chuckled. "I guess you get the couch. I wonder if we'll have a steady rotation when one of us pisses her off."

"Good night. Sorry I woke you," Adam said as he turned to leave.

He eased the door shut behind him and stared down the hall at his locked door. It was nothing a screwdriver wouldn't fix. Maybe it was time he and Holly had a little time alone.

A few minutes later, he quietly slipped into his bedroom. Holly had left the lamp by the bed on and the soft glow poured over the bed. He set the screwdriver down on the dresser and shrugged out of his clothing.

He walked to the bed and looked down at Holly's curled up body. Only her face peeked out from underneath the covers. A face that was red and blotchy. His chest tightened at the evidence of her tears.

He gently pulled back the covers and climbed in beside her. He pulled her tightly into his arms, liking the way her soft curves melted into his hard body.

She stirred and opened bleary eyes. They flared in surprise when she saw him.

"How did you get in here?"

"Quite easily actually. Why did you lock me out?"

She looked away. He trailed a finger over a lock of her hair that rested on her neck.

"I just needed some time alone," she said softly.

"That's understandable, but you don't have to lock the door to get your point across."

She looked back at him again, her eyes troubled, uncertainty lurking in their depths.

He sighed. Ethan was right. He should have just explained his involvement with Lacey from the get-go. Then maybe he'd be sliding his dick into Holly's pussy instead of lying here with a raging hard-on about to become embroiled in sensitive talk.

He checked his impatience and cupped her cheek in his palm. "Listen to me, baby. There is nothing going on between me and Lacey. I'm sorry if you got the wrong impression."

Holly shifted and pulled the sheets up higher around her. The gesture looked protective in nature but instead of making her look stronger, it only made her seem more vulnerable.

"I don't understand."

Her voice came out soft and breathy, the kind that would make a man instantly hard. If he wasn't already. She was everything soft and feminine, what a woman should be.

"What don't you understand, baby?"

She looked away again. "Why didn't you choose her?"

Adam frowned. That wasn't what he expected her to say.

"She's everything I'm not," Holly continued. "She's strong, tall, pretty. I bet she doesn't need anyone."

Adam leaned back against the pillows, taking Holly with him. He cradled her against his chest, and she laid her cheek on his shoulder. He stroked his hand up and down her arm.

"I won't lie to you. There was a time when I was attracted to Lacey. I even went as far as to bring her home, introduce her to Ryan and Ethan. But I knew immediately that she wasn't the one. I didn't feel a connection with her. Not like I did with you, and it was obvious the others didn't either. Ryan outright despised her on sight. I still haven't figured out why. Ethan, well, he was indifferent. I stopped seeing her directly after that."

Holly stilled against him. He could feel another question coming. One that apparently was difficult for her if her body language was any indicator.

"Ryan said...he said you were a sucker for a woman in distress."

The light bulb went on immediately. Adam sat up, dragging Holly up with him. He cupped her chin in his hand and forced her to look him directly in the eye.

"Baby, I'll always protect you, but that isn't why you're here. Ryan's a dumbass. He talks to hear his head rattle, I swear. If you want an explanation as to why you and not her, well I don't know. I can only tell you what I feel here."

He clenched his other hand into a fist and thumped his chest. "It's you, baby. And maybe in time you'll believe that."

Her eyes glittered suspiciously in the lamplight.

"I want it to be me."

"But?" There was clearly a but in her statement. Doubt clouded her voice, and it made him uneasy.

"I'm scared of making the wrong decision. Again."

"Does it feel wrong?"

She didn't answer immediately.

"Holly?"

"No, it doesn't feel wrong. That's what scares me."

Adam let out a small sigh of relief. He could fight uncertainty. He couldn't fight a made up mind. Ethan's words echoed in his mind. Was he right? Did Adam already love her? It was hard to separate his satisfaction with finding the woman who would complete their family and the idea of love.

He knew one thing. He wasn't letting her go. If that meant he loved her, then maybe Ethan was right. And he'd try his best to make her love them as well.

He slid his hand down her side and over her hip. "I want to make love to you," he murmured. "I've thought of little else all night."

She stared up at him, her bottom lip caught between her teeth. He saw hesitation in her expression, but he also saw desire. Was she still afraid of him?

He lowered his head to hers, meeting her lips with his. She tasted sweet. Just like she looked. He wanted to feel those lips around his cock, her wet mouth sucking him deep. He was ready to explode just thinking about it.

"Take your clothes off," he said hoarsely. "I want to watch you."

She rose up on her elbow then slowly scooted off the bed. She stood for a moment, staring at him, her bottom lip tucked between her teeth. Then her fingers began to fumble with her pants.

He propped up on his elbow and watched as the smooth skin of her legs came into view. His fingers itched to touch her.

She began unbuttoning her shirt, her hands working down as the shirt loosened around her breasts. When she parted the shirt, he sucked in his breath. Damn she was beautiful. She had perfect breasts. They bobbed and swayed as she shrugged completely out of her shirt and let it fall to the floor.

He crooked his finger at her. "Come here."

She crawled back onto the bed, her eyes bright with desire. Her lips wavered inches from his and then she kissed him. He ran his hand over her shoulder then down her side and underneath her breast. He cupped it in his hand, loving the feel, how it filled his palm.

His dick was hard as a rock, and it was becoming more painfully engorged by the minute. There was no part of his body that didn't scream out for her.

He continued to taste her, loving the raspy sounds of her breath as they skittered across his lips. But he wanted those lips around his cock, could think of little else.

Cupping his hand around the back of her neck, he slowly, but firmly eased her down toward the juncture of his thighs. With his other hand, he circled his fingers around the base of his dick and guided it toward her waiting mouth.

He groaned as her wet tongue slid down the length of his cock.

"Oh, baby, you feel so damn good."

Her hair fell forward across his thighs. He moved his hand from his cock and tangled it in her hair, holding her in place as his hips jerked forward.

Slow and easy, she took him deeper, her tongue swirling around the head. He butted against the back of her throat then withdrew so she could catch her breath. She was magnificent.

She made small sucking noises as she coaxed him deeper. Her tongue rasped erotically over the vein on the underside of his dick. He closed his eyes and clenched his jaw as tight as he could.

He stroked his hand down her back and over the globes of her ass. He slid his finger into her wetness, and she flinched in reaction. He smiled as she took him deeper. They were driving each other crazy.

He burrowed his fingers deeper, seeking her swollen clit. He began to rotate his finger, parting the folds, baring the flesh for his touch.

He withdrew and ran his fingers up again, delving into the cleft of her ass. She tightened in reflex as he ran a finger around the puckered opening to her ass. God, she was tight.

He took his hand away and tangled it in her hair, pulling her away from his cock. Just the thought of plunging into her ass nearly made him come right then and there.

"Lay back," he commanded, rotating over her body.

She fell back, her mouth swollen, her eyes glazed with heady desire. Her legs fell open and he crawled between them, cupping her ass in his hands, spreading her.

In one hard thrust, he was inside her. She cried out, he cried out. Her hands clawed at his shoulders, pulling him closer. He smiled and bent down to capture her mouth with his.

"Do you trust me?" he whispered against her lips.

"I do."

He slowly withdrew. "Turn over."

When she complied, he stood up and walked across the room to the bathroom. He rummaged in the drawer for a tube of KY then walked back into the bedroom.

He smoothed a hand over her buttocks. "Scoot back," he murmured.

He positioned her at the edge of the bed on all fours, her ass to him. He squeezed some of the KY onto his fingers then gently slid his hand between her ass cheeks. She moaned softly when he eased one finger into the tight opening.

Holly's eyes flew open when his finger breached her ass. A multitude of sensations washed over her. A little fear, a lot of longing, a little pain, and a whole lot of pleasure.

She braced herself on one hand and smoothed the other over her stomach and to her pelvis below. Her fingers found her clit, and she began moving it in a circular motion. Pleasure rocketed through her abdomen.

His fingers left her for a moment and then she felt the head of his penis press against her sphincter. Slowly, ever so slowly, he pushed forward, allowing her to adjust to the sensation.

Her fingers stroked harder as she sought to offset the burning. She moaned deep in her throat. Then with a soft release, she felt him gain entrance.

She heard him say something unintelligible and then he sank all the way into her. She'd never felt such an exquisite fullness. Ryan's words filtered back to her. *Adam in your ass, me in your pussy.* God, what would it feel like to have them both so deeply within her?

Adam began to thrust in and out. She was at a complete loss as to how to describe the overwhelming pleasure. It was part pain, part delicious ecstasy, and they combined to send her spiraling into the most excruciatingly, wondrous agony she'd ever endured.

His hips pressed into her buttocks, and she knew he was as deep as he could possibly go, and yet, she wanted more. She pressed back against him, rocking her hips in time with his thrusts.

Her orgasm blossomed and grew until it consumed her. She needed it. She was going to fly apart at the seams.

Behind her, Adam cried out, and then she felt the flood of his release. And then she shattered. She buried her face in the covers to keep from screaming. Adam's hands gripped her hips tightly, holding her against him as he finished.

Her entire body quaked, shivered, convulsed. She fell limply to the bed as he withdrew. She closed her eyes, her breath coming in torturous gasps. Then she felt a warm cloth wiping over her tender flesh.

"Are you all right?" Adam asked huskily.

She nodded, unable to form a coherent response.

The bed dipped and then Adam gathered her in his arms. He kissed the top of her head and held her tightly against his chest. His heart beat wildly against her cheek.

"You are the most amazing woman," he whispered. "No one has ever made me feel like this."

Nothing he could have said would have evaporated her fears as quickly as that simple statement. Suddenly, Lacey was gone from her mind and her worries. She wrapped her arms around Adam's waist and closed her eyes. For the first time, she really believed that she might just hold the hearts of three men, and that they held hers.

Chapter Fourteen

Sinful, delicious sensations woke Holly up. She opened her eyes to Adam's broad chest. She was flung across him carelessly, and she smiled to think how possessive she must look. A woman staking her claim.

"Aah, she's awake."

She turned her head to see Ethan beside her. His hands stroked over her back, down over her behind and back up again.

And what a way to wake up.

A look to the end of the bed revealed Ryan. A bare-chested, incredibly sexy Ryan.

She looked up to see Adam staring down at her, lust emblazoned in his eyes.

He grinned. A predatory, all male grin. One that said he had his woman right where he wanted her. "We've been waiting for you to wake up."

"I just bet you were."

Adam bent his head to kiss her. She felt Ethan's lips press against the small of her back, and she shivered as goose bumps traveled up her spine.

Then Adam scooted out from underneath her and stood up beside the bed. He held out a hand to help her up. When she'd stood, Ryan peeled off his shorts, crawled onto the bed and laid crossways over the sheets, letting his legs dangle off the side, his feet planted on the floor.

"Come here," Ryan directed, holding out his hands for her.

She needed no further urging. She knew what was coming. She quivered from head to toe as she straddled Ryan. She looked down into his eyes, eyes that blazed into hers. She splayed her hands across his hard chest and lifted her bottom just enough that she could cradle his straining cock between her legs.

A sheen of sweat beaded on Ryan's forehead. "Tease," he ground out.

She smiled, delighting in her power. Slowly, she sank down onto him, taking him deeply inside her. She closed her eyes and let herself feel every delicious inch of him.

He gripped her hips in his large hands and held her tightly. She began a slow, sensuous ride. The bed dipped again as Ethan came to her on his knees. She rolled her tongue over the head of his erection then sucked it into her mouth. Ethan's breath came out in a hiss as he slid further beyond her lips.

Behind her, she felt Adam step between Ryan's legs, and her heart sped up. Ryan moved his hands from her hips and cupped her buttocks in his palms. He massaged them then spread them as the broad head of Adam's cock nudged her opening.

He eased lubricant around the puckered opening then pressed forward as gently as he had the night before. She felt the muscle tighten in resistance then give way under his persistent push. She cried out around Ethan's penis as Adam surged forward with one determined thrust.

They were all a part of her, all buried deeply within her. She couldn't move, couldn't process the bombardment of ecstasy. Ryan helped her, moving her hips as he and Adam set the pace, thrusting in unison. Ethan stroked into the wet depths of her mouth, and she wrapped her hand around his cock, wanting him deeper, wanting all of him.

She was fast losing control. She moved in mindless rapture, allowing Ryan to control the pace.

Adam stiffened behind her. He pressed against her as tightly as he could and then she felt him explode inside her. But still Ryan thrust into her pussy. When Adam gently slid from her, she moaned in protest. She was close to the most explosive orgasm of her life, and she didn't want to lose the sense of fullness that was fast driving her over the edge.

Ethan pulled from her mouth and quickly moved behind her. Almost before she could adjust to the loss of Adam, Ethan slid into her in one long stroke. She screamed at the sensation. No preamble, no gentle coaxing. One minute he was nudging at her back entrance and the next he was fully seated within her.

"That's it baby, feel," Adam murmured next to her. His hands stroked over her breasts, loving her, urging her on.

Ryan and Ethan surged into her, and she threw back her head, her mouth open in one long cry of triumph. This was it. This was what she'd waited for her entire life. A sense of belonging. True belonging. She was theirs, but by God they were hers as well.

"Come with us," Ryan whispered, as his mouth closed around her nipple.

"Oh God, yes!"

She bucked wildly between them. Ethan drove powerfully into her behind, his hands gripping her hips, holding her against him.

Her pussy tightened around Ryan's cock, her stomach clenched in red hot need. Waves of explosive pleasure rained down over her. She gripped Ryan's shoulders and screamed as her orgasm claimed her.

Ryan's big body shuddered beneath her, and Ethan bucked against her ass as they poured themselves into her.

She fell forward, and Ryan caught her against him, wrapping his arms tightly around her. She rested against his chest, breathing deeply, trying to catch her breath. She curled her arms around Ryan and buried her head in his neck.

Behind her, Ethan withdrew. He bent and kissed the small of her back. "I'll be right back, doll, don't move."

As if she could.

Soon a warm cloth soothed over her skin.

Ryan rolled her beneath him and gently withdrew from her quivering pussy. He propped himself on his forearms so as not to crush her with his weight then bent and kissed her.

"You're ours," he said simply.

The words slid over her like warm honey. Comforted her in a way nothing else could. She was theirs.

"Stay with me," she whispered. She yawned sleepily.

Ryan gathered her in his arms then pulled the covers over them both. "Go to sleep. I'll be right here."

Chapter Fifteen

Adam peeked into the bedroom to see Holly still sleeping soundly in the bed. He smiled. She looked like a sated kitten, curled up with her arms around his pillow. It was amazing that in such a short time he couldn't imagine life without her.

He knew via his own upbringing that such a situation could work and work well for all parties involved, but seeing it, experiencing it firsthand was more validating.

And speaking of, he needed to phone his parents. They'd be interested to know about Holly, and he nor Ethan and Ryan had talked to them in over a month.

He quietly withdrew from the bedroom and walked down the hall to the living room.

Ethan looked up from the computer. "She still sleeping?"

Adam nodded. "I think we wore her slap out."

Ethan smiled and Adam marveled at how settled and content his brother looked. "You seen Ryan? I thought we'd call Mom and let her know about Holly."

Concern flared in Ethan's eyes. "He went out to the barn. I think he's in a lot of pain today, though he wouldn't say so. Got pissed off at me when I asked."

Adam swore. Ryan had been doing so much better lately. Much of the darkness in his eyes had faded, and he knew Holly had everything to do with it, but Ryan had improved physically as well since his return from Iraq. He was a far cry from the battered shell of a man Adam and Ethan had collected from the Army Hospital a year ago, but his leg still bothered him on occasion.

He turned and strode from the living room toward the back door. Not bothering with his coat, he crossed the short distance from the cabin to the barn. He slipped inside and saw Ryan sitting on a hay bale in the back. As he drew closer, he could see Ryan's face drawn in pain. Sweat beaded Ryan's brow, and he was pale.

Ryan was bent over massaging the area above his knee. When Adam was a few feet away, Ryan looked up and saw him. He dropped his hands and stood up. Ryan cried out as his leg buckled. Adam reached over and yanked his brother up against him to prevent him from falling.

"I'm fine," Ryan gritted out.

"No, you're not fine, damn it. Stop trying to hide from the rest of us, for God's sake."

"Just leave it, Adam. I can deal with this on my own."

"You could," Adam agreed. "But don't be stupid. Ethan and I are here to help. And now Holly."

"I don't want her to know," Ryan said fiercely.

Adam blinked in surprise. "Here, sit down," he said, shoving Ryan back down onto the hay. "Now what the fuck is your problem?"

Ryan rubbed absently at his leg.

"Is there anything I can do? Do you want a pill?"

Ryan shook his head. "I don't want any fucking pills. It's just a bad morning. I don't know why the fuck it hurts. It just does."

"Maybe we should take you back to the doctor, let him check you out again."

"There's nothing he can do."

Adam sighed and ran a hand through his hair. "Damn it, Ryan, don't be so fucking difficult. I wish you'd talk to me. I still don't have a goddamn clue what the hell happened over there."

Pain lashed across Ryan's face before his eyes turned cold and stony. "There's nothing to talk about. I'll get over it."

Adam knew the subject was officially closed. Ryan could be a brick wall when he put his mind to it. He'd like nothing better than to kick his little brother's ass, but it wouldn't do a damn bit of good. Ryan wouldn't budge. Not until he was ready.

"I was going to call Mom and Dad. Thought you might want to talk to them."

Ryan waved his hand. "You go ahead. I'll be there in a minute."

Adam started to argue, but Ryan stopped him.

"Just go. Please."

It was the please that did it. Ryan rarely said please, and pain edged his voice. Adam knew he didn't want to be weak in front of his brothers. Anger choked him. Anger at whatever the hell had destroyed so much in his brother.

Adam turned around and walked out of the barn.

Holly burrowed deeper under the covers, not wanting to leave her warm nest. She was tired, deliciously exhausted, and she had about as much motivation to get up and move as she did a trip to the dentist.

She closed her eyes and relived the ecstasy she'd experienced as the three men had made love to her. Alone they were a force to be reckoned with, but together they were positively mind-blowing.

She missed them already. That feeling drove her out of the bed as she went in search of them. She pulled on one of Adam's discarded shirts and let it fall to her knees. She walked barefooted down the hall, hoping to find one of them in the living room so she could indulge in a good snuggle session.

She found Ethan on the couch. He smiled at her and patted the spot beside him. She immediately curled herself around him, loving the warmth that emanated from his body.

"Want a blanket?" he asked as he wrapped his arms around her.

She shook her head. "You're fine." She burrowed further into his arms until his heat had soaked into her body. "Where is everybody?"

"Ryan's out in the barn and Adam's on the phone in the kitchen."

"Who's he talking to?"

"Our parents."

She stiffened. Until now she hadn't given their parents a single thought. They'd existed as a non-entity. She remembered Adam mentioning them once when he explained that his mother, like her, participated in a relationship with three men.

"Something wrong?" Ethan asked.

"Your parents...do they know about me?"

He smiled down at her. "They do now."

She couldn't control the look of dismay, and she knew Ethan saw it.

He arched an eyebrow. "You look less than thrilled."

"Do they know everything?"

Ethan continued to stare at her. "I'm sure Adam has filled them in on the situation."

Holly groaned. "Not the image I want to present to your parents."

"Oh hush. They'll love you. They'll be thrilled we found you."

Adam walked in holding the phone to his ear. "All right, Dad. I'll give you to Ethan, and I'll talk to you later."

He handed the phone to Ethan, and Holly moved away. She felt awkward being talked about. She headed to the kitchen to escape the conversation. As she poured a glass of juice from the fridge, Ryan stepped in the back door.

She smiled shyly at him. "Good morning."

Pain glittered brightly in his eyes, and he limped as he walked.

"Ryan, what's wrong?" she exclaimed. She set her juice down and rushed over to him.

As soon as she touched him, he stiffened. "I'm fine."

She backed off, hurt at his demeanor.

He closed his eyes and put out a placating hand. "I'm sorry. I'm fine, really."

She curled her hand back around her juice and maintained her distance. She didn't know what to say, so she said nothing.

Ryan stared at her for a long moment then limped into the living room. His rebuff stung, but more than that, she wondered what had happened.

She sipped at her juice and sighed. Living with three unique personalities could get exhausting. If she were more secure in the relationship maybe she wouldn't be on eggshells all the time, but she was still learning all three of them.

Ethan was so open, and Ryan was his complete opposite. Reserved, shut off from the rest of the world. And Adam, well, she was still trying to figure him out, too.

"Don't take it personally," Adam said.

She looked up to see him standing in the doorway Ryan had left through.

"What's wrong with him?"

Adam opened the fridge and took out a beer. He popped the cap and took a long swig. "It's his leg. He got a leg full of shrapnel over in Iraq. Did a lot of damage. He's getting better, but it still gives him a lot of pain from time to time."

"And he won't talk about it to anyone?" she asked.

Adam shook his head. "I wish to hell he would."

Holly set her glass down and ran her finger around the rim. "Your parents. They're like us, aren't they?"

Adam nodded.

"So they won't think anything bad about me."

She tried not to make it a question, but somehow it came out inquiring anyway.

Adam smiled. "Relax, baby. They'll love you."

Ethan ambled into the kitchen. Adam looked up from his beer. "You done with Mom and Dad?"

"Yeah, Ryan's talking to Mom now. I expect he's getting an earful. She's pretty worried about him."

Adam looked over at Holly again. "You probably ought to get packed up today. We'll head out early in the morning."

She smiled. "Not much to pack."

"We'll remedy that in Denver," Ethan said. "We'll take you shopping for whatever you need."

She grinned mischievously. "Even underwear?"

"Especially underwear," Ethan replied.

"If I had my way, you wouldn't wear underwear," Adam murmured close to her ear.

Ryan walked into the kitchen, his features drawn. He slid the phone across the bar then turned and limped out.

Holly followed his progress, her heart aching at the pain in his expression. What would it take to get beyond the barriers he'd erected?

She wasn't sure what had awakened her, but her eyes fluttered open and searched the darkness for what had disturbed her sleep.

Holly strained her ears for the source of the noise she'd heard. A low moan filtered down the hall then an inarticulate cry. She sat up and glanced frantically around. Adam and Ethan were sound asleep in bed next to her, but Ryan was gone.

As carefully as she could so as not to wake the guys up, she eased from the bed. The house was chilly, and she shrugged on Adam's flannel shirt for warmth.

She padded down the hall toward the noise, ending up at Ryan's door. She pushed it open and peered inside. Ryan was on the bed in a tangle of sheets. The comforter was twisted and lay discarded on the floor.

He moaned again and stirred restlessly, his head shaking from side to side.

"No," he said in a thick voice. "God, no. Stop for God's sake, she can't take any more."

Holly moved closer, shocked to see Ryan's face bathed in tears. Her chest constricted painfully. She sat down on the bed next to Ryan and put her hand on his forehead.

"Ryan, it's okay. It's me, Holly. Wake up."

He let out a torturous cry, the sound hitting her directly in the heart. She wrapped her arms tightly around him, pulling him against her. She held him, rocking back and forth, running her hands through his tangled hair.

In response, he curled his arms around her, squeezing her tightly against him.

"I'm here, Ryan," she whispered. "You don't have to be afraid any more."

"Holly?"

His voice was muffled by her chest. He sounded confused. Uncertain.

She trailed her fingers through his hair, soothing him. "I'm here."

He tensed in her arms then pulled slightly away. "I didn't mean to wake you."

But she wouldn't let him shove her away. "Talk to me, Ryan," she said softly. "What happened to you?"

He leaned back closing his eyes. She followed him down to the pillow, curling her arm around his stomach. She waited, not pressing him. She sensed an internal battle raging.

He scrubbed a hand over his face and took a deep breath. "We got caught with our pants down behind enemy lines. Our mission went down the toilet in a matter of minutes. Most of my

153

team managed to get out but I got a leg full of shrapnel from a mortar round. I fell behind. They fucking left me there."

She sucked in her breath. Granted she knew next to nothing about military matters, but wasn't their creed never to leave behind a fallen comrade?

His breath came out wavery, and she knew he struggled to keep his emotions in check.

"I wanted them to go. I didn't want to weigh them down. But they left me. I was captured and taken to a shit hole."

His words came out rambling, in a rush as if he had a hard time formulating his thoughts. This was likely the first time he'd talked about the experience at all.

"For two weeks, I saw and endured things I never imagined."

His voice came out in a croak, breaking at the end.

"There was one soldier. She was British. They wouldn't leave her alone. They enjoyed tormenting her. After six days, she died and they left her there to rot."

Tears streamed down his cheeks. She held him closer, kissing his chest, trying to keep her own tears at bay.

"After she died, they turned their attention to me and another American soldier being held there. My leg was infected. I was running a fever and half out of my mind, but I'll never forget the *pain*."

He broke off again, his chest heaving with unspent emotion.

She pressed her forehead to his, her tears mingling with his. She hugged him to her, desperately wanting to alleviate his pain.

He wrapped his arms around her and buried his face in her breasts. "I need you."

She let him shove her shirt over her head, and soon they were naked, flesh pressing tightly against flesh. She kissed him hotly, allowing the full breadth of her passion and loving to flow into him.

Tonight she was the aggressor, making love to the man of her dreams. Their tongues mated and dueled. She rained a trail of kisses down his jaw to his neck and then down his chest to his taut belly.

His hands tangled in her hair, pulling her closer, holding her tightly. Her hands smoothed over the hard planes of his body, touching, feeling, showing him her love.

She straddled him, cupping his hardness in the cradle of her pelvis. She bent forward, sinking her hands into his hair. She pulled him to her mouth, kissing him fiercely. Then she reached down and grasped his cock, guiding him into her hot wetness.

Her fingertips trailed down his chest as she rose up, threw her head back and began to ride. He cupped her breasts in his rough palms, thumbing her nipples, plumping the soft flesh in his hands.

They rode fast, hard, each reaching for the waiting pleasure. She could feel him tighten beneath her, deep inside her, and knew he was close to his release. She felt the pinch of her abdomen, the wonderful pressure as it built, spread and finally burst into an explosion of color and ecstasy.

She leaned forward, panting against his chest as she bucked and writhed in her orgasm. Then she felt the flood of semen into her womb. He wrapped his arms around her, holding her close, murmuring things in her ear she couldn't make out.

He shifted enough that they rolled so she was cradled in his arms. He stroked her hair and kissed her forehead. "I love you," he whispered.

She tucked her head underneath his chin, letting the words spill over her. She knew he didn't utter them lightly. She didn't say anything. She just held him until she felt the even breathing of sleep overtake him.

Chapter Sixteen

Adam shuffled into the living room, looking around for the others. For the first time in longer than he could remember, he'd slept past dawn. He'd joked about wearing Holly out, but the truth was, she was exhausting him. He grinned and flexed his tired muscles. A man could only dream of that kind of tiredness.

He continued into the kitchen, expecting to see everyone there. However, Ethan was the only one there.

"Mornin'," Ethan said around his mug of coffee.

"Where's Ryan and Holly?"

"In the barn."

Adam slouched down at the bar. "The barn? They going riding? We need to be hitting the road."

Ethan's lips curled into an amused grin. "He's teaching her self-defense moves."

"Huh?"

Ethan shrugged. "They've been at it for the last hour."

Adam grunted. "Ryan must be feeling better."

Ethan set down his mug. "Holly got up last night after Ryan went to his room. When I got up this morning, they were wound as tight as two springs around each other. Ryan looked more at peace than I've ever seen him."

Adam's heart lightened at that announcement. Maybe Holly was chasing the demons from Ryan's soul. Lord knows he'd lived with them long enough.

He leaned forward on the bar, crossing his arms in front of him. She was nothing short of a miracle. To all of them.

"She's incredible," Ethan said.

Adam looked up and knew Ethan had read his thoughts, knew they were of Holly. He nodded. "That she is. I can't believe we've found her."

He couldn't describe his sense of awe. He knew his brothers had harbored their share of doubts as to whether or not they'd ever find the woman that would complete them, but he'd known they would. Felt it. He just hadn't known when or how.

"I hope Cal can take care of the divorce as quickly as he thought," Ethan spoke up. "We're going to have to be careful, Adam. I don't see her husband being willing to walk away so easily if he knows she can destroy him."

Adam nodded, a knot of concern growing in his stomach. "I've had the same thought."

The door to the kitchen burst open and Holly stumbled in giggling, Ryan right behind her. Adam watched the ease on their faces. No torment, no darkness edged their eyes. Ryan looked *happy.*

Holly flashed him and Ethan broad smiles then she threw herself into Adam's arms. He caught her in surprise, and she burrowed into his chest, shivering even as she laughed.

He kissed the top of her hair and wrapped his arms tightly around her. He looked at his brothers over the top of her head and saw in their eyes how affected they were by Holly's presence.

"You ready to hit the road?" Adam asked as he pulled Holly away from his chest.

She wrinkled her nose and grinned. "Only if I get to ride up front."

He laughed and kissed her chin. Then he swatted her on the butt. "Go get your bag and we'll head out."

The drive to Denver went quickly. Holly enjoyed the scenery, the peace of feeling safe and secure. She hoped getting a divorce was as simple as the brothers made it appear. In the back of her mind, she wondered if Mason would really let her go so easily.

As they pulled into a downtown hotel, Holly gazed around in awe. Then she glanced sideways at Adam and quirked her lips into a smile.

He raised an eyebrow.

"I wouldn't have expected you guys to want to stay here. Downtown."

He smiled. "We're not complete backwoods hicks. Don't get me wrong. We're a lot more comfortable *out* of the city, but we thought you'd like this, and plus, Cal's office isn't far from here."

"And we're near shops," Ethan said leaning forward from the backseat. "So you can do whatever shopping you need to do before we go back."

"How long are we staying?" Holly asked.

"A few days," Adam said as he opened his door. "Thought we all might enjoy the break."

Holly, Ethan and Ryan waited as Adam went to check in. A few minutes later, he returned and pulled the Land Rover forward into the parking lot.

"Let's go in, get cleaned up then we can go get something to eat," Adam said as he turned the engine off.

"A steak maybe?" Holly asked hopefully. Her mouth watered at the thought of a nice thick ribeye.

Ryan chuckled. "No worries about her fitting in."

They climbed out and Holly shivered at the shot of cold air. Ryan curled an arm around her and pulled her close to his side as they hurried for the entrance.

They all crowded into the elevator and Adam pushed the button for the top floor. They got off and walked down the hall to the end. Adam opened the door and Holly eased past him into the room.

She sighed appreciatively at the large suite. To the right, a bathroom complete with Jacuzzi and shower, to the left, doorways to two bedrooms. Ahead was a cozy sitting room with a couch and two chairs, a big screen TV and cocktail bar.

"Want me to draw you a bath?" Ethan asked her.

She shook her head as she wandered through to one of the bedrooms. "Just a quick shower. I'm starving."

She hurried into the large bathroom and turned on the shower. Then she dug around in her suitcase and pulled out a pair of jeans and a shirt along with a fresh change of underwear. She smiled ruefully at the plain Jane white briefs and bra. When she hit the shops, lingerie was going to be one of the first things she bought.

Thirty minutes later, she came out of the bathroom to where the guys were watching TV. "Ready?" she asked.

They stood and headed for the door. Downstairs, they walked out to the Land Rover and climbed in.

"They have a good steakhouse not far," Adam said. "Has great atmosphere. Laid-back."

"Sounds good," she said enthusiastically.

In truth, she didn't care where they went. The thought of a juicy steak had her positively slobbering. If she wasn't careful, she'd have to wipe the drool off her chin.

They soon pulled into a crowded parking lot. A large rambling old-style restaurant spread out across two lots. It was fashioned like a southern bayou cabin with cedar wood and a front porch boasting knobby rocking chairs.

Holly walked to the entrance, her arms snug around the waists of Ryan and Ethan. This was her first true outing with the three of them, and she felt self-conscious, but at the same time, devilishly happy. What woman wouldn't be green with envy? She had three of the most drop-dead gorgeous guys in the entire state of Colorado all to herself.

Adam gave their name to the woman manning the front, and within seconds, she was shepherding them to a table in the far corner of the room.

Ryan held out her seat for her, and Holly sat down next to Adam. The waitress came by and they rattled off their drink orders while they started looking over the menu.

Adam curled a hand around Holly's neck and massaged gently. She loved his touch. Loved that he touched her so often. They all did. It comforted her in ways words never could.

She leaned back in her chair and absorbed the surroundings. In the middle of the room, a zydeco band cranked out upbeat Cajun songs. Smiling couples navigated the tiny dance floor in various stages of the two-step.

"Wanna dance?" Ryan asked with a slow, sexy drawl.

She arched an eyebrow in surprise. "You dance?"

He gave her a wounded look. "My mama taught me to dance just fine."

Holly laughed and scooted her chair back. "By all means, let's dance. I can't two-step, but if your mama taught you, you can teach me."

Ryan led her onto the floor, his hands curving possessively around her hips. His fingers splayed out over the curve of her ass and tucked into her back pockets. He pulled her close to him, until she fit perfectly in his groin.

"Aren't we too close for the two-step?" she murmured.

"Who cares," he growled into her ear. "I like you just where you're at."

She felt his cock swell against her belly, and a thrill shot through her system. Her knees went weak with wanting. She trembled against him and wrapped her arms around his waist.

He nuzzled his face into her hair and blew gently over her ear.

"You are evil," she whispered. "Don't think I won't get you back."

"I live in hope."

She laughed.

Feeling bold, she slid one hand between their bodies, wiggled her fingers into the waistband of his jeans and down to his hard cock.

"Jesus, woman."

He mashed their bodies closer together, and she laughed again.

"Afraid someone will see?"

His response was to fuse his lips hotly to hers. She was robbed of air as Ryan feasted hungrily on her mouth. When he pulled away, his eyes glittered with desire, molten lava about to explode.

"That answer your question?"

A tug at her waist prevented her reply. She turned to see Adam cutting in, a cocky expression on his face.

"You're hogging her, little brother."

"Later, babe," Ryan said, promise etched in his eyes.

Adam tugged her into his arms, a wicked grin on his face. "You two trying to make it on a public dance floor?"

She blinked innocently at him.

"Oh, I saw your hands down his pants, baby."

"Jealous?"

He grinned. "Hell yeah. Only I don't want your hands there. I want those sweet lips wrapped around my dick."

Her body jolted at his explicit words. Her nipples hardened to the point of aching. He smiled a slow, satisfied smile. "Are we turning you on, baby?"

"Is this a plan y'all have hatched?" she demanded. "Try to make me as horny as possible in the middle of a restaurant?"

"Is it working?"

"Hell yes," she muttered.

He chuckled and nipped playfully at her ear with his teeth. "Good."

Another tug at her waist, and she moaned in protest. "This isn't fair and you both know it," she complained.

"Are you wet?" Ethan whispered as he took her into his arms. "Are you imagining the three of us licking, sucking, biting, fucking...?"

She groaned low in her throat. "Oh my God, you have to stop," she said weakly. "Can't we skip dinner?"

He laughed, low and husky. "Oh no, doll. We have all night."

She closed her eyes and thunked her head against his chest. "I'm so going to make you all pay for this. I'm gonna give prick tease a whole new definition."

He threw back his head and laughed. "Somehow I think I'll enjoy whatever punishment you come up with."

He picked his head up and looked over her shoulder. "Food's here."

She looked over to where Adam was motioning to them.

She walked back over and wilted into her chair. She shot them all dirty looks and ignored their innocent grins.

"Ohh, this smells heavenly," she said as she sniffed the delicious aromas floating over the table.

"Try mine," Ryan offered, holding a fork out to her.

She examined his offering. "What is it?"

"Bacon wrapped shrimp in butter sauce."

"Mmmmm." She opened her mouth and he gently tucked it between her lips.

"Such a sweet mouth," he murmured.

He extended his finger and wiped a small bit of butter from her lip then slid his finger into her mouth. She sucked at his finger, swirling her tongue around the tip.

"Witch."

She withdrew, smirking at him.

She cut into her steak and savored each and every bite of the tender meat. In between bites of her own food, the men gave her samples of their entrees, each one given with a dose of sensuality that left her weak and aching. She'd never existed in such a haze of sexual awareness. Each look, each touch sizzled and burned, awakened a powerful yearning within her.

She knew they were drawing attention from nearby tables, and she didn't care. Let them look. How could she possibly feel awkward about something that felt so intrinsically right? Never in her life had she felt with such absolute conviction that she was where she needed to be.

"What are you thinking about, doll?"

She smiled at Ethan, allowing the full force of her contentment to shine.

"I was thinking how perfect this evening is."

"And to think it's just getting started," Ryan murmured.

Adam slid his hand over to rest on her thigh. His thumb drew lazy circles above her knee, and his fingers slipped further between her legs.

"I'm glad you're having a good time, baby."

She leaned back in the chair, her glass of wine in hand. She sipped leisurely at it.

"Anyone up for dessert?" she asked.

Three pair of eyes sizzled over her skin. She shivered in reaction.

"I know exactly what I want for dessert," Ethan drawled.

Her cheeks blazed, and her legs clenched together to squelch the unbearable tightening in her pussy.

"I can't wait to taste you," Ethan whispered. "So sweet. Soft."

"Maybe we should go," she mumbled.

"Something wrong?" Adam asked.

She shot him a dirty look. Then she leaned over, brushing her breasts against his arm. She dipped her hand low, slid it over his thigh, between his legs until she cupped his bulge in her hand. She squeezed gently, kneading and fondling.

"Not a thing," she said sweetly.

He stood and hauled her up next to him. "Never let it be said I didn't accommodate a lady. Let's go."

The ride home was quiet. Tension radiated throughout the vehicle, and Holly's legs stayed tightly pressed together. Her clit pulsed and hummed. If she so much as touched herself there, she'd go off like a rocket.

When they arrived at the hotel, she walked to the elevator on shaky legs. Once inside, Ryan pulled her against him, his hands fumbling with her jeans.

"Off," he ordered.

"We're in an *elevator*," she whispered.

He gave her a wicked grin as the elevator did a slow rise to the third floor. "Don't make me rip them off you."

She swallowed then quickly shucked her shoes and jeans. *Oh God, don't let anyone be going up!*

Ryan unbuttoned his jeans, pulled them down then hoisted Holly up in his arms. In the time the elevator climbed to the sixth floor, he had sunk his cock deep inside her.

She wrapped her arms around his neck and buried her face in the curve of his shoulder. His palms cupped her ass, squeezing, lifting as he plunged deeper.

She wasn't going to last. She was too aroused from the night of teasing.

The elevator whooshed open and Ryan started forward, his steps measured as he worked around his jeans that were pulled down to his hips.

She'd never experienced such a rush. Ryan buried deeply within her pussy, walking down a public hallway of a hotel, knowing someone, anyone could walk out and see them at any time.

Adam walked in front, and behind them, Ethan carried Holly's shoes and jeans.

She moaned, biting her lips to keep the cries of pleasure at bay. She gripped Ryan harder and rocked her hips closer in to him.

Adam opened the door and Ryan walked inside, carrying Holly. Ryan pressed her to the wall next to the bathroom, reminiscent of their interlude in the barn. Holly couldn't hold on any longer.

Her stomach tightened, her pelvis constricted, every muscle in her pussy exploded in pleasure. She cried out as Ryan's mouth smashed into hers. He rocked her against the wall, driving harder.

She was adrift in mindless pleasure, her body drawn as tight as a bowstring. And still she kept climbing.

Ryan's mouth slid down her neck, nipping and sucking as his hips rocked between her thighs.

"Let go," he whispered. "I'll catch you. I'll always catch you."

His words, so heartfelt, were her complete undoing. She splintered into a hundred different pieces, each going a different direction. The room blurred and slipped out of focus, and she went limp against Ryan.

He gathered her tighter in his arms, his body going rigid as his own release gripped him. Slowly, with extreme care, he lowered her until her legs released his waist and her feet hit the floor.

As Ryan stepped away, Adam curled an arm around her waist and guided her toward the bathroom.

"First a nice, hot shower. Then we have plans for you."

"You mean there's more?" she asked weakly. Honestly, if there was much more, she was going to live a very short life. How much pleasure could one woman stand?

He kissed the tip of her nose. "Oh yeah, baby. The night is just beginning."

Chapter Seventeen

Holly closed her eyes as Adam gently washed her body under the hot spray of the shower. He kissed and sucked in between rubs and strokes until she was very nearly out of her mind with pleasure.

When his hands slipped between her legs, delved into the soft folds surrounding her clit, her entire abdomen clenched and spasmed. He ran his fingers through the layers, thumbing her clit as he gently soaped the curls.

"Please," she begged.

"Please what?" he asked as he removed his hand.

"Oh God, don't stop!"

He chuckled and reached over to turn the water off. He stepped out of the shower, and she watched in unabashed appreciation as water beaded and ran down his muscular body.

He quickly ran a towel over his naked skin then reached back into the shower for her. He wrapped the large towel around her body and pulled her into the front of the bathroom. He dried her skin then her hair then tossed the towel aside, leaving her naked in front of him.

He wrapped his big hands around her waist and hoisted her up onto the counter by the sink. She looked at him in surprise as he gently spread her legs, baring her pussy to his hands and his eyes.

"I've wanted to do this for some time," he said as he reached into the small overnight bag that housed their toiletries.

She watched in fascination as he took out a razor and a small can of shaving cream.

"Just the thought of your pussy all pink and bare, smooth and soft...makes me hard every time," he said in a husky voice.

She shivered, small goose bumps dotting her skin.

He slid a finger into her wet center then moved it upward, parting her folds as he went. Then he bent his head and sucked her clit into his mouth.

She nearly shot off the counter, her body convulsing at the out of control sensation that shot through her belly.

He lifted his head back up and grinned.

"You're so mean," she complained.

He laughed then wet a washcloth in the sink beside her. She closed her eyes and leaned her head back against the mirror as he began applying the cream to her pussy.

His strokes were feather light, each one making her clench her teeth a little harder. Teasing, soft, not hard enough to make her come, each touch drove her crazier with lust.

Several torturous minutes later, he stepped back. He ran a finger over her bare skin and murmured his satisfaction.

"Ethan and Ryan are going to be very pleased," he said.

"And you?" she asked softly.

"Oh baby, I couldn't be any more pleased with you."

He reached forward and plucked her off the counter and carried her into the sitting area of the suite.

Ethan and Ryan both sat sprawled on the couch. Naked. Looking so absolutely delicious, she wanted to run her tongue over their entire bodies.

And then it hit her. She had to be dreaming. None of this was *real*. She'd wake in a few hours, be back in the mess that was her life, drenched in sweat from the most wonderful dream she'd ever had in her life. Depressed as hell because it was all a fantasy.

Ethan must have seen the dismay on her face. His eyes darkened in concern. "What's that look for, doll?"

She glanced between both of them, then to Adam who still held her tightly in his arms.

"Is this real?"

She had to ask. What woman could possibly believe such a fantastic thing could happen to her?

Adam's hand slipped over her hip and pinched hard on her ass.

"Ow!" she exclaimed. "What was that for?"

He laughed. "I pinched you. Still think you're dreaming?"

She shook her head in amazement. "If I am, I hope I never wake up."

"Put her down, Adam," Ryan drawled. "I want to see the finished product."

She slid down Adam's body until she was on her feet. Ethan crooked his finger at her, and she walked to where they sat on the couch.

She felt bare. Exposed. The current of air that blew over her bare skin tickled and tingled.

Ethan leaned forward, sliding a finger over her belly, around her navel, down the centerline of her body to the newly shaved skin of her pussy.

"Just like I imagined. Pretty. Pink. So soft. I can't wait to taste you."

Ethan pulled her down to him until she straddled his big body. He sucked one taut nipple into his mouth then the other. Then he swung her over until she lay on the couch between him and Ryan, her head on Ryan's lap. Ethan slid down until his mouth was level with her hips.

Firmly, with hands that sent sensation racing up her body, he parted her thighs. He blew gently over the swollen skin. A chill crawled up her spine until she shook to rid herself of it.

His tongue darted out, and she moaned as it made contact with her quivering pussy. He used his fingers to part the flesh, and his tongue delved deeper.

"Sweet. So sweet," he murmured.

He folded her legs and pushed her knees to her chest, completely baring her to his touch and sight. His fingers explored her, then he sank one inside her. Withdrew. Then two took the place of one.

He moved his fingers back and forth as he sucked her clit into his mouth, swirling his tongue around the taut flesh. She quivered and shook, her legs going weak, her belly convulsing.

Ryan's hands went to her breasts, tweaking her nipples until they were stiff and erect. Adam stood to the side, his arms folded across his broad chest.

Ethan continued his sensual assault between her legs, until her entire body was bathed in sweat. She arched into him, so close to coming again.

Then his head came away. Ryan's hands fell to the couch. Her body heaved with exertion. She started to protest, but Adam was there, pulling her up.

"On your knees," he directed, helping her into position. "There. Put your hands on the back of the couch. Let your feet dangle off the edge of the cushions."

She positioned herself according to Adam's instructions, kneeling so that her head faced the back of the couch. Her hands slid over the edge as she looked away from the men.

Adam walked around until he faced her. His cock was inches from her mouth. She moved toward it, wanting to taste him, wanting him to slide it to the back of her throat.

His soothed his hands through her hair, caressing her face, running the tips of his fingers around her lips.

Behind her, she felt hands move over her buttocks, dipping into her pussy, spreading her legs. She burned with need.

Adam gathered her hair in one hand, collecting it in a makeshift ponytail at the back of her head. With the other hand, he guided his cock into her mouth. She closed her eyes and savored the taste and feel of him sliding along her tongue.

"Yesss," Adam hissed out. "You feel so good, baby. Just like that. Take it deep."

As Adam began to work his cock in and out of her mouth, Ethan slid into her pussy. She made soft sounds of appreciation as the two men worked in unison. They were exquisitely gentle. She gave up complete control to them, allowing them to set the pace. She merely felt. Enjoyed the thrill of their seduction.

Adam let his hand fall, allowing her hair to cascade over her shoulders. Then he withdrew from her mouth, and she whimpered in protest.

Ryan walked around to replace Adam. Adam disappeared from her view as Ryan sank into her mouth. Ethan caressed her hips, holding her as he slowly thrust within her. Then he too withdrew, and cool air blew over her exposed pussy.

Then she felt Adam's hands close around her waist. They skimmed the surface of her skin and settled possessively on her buttocks. He massaged then spread her ass cheeks and settled his lubricated cock at her anal opening.

The broad head of his penis penetrated the tight muscle and sank inward with a soft pop. Inch by inch, he pressed forward until his taut abdomen rested against her behind.

She licked and nibbled, swirled her tongue around Ryan's cock as he sank his fingers into her hair. She was buffeted between the two men, their cocks deeply within her body.

Her hands curled tightly around the edge of the couch, her fingers bloodless from the pressure. Suddenly Ryan withdrew. Her head came up in surprise as Adam grasped her by the waist and picked her up, his dick still seated within her ass.

"Easy, baby," he murmured. "I won't hurt you."

He turned until she was faced away from the couch and then he slowly eased himself down until he sat on the couch, her on top of him.

He leaned back, spreading her legs. The fullness in her rear was all consuming. Hot. The pinch of pain was heady. She rode a fine line between the most unbearable pleasure she'd ever experience and the bite of erotic pain.

Ryan stepped between her widespread legs and fisted his cock with one hand. She finally understood the position Adam had put her in.

She relaxed her body against Adam's chest, letting her head fall back until her cheek rested against his.

Ryan bent and pressed the head of his dick to her pussy, exerting pressure until he slid into her tightness. The fullness was more than she'd ever experienced. Ryan leaned into her until she was sandwiched tightly between him and Adam. Then Ryan began to thrust.

They fit together like a dream. Adam cradled her body with his, absorbing the motion of Ryan's thrusts along with Holly.

"You're so beautiful, so giving," Adam whispered against her ear. "You were made for us."

She reached back and curled her arms around Adam's neck, stretching between the two men. She closed her eyes as Ryan's mouth found her nipple.

She tuned into the multitude of sensations wracking her body. Currents of fire arced through her like a bolt of lightning.

"Come for me," Ryan said. "I want to watch you."

Cradled between the two men, their bodies worshipping hers, Ryan's husky words washing over her like fine wine. She let go. Allowed herself to free fall into the dark abyss that rushed up to claim her.

She felt tugged in forty different directions as her body jumped and spasmed. She closed her eyes to black out the splashes of color so bright in her vision.

It was if someone cut a tightly pulled rubber band. Her body melted into Adam's. She heard soothing words against her ear, but couldn't make sense of them.

Hands stroked up and down her slick body as Ryan pulled gently away. Adam rotated her underneath him, her belly flat to the sofa. He pushed forward, thrusting slowly into her. Once, twice and then she felt his release flood into her. Then he eased from her.

"My turn," Ethan said above her as he scooped her into his arms.

She sagged limply against him, wondering what else they could possibly do that could top this.

Ethan walked into the bedroom and laid her on the bed. Something warm and slick splashed onto her back. Then gentle hands began to massage her tired muscles.

She moaned in pure satisfaction. So she was wrong. It *could* get better.

Chapter Eighteen

Holly wiped the palms of her hands on her jeans as they stood in the reception area of the lawyer's office. So much was riding on what the guys' friend would tell them.

Logically, she knew there was nothing Mason could do to prevent the divorce. Make things difficult? Yes. But he could not simply prevent it from happening. She hoped her threat was enough to persuade him not to contest.

Her money was another issue, but her parents had put it in trust, and unless she *gave* the money to Mason, he had no claim on it. But it didn't mean he wouldn't try.

She closed her eyes and shuddered. Would she ever be free of her horrible mistakes?

Warm, comforting hands squeezed her shoulders. Ethan. Already she could recognize his touch. Distinguish it from Adam's or Ryan's.

"You're worrying too much, doll. We'll take care of this. I promise."

She turned around and smiled weakly. "I want it to be over with."

"I know. And it will be."

A tall, well-dressed man appeared in the waiting room. He crossed to where Adam stood and extended his hand.

"Adam, it's damn good to see you again."

"Cal," Adam returned.

Cal turned to shake hands with Ethan and Ryan then settled his gaze on Holly.

"You must be Holly." He smiled warmly at her, and she relaxed some.

She extended her hand and shook Cal's. "Thank you for seeing us."

"My pleasure." He turned and extended a hand toward the hallway. "If you'll all come this way to my office, we can get started."

Adam reached for Holly, and she went willingly into his embrace. His hand squeezed her waist comfortingly as they followed Cal into a large, expensively furnished office.

Cal gestured for them to sit down then settled behind his mahogany desk. "Adam has filled me in on most of the details." He looked up at Holly. "May I call you Holly? Somehow I don't think you'd like to be called Mrs. Bardwell."

"No, please, call me Holly," she said huskily.

He smiled. "Okay, Holly." He opened a folder and pulled out a sheaf of papers. He slid them along the polished surface of the desk in her direction.

"I'll have you look over and sign these so I can get the ball rolling. Your case is pretty straightforward. If there aren't any complications or objections, you're divorce can be final in as little as ninety days. Obviously if problems arise, it will go longer."

Holly stared down at the papers in front of her. It sounded so simple. Ninety days. She could be free in three months.

"What if...what if he doesn't agree?" she whispered. "I mean what if he won't sign the papers?"

She looked up at Cal, trying to keep the fear from her expression. She wanted to appear calm and confident, but inside she was a wreck.

"Then we kill him," Ryan muttered.

Cal chuckled. "As much as I like Ryan's idea, we'll leave it in the hands of the legal system. Once your husband is served, he can do one of three things. He can sign the papers, he can ignore them or he can hire a lawyer and show up in court to contest."

He leaned forward and put a hand over Holly's. "No matter what he does, though, he can't prevent you from divorcing him. All he can do is delay the inevitable. Remember that."

Holly blew out her breath. "Thank you." It was all she could manage without betraying how badly she was shaking. She felt like standing up and yelling. Finally she was taking a proactive stance in deciding the course of her life. And it felt damn good.

She glanced sideways at Adam, Ethan and Ryan, unable to keep the small smile from tugging at her lips. Then she looked back at Cal. "Is that all? I don't have to do anything else?"

"No," Cal said.

She paused for a moment and took in several steadying breaths. "Will I...will I have to face him in court?"

"No."

The answer came from at least three different sources and she turned in all directions.

Cal chuckled. "No. If he opts to go to court that is his prerogative, but you aren't asking him for anything. There's nothing to dispute, so I doubt he'll want to appear, and if so, I will appear on your behalf as your counsel."

She smiled, felt her entire face relax. The more she tried to contain her joy, the wider she felt her face split. Adam slipped a hand up and down her back then rested his palm on her shoulder and squeezed.

Cal looked intently at her. "This will end soon, Holly. You have my assurances."

A tear slipped down her cheek. She wiped it away impatiently, not at all sure *why* she was crying. She was thrilled. She was relieved.

"Thank you," she said again.

Adam stood beside her and reached across the desk to shake Cal's hand. "We appreciate everything, Cal."

Cal also stood. "I'm glad to do whatever I can. You know that. I'll be in touch."

Holly followed the men out of the office. Ryan hung back in the hallway and immediately pulled her into his arms. She hugged him back, feeling just as relieved as he seemed to be.

"Want to find a salon now?" Adam asked as they stepped out into the cold air.

She bobbed her head enthusiastically. They walked over to the Land Rover and Holly slid into the front seat. She let out a long whoosh of air and briefly closed her eyes.

"Feel better?" Ethan asked from the back.

She opened her eyes and swiveled her head to look at him. "You don't even know," she said softly.

"I know I feel better," Ryan muttered. "The sooner she no longer bears that bastard's last name, the better."

Holly wrinkled her brow. She hadn't considered the issue of last name. Once she was divorced, would she resort to her maiden name? She didn't see how she could take Colter since it wasn't exactly legal to marry more than one man. But at the same time, she wanted to belong to them, didn't want to be viewed as merely a lover or a girlfriend.

"What are you thinking about, baby?" Adam murmured as he started the engine.

She paused not wanting to admit exactly what had crossed her mind. It seemed presumptuous at best. She hated the insecurity that crept in despite her best efforts to keep it at bay.

She opened her mouth to respond, but couldn't make the words come out. "Nothing," she said with a slight stammer.

Adam braked and shoved it into park halfway out of the parking place. "What are you afraid of? What is it you won't say? You have to know you can tell us anything."

She swallowed. "It's ridiculous."

Adam cupped her chin, rubbing his thumb gently over her jaw. "I hate that you worry so much around us. Now tell me."

"The whole name thing," she mumbled. "I just wondered."

"Wondered what?" Ethan asked leaning forward in his seat.

"I kind of liked the idea of being a Colter," she said, her cheeks flaming. "But I know it isn't possible."

"What?" Ryan demanded. He grasped the back of her headrest and pulled himself forward until he met her gaze. "Why isn't it possible?"

Ethan and Adam also wore questioning expressions.

"I can't exactly marry all of you. Legally. That is if you'd even want marriage. Oh hell, I'm making a mess of this," she muttered, closing her eyes.

"Baby, do you doubt how much we want you?"

She hesitated for the briefest of moments then finally shook her head.

"As soon as possible you *will* have our name," Adam continued. "Call me old-fashioned, but you belong to us. We want you to be a Colter."

"But how?"

He smiled at her. "You're over thinking this, baby. It's quite simple. You'll marry one of us in a legal ceremony."

Her mouth rounded to an O. How stupid of her. That idea had never occurred to her and yet it made perfect sense.

"Hell, I like the idea that she's finally talking about us in a permanent sense," Ethan said.

She glanced back at him to see his eyes twinkling. Truth be known, she'd surprised *herself*. Was she a masochist to jump into another relationship on the heels of extricating herself from her first big disaster?

This wasn't a mistake. Couldn't be a mistake. She wouldn't allow herself to think it.

Adam pulled out of the parking lot and drove off down the street. A few minutes later, he pulled into the lot of a sleek-looking hair salon.

Holly looked over at him in surprise.

He smiled back. "I asked for recommendations. This place came up several times."

She leaned over and kissed him full on the lips then quickly piled out of the Land Rover.

"Hey, it was my idea to ask," Ethan grumbled as he slammed the back door.

Holly grinned and gave him a chaste kiss on the cheek. She walked ahead of them into the salon and was greeted by a cheerful lady who looked to be in her forties.

"I don't have an appointment," Holly began.

"What's your name, honey?" the woman asked.

"Holly Bar...just Holly," she said.

The woman jotted down something on a pad of paper then beamed up at Holly. "Well, you're in luck, Holly. I can take you right now. My name's Jolene. Come on around and let me get you settled in. Then we'll talk about what you need done, though I can tell you definitely need some color."

Holly blinked as the woman herded her around the counter, chattering brightly the entire way. She glanced back at the men who had taken seats in the small waiting area. Adam smiled back at her then winked.

Jolene whipped a cape out and secured it around Holly's neck then ran her fingers through Holly's shoulder length hair. "Honey, I hate to be the one to tell you this, but you need to fire your stylist. This is one of the worst dye jobs I've ever laid eyes on."

Holly smiled. "I'm afraid I did it. I was in a hurry. Messed it up. Can you fix it?"

"Do you want to go blonde?"

"No, I'd like my natural color back."

Jolene studied the strands of hair in her hands for a minute. "Sure, I can fix it, honey. Don't you worry about a thing. Come over to the sink and let me wash it for you."

Several minutes later, Holly sat back in the chair, her hair damp from the washing. Jolene began combing her hair out and Holly relaxed.

Jolene leaned forward and in a loud whisper said, "Now, honey, I'm not one to pry, but you have to tell me which one of those gorgeous hunks is yours."

Holly froze, a smile hovering on her lips. For a brief moment, she considered just pointing out one of them, but why should she care what this woman thought of her?

"They all are," Holly said softly.

Jolene's brows shot up. "All? Oh honey, tell me you're joking. Surely no woman is that lucky!" She shot Holly an exaggerated wink in the mirror.

Holly chuckled then blushed.

"You're serious, aren't you?"

Holly nodded.

Jolene shook her head. "Lordy. You have to tell me how you do it. I'd give my eyeteeth for two, much less three men who looked like that."

Holly stared at her in amazement. There was no shock or outrage in the woman's voice.

"Well, never mind, honey, you're obviously telling the truth. Would you look at the way they're looking at you? Like they could eat you up for lunch." Jolene sighed wistfully. "There was once a time when a man looked at me like that."

"What happened?" Holly asked, curious at the longing in the other woman's voice.

"Oh, we wanted different things. Or at least I thought I did. I just couldn't accept what was staring me in the face. Lean back, honey, let me get this cotton around your forehead."

Holly dutifully leaned back and waited for her to continue.

"He finally got tired of waiting, I guess. Took off on his Harley and I never saw him again."

"Oh, that's too bad," Holly said. "You don't know how to find him?"

Jolene looked startled. "Well, I never considered trying to find him. Of course, that was years ago. He's probably married with a passel of kids by now."

"Maybe," Holly murmured.

Two hours later, Jolene whirled Holly around in her chair to face the mirror.

"There you go, honey. What do you think?"

Holly stared back at her reflection. "It's me," she whispered. No streaks of blonde shone in her light brown hair. The ends had been trimmed and the tresses gleamed in the soft light.

Jolene beamed back at her. "I thought you'd like it."

Holly stood and impulsively hugged the older woman. "Thank you."

Jolene steered her toward the waiting room. "Go see how your young men like it."

Holly walked over to where the brothers sat. Adam stood and reached for his wallet.

"You look beautiful, baby."

She smiled and ducked her head. She glanced over at Ethan and Ryan who also nodded their approval.

"Want to hit the shops and buy you some clothes?" Ethan asked. "There's several down this street."

"I'd like that," she replied.

She'd also noticed a boutique specializing in lingerie. A small smile curved her lips and she bit the inside of her cheek so as not to betray her thoughts. She'd love to buy a sexy new outfit and surprise them.

Ryan held out her coat for her and she slipped it on. As they walked out, Holly caught Jolene's eyes, and the hairdresser threw her a saucy wink and a thumbs up.

At first, Holly hurried through the shops, sure that the men would be bored silly watching her clothes shop, but she soon realized they enjoyed seeing her try on new things.

Her last stop was the lingerie store, and she made the excuse that she needed bras. Inside, she picked out two sexy outfits and grinned in delight at the idea of surprising them when they returned home.

When she stepped back out, Ryan and Ethan reached for her bags.

"Adam's gone over to warm up the Rover," Ethan explained as they stepped out to cross the street.

They hurried forward. Out of the corner of Holly's eye, she saw a sedan pull out from where it had been parallel-parked. She blinked in surprise when it barreled out into the street. Straight for them.

Ryan and Ethan were a step in front of her, and she threw all of her weight into their backs, desperate to shove them out of the way. In the distance, she heard Adam shout.

Ryan and Ethan stumbled forward just as the car careened by. Pain exploded in her hip as she felt the hard bumper glance off her leg. She went sprawling, her hands out to brace her fall.

Chapter Nineteen

Adam watched in horror as the car struck Holly and sent her spiraling to the street. He yelled her name again as he ran for her. Ryan and Ethan knelt beside Holly, and he shoved his way in. His breath caught in his throat when he saw her beautiful eyes open and stare up at him.

Her face contorted in pain, and she struggled to get up.

"No!" he shouted. "No," he said in a lower voice when she winced at his tone. "Stay there, baby. Oh my God, are you okay?"

He yanked his cell phone out of his pocket and punched in 911.

"No, Adam, don't," she protested, holding her hand up. "I'm fine, really. It's just my hip. The car mostly missed me."

Mostly. Jesus. Was she trying to give him a heart attack?

"What the hell was that idiot doing?" Ryan demanded, his voice shaking as he stroked over Holly's hair.

Adam shot Ryan a quelling look. The hit-and-run was no accident, and he didn't want Holly more afraid than she already was.

"Holly, we need to call an ambulance," Ethan said gently. "You could be hurt."

By now a small crowd had assembled up and down the street. Adam heard the wail of a siren.

"I don't want to go to the hospital," Holly said, her eyes pleading with Adam. "Let me get up. I'm only a little banged up."

He wavered a moment, his concern for her overriding all else. She moved against Ryan's hand, trying to squirm her way up.

"Easy, baby," he cautioned.

Adam reached down and lifted her easily into his arms.

"Can you stand?" he asked, unwilling to set her down yet.

"I'm fine, really. Just a little shaken."

With great care, he set her down on her feet. Ethan's hands came out to steady her as she wobbled the slightest bit. She rubbed her hip with her hand, her fingers catching in the torn material down her leg.

"These were my favorite pair of jeans," she said ruefully.

Unable to stand it a moment longer, Adam crushed her to him, his arms holding her tightly against him. He drew in several steadying breaths, trying to calm the adrenaline that buzzed through his veins.

Some son of a bitch had just tried to kill her. He'd bet his entire cabin that it was her soon-to-be-ex-husband. He stared over at his brothers and saw answering rage in their eyes. He put a finger to his lips and they nodded their understanding.

A police cruiser roared up seconds later, followed quickly by an ambulance. People crowded round as the paramedics examined Holly and the cops questioned everyone.

An hour later, Holly signed no transport papers, and the crowd began to disperse. The responding officer took the last statement and climbed into his cruiser.

Holly's eyes were etched with pain and fatigue. Adam knew she hadn't been completely honest about the extent of her injuries, and he planned to remedy the situation immediately.

He tossed the keys to Ethan. "You drive."

He bent and picked Holly up into his arms and cradled her gently against his chest. She didn't protest, only expelled a weary sigh as she rested her head on his shoulder. He walked over to the Land Rover and eased into the backseat with her.

Ryan turned around in the front seat, his eyes bright with worry. "Are you all right, Holly?"

She stirred in Adam's arms and put out her hand to touch Ryan's arm. "I'm fine. I promise. Just a little shaky now that it's all over with."

But even as she offered Ryan reassurance, Adam could feel the tension in her body, see the pain in her eyes. He knew Ryan could see it too.

At the hotel, Adam carried Holly to their suite and laid her on the bed. He wanted to see her injuries, make sure she was truly all right.

Ethan and Ryan crowded in as Adam slowly pulled her tattered jeans away from her body. His hands trembled in rage as he saw the large bruise already forming on her hip and upper leg. Blood from a three-inch gash smeared her pale skin.

Holly lay still on the bed, her eyes closed as Adam took stock of her injuries. He hated to disturb her, but he needed to know if she hurt anywhere else.

"Baby," he said softly.

She opened her eyes, her eyelashes fluttering delicately against soft skin. She looked so damned vulnerable.

"Are you hurt anywhere else?"

She shook her head slowly.

"We need to clean this up," he said. "If I draw you a bath, can you soak for a bit and let me clean your leg?"

She nodded.

"I'll go run the water," Ethan said. He trailed his hand down her cheek then bent down and kissed her forehead. "Be back in a sec, doll."

Adam watched as Ethan walked away with clenched fists. His brothers were as eaten up with worry as he was. And with anger.

"Let's get you out of the rest of your clothes," Adam said.

He eased the shirt over her head, careful not to move her more than necessary. Ryan sat at her head, smoothing his hand over her hair.

Adam felt her begin to tremble. At first, tiny quakes shuddered over her body, but then she began to shake in earnest. Tears leaked from beneath her eyelids, and Adam's chest tightened.

He bent over and pulled her naked body into his arms. "You're safe now, baby."

She hiccupped softly, her breath snagging as she sucked in.

"I don't know what's wrong with me," she said as she scrubbed at her face.

Ryan scowled. "You had a terrible fright."

"Her bath is ready," Ethan said from the door.

"Come on, baby. A nice, hot bath will make you feel better."

Adam stood up and carried her into the bathroom. He set her gently down into the sudsy water. She hissed in pain as the water hit her leg.

Adam cursed under his breath. "I'm sorry."

She slumped against the back of the tub, eyes closed. "You were right. This feels wonderful."

"You're going to hurt tomorrow," Adam said as he knelt beside the tub.

"I hurt now," she said wryly.

Adam reached down with a washcloth and gently began to clean the cut on her hip.

She turned troubled eyes on him. "You think it was him, don't you?"

He didn't pretend to misunderstand. "Yeah, baby, I do."

She sank lower in the tub, her shoulders hunched in defeat. "He could have killed Ryan and Ethan."

"He could have killed *you*," Adam growled.

"I couldn't stand for anything to happen to one of you," she said.

"And we couldn't stand for anything to happen to you. Now come on, I'll dry you off and put you to bed."

He lifted her from the tub and wrapped a big fluffy towel around her. When they left the bathroom, Ryan caught Holly in his arms and hugged her tightly.

"You scared me," Ryan said gruffly.

Holly stretched on tiptoe and curled her arms around Ryan's neck. She felt incredibly safe in his arms, like nothing could touch her.

"Make love to me," she whispered.

"I don't want to hurt you," Ryan said against her ear.

"You'll be gentle," she said with absolute conviction. She knew of anyone, these men would never hurt her. "I need you."

"Come to bed," he said, tugging her forward.

She went willingly and allowed him to remove the towel that covered her body. He pulled back the covers and gestured for her to get in. She nearly groaned aloud as the soft linens enveloped her.

She glanced up to see Adam and Ethan standing beside Ryan. Ryan shrugged out of his shirt and climbed in beside her. Adam walked around to the other side of the bed and sank down behind her. Ethan sprawled across the end of the bed, propping himself up on his elbow.

They weren't going to make love to her. Even as a teeny bit of disappointment tugged at her, fatigue settled in. She burrowed against Ryan's hard chest and sighed in contentment as his strong arms curled around her.

Warm lips sent a shiver up her body as Adam gently kissed her bruised leg.

"Go to sleep, baby," he murmured. "We'll be right here."

She closed her eyes, reveling in their warmth and strength. She couldn't allow herself to think about what could have happened today. As much as she feared the decision to stay with the brothers, she knew she couldn't live without them.

But what if her staying was what brought them harm?

Chapter Twenty

"We could have lost her today," Adam said. Anger still surged hotly through his system. He wanted to kill someone. With his bare hands.

He turned to stare at his brothers. "We can't stay here. We can't protect her here in the city. It's too open."

"I agree," Ryan said in a steely voice. "We should get back home."

The three brothers paced the living room of the suite like caged predators. Holly slept a few feet away in the bedroom, the door ajar so they could hear if she wakened.

"The question is, what are we going to do about her husband?" Ethan said.

"We protect Holly and wait for Cal to do his job," Adam said.

Ryan scrubbed through his hair impatiently. "Something has to be done. We can't sit around with our thumbs up our asses. You and I both know this isn't over."

"I'm well aware of that," Adam said, trying to curtail his irritation. He knew Ryan was as worried as he was. "We go home and keep our guard up. He's at a disadvantage on our turf. No one knows those mountains better than we do. When we're out here in the open, we're little better than sitting ducks."

Ethan nodded in agreement. "I saw something in Holly's eyes I didn't like tonight. More than fear. It was the knowledge that something she did could have harmed us. I don't want her thinking that way."

"She didn't *do* anything," Ryan snarled.

Ethan held his hands up. "I didn't say she did, Ryan. Back off. I just know what she's thinking, and I don't like it. She thinks she's the reason for all of this."

"Enough," Adam said. "The important thing is we get Holly back to the cabin and make damn sure one of us is with her at all times. We don't want to do anything that could complicate a divorce. As soon as it's final, then we can figure out the best way to deal with the asshole."

A sound from Holly's room called a halt to the conversation.

"I'll go," Ryan said. Before Adam or Ethan could respond, Ryan strode across the room.

"He loves her," Ethan said quietly.

Adam nodded, satisfaction filling his chest. Getting close to Ryan was as hard as peeling a pit bull off your ass, but once Ryan allowed someone in, he embraced them wholeheartedly. And he was fiercely protective of those he loved.

"He'll watch over her well," Adam said.

"We all will," Ethan corrected.

Adam checked his watch. Two A.M. But he wasn't going to sleep much tonight. If it weren't for the fact Holly needed to rest, he'd head them all out now and get out of town. Back to their cabin.

"Why don't you get some rest?" Ethan offered. "I'm wide-awake. I'll hang out here and make sure everything stays quiet."

Adam expelled his breath in a long whoosh. "All right. I doubt I'll sleep, but I'll kick back for a few hours. We'll drive home in the morning."

Adam shuffled into the bedroom. He glanced over to see Ryan wrapped around Holly, their legs entwined. Ryan's hand rested possessively on Holly's hip, his fingers splayed out over the curve of her ass.

Ryan opened his eyes and stared at Adam from an angle. Adam lifted his brow in silent question. Ryan nodded, signaling all was well with Holly. Adam shucked his boots and jeans and quietly crawled into bed on the other side of Holly.

She stirred restlessly beside him, scooting her backside into his stomach. He kissed her bare shoulder then nuzzled his face around her hair before relaxing onto the pillow.

But when he closed his eyes, all he saw was the car hitting Holly. Over and over. His heart raced and a knot grew in his throat. How close they'd come to losing her.

He'd been lax, they all had, but it wouldn't happen again. He'd sworn to protect Holly from the moment she'd appeared in their lives. And already he'd failed her.

Holly eased out of the bed, wincing as her leg bore the full brunt of her weight. She contorted her body, looking down at the dark purple bruise and the tender gash that slanted diagonally from her hip.

Warped amusement burbled up. Her first thought had been she felt like she'd been hit by a car. At least now she had good reference for the old cliché.

She stretched and rotated her shoulder. She felt old and decrepit, as stove up as a ninety-year-old woman. But at least she was alive. No thanks to Mason.

She limped toward the bathroom, wondering where the guys were. The digital clock on the bedside table told her it was early. She carefully dressed, brushed her teeth then ran a brush through her hair. She still looked like hell, but at least she felt marginally better.

A noise at the door caused her to look up. Ryan stood in the doorway to the bathroom, staring intently at her.

"I thought I heard you. How are you feeling?" he asked.

She smiled. "Stiff and sore, but considering the circumstances, it could be a lot worse, so I'm grateful."

Warring emotions swirled in Ryan's eyes. Anger, concern, and what looked like fear. She put down her brush and walked silently into his arms. She wrapped herself around him, hugging him tightly.

"I'm okay, Ryan. Really."

Strong arms nearly squeezed the life out of her. Against her cheek, his heart thudded in his chest.

"I don't know what I'd do if anything happened to you," he said hoarsely.

She leaned back, tilting her head up to look at him. "But nothing did," she said lightly.

He cupped her cheek in his hand then leaned in to kiss her.

"I love you," he murmured against her lips.

She opened her mouth to respond, but the words stuck in her throat. Instead, she kissed him back, allowing their tongues to mingle and swirl.

He pulled away then rested his forehead on hers, their noses and mouths barely an inch away. "I haven't felt that kind of fear since I left Iraq," he admitted.

She reached up and tangled her hand in his hair, smoothing it over his ears. She bumped and rubbed her nose to his playfully. Then she kissed his lips. "Let's put it behind us and go home," she said.

Fire ignited in his eyes. "Home sounds damn good to me. Adam and Ethan have already packed."

"Let me get the rest of my things then," she said.

"You go on out and let the others know you're okay. I'll finish packing for you," he offered.

She smiled and ran her hand over his cheek once more. He caught her hand and kissed each fingertip before allowing her to pull it away.

She left the bathroom smiling. Not even the pain and stiffness in her hip could overshadow the happiness she felt. When she entered the living area of the suite, Adam and Ethan both looked up from where they sat.

Ethan stood and met her halfway, enfolding her into his arms. "How are you feeling today?"

"I'm okay, just a little sore."

He urged her over to where Adam sat, and she curled onto the couch between them.

"Sorry to cut our trip short, baby, but I think it's best if we head home this morning," Adam said, regret creasing his brow.

"I'm ready to go home," she said firmly.

He smiled. "I'm glad. Glad you think of it as home."

Ryan trudged out of the bedroom, suitcase and carry-on bag in hand. "Everything's out of the bedroom," he announced.

Adam turned back to Holly. "I thought we could get something to eat on the way. I'd like to get out of town as soon as possible."

"That's fine," she said. "I'm ready when you all are."

She eased up from the couch. Ethan stood beside her and wrapped an arm around her waist.

"Ryan and I'll go down with the luggage and warm up the Land Rover. Give us a few minutes then meet us out front. I'll pull around to the entrance," Adam said.

Ethan nodded, and Adam and Ryan collected the bags and walked out.

"You sure you're feeling okay today, doll?" Ethan asked.

She nodded. "I'm sore, but the more I move, the better I feel."

He kissed her forehead. "I'm sorry we didn't look out better. It should have never happened."

She scowled at him. "It's not your fault. Any of yours." She sighed and leaned further into his embrace. "I just hope it's over soon."

"It will be, doll. It will be."

Chapter Twenty-One

They arrived in Clyde by noon and Adam pulled into the small parking lot of the sheriff's office. Holly looked less than thrilled when she realized where they'd stopped.

"We need to tell Lacey what's going on so she can be on the lookout for Mason," he explained. "If she sees him, she can let us know. Added protection."

"But will she?" Holly asked softly, turning her wide eyes on him. "Tell us, I mean?"

The question hung between them, hovering in the air.

"I don't see why we need to involve her," Ryan spoke up.

Adam ignored Ryan. "Do you trust me, baby?"

"You know I do," Holly said. "It's her I don't trust."

"Then know I'd never do anything to endanger you."

Holly stared back at him for a long moment then nodded.

Satisfaction rolled and flexed inside him. He reached over and squeezed her hand. "Come on, this won't take but a second."

Holly sucked in a deep breath and opened her door to get out. Personally, she'd rather pluck her fingernails off one by one than have to deal with the jealous redhead.

The four trekked into the small building and Lacey looked up from where she sat behind her desk. She lifted a brow in question as Adam strode across the floor toward her.

Holly hung back, and Ryan slipped his arm around her neck, letting his hand dangle loosely over her shoulder.

Lacey stood, her eyes warily glancing over Adam and beyond to where Holly, Ryan and Ethan stood.

"Adam," she said nodding in his direction. "What can I do for you?"

"We've got a problem, Lacey. We could use your help."

"What kind of problem?"

"Mason Bardwell," Adam said harshly. "We have reason to believe he's trying to kill Holly."

Lacey leaned back against her desk and folded her arms across her chest. "You sure about that, Adam?"

"I'm sure. Now can we expect help from you?"

She swept her gaze up and down Holly before her eyes darted back to Adam. "Yeah, whatever I can do. You know that."

"I need to know if you see him," Adam said. "Immediately."

"Don't want me to detain him?" Lacey asked. "You want to press charges?"

"We don't have proof. Yet," he added.

"You gonna hole up at the cabin then?"

Adam nodded. "For now. Until we're sure Holly's safe."

Something that looked remarkably like hurt flashed in the other woman's eyes. Holly felt a pang of sympathy. It was obvious Lacey had feelings for Adam, and just as obvious that he didn't return them.

"I'll keep my eyes open, and I'll tell my deputies to do the same," Lacey said. "But if he shows up, don't do anything stupid, Adam. You call me."

"We'll do whatever it takes to ensure Holly's safety," Adam said evenly. "I won't make any promises as to how that happens."

"Good enough. I'll check in on y'all when I'm up there next."

"Thanks, Lacey. We appreciate it."

He tipped his Stetson in her direction then turned to face Holly and the others. "Let's get on home now."

Holly glanced back at Lacey one more time before she followed the guys out. Unmistakable dislike glittered in the other woman's eyes, and Holly didn't look away, unwilling to be intimidated. Finally Lacey's gaze fell, and Holly walked out.

"We should stop by Riley's and ask him to keep a look out as well," Ethan said as they piled into the Land Rover.

"Good idea," Adam said. "I'll stop and run in. You all can wait in the truck.

Thirty minutes later, they drove out of Clyde after stopping at Riley's. When they finally pulled into the drive of the cabin, Holly expelled a long sigh of relief. She'd never been so happy to be anywhere before.

She walked inside with the guys and promptly sagged onto the couch. She reached for the afghan strewn to the side and pulled it up to her chin.

"Cold, doll?" Ethan asked.

She nodded and snuggled deeper into the couch.

"I'll build a fire."

"I'll case the perimeter," Ryan said.

"I'll go with you," Adam said. "I need to check on the horses anyway."

201

Holly watched as they walked out the back door then she turned to Ethan and arched her brow. "Case the perimeter?"

Ethan chuckled. "It's Ryan's way of saying he's going to check out the property, make sure nothing's been disturbed and probably set a few traps."

"Traps?" she echoed.

"He's ex-military, doll. He thinks like a soldier."

"Do you think he'll come for me here?"

His eyes softened. "I don't know, but if he does, we'll be prepared." He headed toward the back door. "I'll be right back. I'm going to get some wood for the fire."

She settled back against the sofa cushions and closed her eyes. She was home. She'd done it. She'd sought a divorce from Mason. The ball was rolling, and all she had to do now was wait until she was free. And then she could begin her life with three men she wasn't sure she could live without.

Over the next few weeks, Holly became more convinced than ever that she had made the right decision. She was happy. Happier than she'd ever been in her life. As great as the sex was, there were plenty of nights when they just enjoyed each other's company. Those were some of her favorite times.

They played games. Talked about good times. Eased further into their lives together. Whatever reservations Holly'd had about committing to three men, they were fast disappearing.

One day after a fresh snowfall, Holly went riding with all three brothers. They took her further up into the high-country where they hunted elk every fall.

There on top of a plateau, Holly understood what it was that had drawn the brothers to the mountains here. She remembered Ryan's statement that there wasn't another place as pretty as the Rockies. He was right. If there was, she hadn't seen it.

Her life had taken such a drastic turn. Never would she have imagined that her spoiled existence would take her to a rustic cabin high in the Rockies. It was only now she realized how fake her entire life had been. Devoid of reality.

She'd floated through her young adult life with no goal, no direction, no aim. Here, in the arms of three men, instead of feeling like she'd traded one dependency for another, she felt alive and free. Capable of making her own decisions. *Encouraged* to be strong and stand on her own.

She sat on her horse, high above the valley and stared out over the horizon. Behind her, she knew Adam, Ethan and Ryan waited, but they didn't rush her, and she wasn't in any hurry to leave the magnificent view she beheld.

There was no explanation for the change she felt blossoming within her. It surged and swelled until it was all-encompassing. It demanded release. Wanted acceptance. Wanted her to acknowledge it.

For the first time in longer than she could remember, she felt completely at peace with the direction of her life.

Adam exchanged looks with his brothers. They all wore expressions of satisfaction. Holly had greatly changed from the scared, wary woman he'd rescued from the ditch. In her place stood a strong, confidant woman.

He was exceedingly proud of her. They all were. He couldn't imagine a better mate for them.

She turned around in her saddle, her brown eyes all soft and warm.

"I don't think I've ever seen anything more beautiful," she said.

Her breath came out in a visible cloud in the cold air. He disagreed with her. He'd seen something more beautiful. He was looking at her.

"I can't wait to see it in the fall when all the aspens are in color," she added.

He smiled back at her. He got a ridiculous thrill every time she mentioned the future. He felt like an adolescent with a first crush. He knew his brothers weren't any more immune than he was.

She nudged her horse away from the ledge and drew abreast of him and his brothers.

"I could stay here forever."

He smiled again at her use of forever. He was turning into a goddamn pussy. And liking it at that. God help him.

"You are staying here, forever," he pointed out. "We can come up here as often as you like."

She smiled sweetly at him, delight shining in her eyes.

"What do you say we head back?" Ethan spoke up. "I'll make us some hot chocolate, and we can play Monopoly. I want revenge for the last time Holly cleaned me out."

Holly's laughter rang out over the mountainside. White flurries began drifting downward, and Holly's eyes lit up in delight.

"More snow!"

They all smiled indulgently at her and turned their horses back toward home. As they continued, the snow began to fall harder. They'd get several inches before it was over with. Added to the six they'd already received, they'd get quite the dump before the night was over.

Chapter Twenty-Two

It had the makings of a perfect evening. The snow had finally stopped falling, leaving the landscape covered in a fresh blanket of white. A fire blazed in the hearth, and Holly sat on the floor playing Monopoly with Ethan and Ryan. Adam shut down the computer and ambled over to sit behind Holly.

He stroked her hair, enjoying her interaction with his brothers. Yes, it was a perfect night. So it shouldn't have surprised him when the phone rang.

He sighed in disgust and dropped his hand from Holly's hair.

"Don't answer," she said huskily, turning to smile at him sweetly.

For a moment, he almost heeded her request. But it could be Cal calling with news, or it could be Mom and Dad. "I'll be right back," he said, dropping a kiss on her upturned lips.

He shoved himself from the floor just as the phone quit ringing. Before he could settle back down, his cell phone started buzzing.

Fuck. Whatever it was, it must be important.

He walked over to the computer desk and flipped open his cell phone.

"Adam here," he said shortly.

"Adam? It's Lacey. Look, I need your help. All of you if you can swing it. I've got a missing kid. Fresh snowfall's made it impossible to pick up any tracks. I could use you."

Adam sighed and ran a hand through his hair. Damn. The last thing he wanted to do was trek out into the cold, but he couldn't very well leave a child out to freeze to death.

"Where do we need to come?" he asked in resignation.

"Meet me in town. We're organizing our search here at headquarters. And listen, Adam. Bring your rifles. We have reason to believe this is an abduction."

Adam shut the phone and looked up to see three pair of eyes watching him.

Holly uncurled her legs and stood up. She walked over to him, worry creasing her brow. "What's wrong?" she asked.

Behind her, Ethan and Ryan also stood, their attention focused solely on Adam.

"That was Lacey," he said. He glanced down at Holly to gauge her reaction.

She frowned slightly but didn't say anything.

"What did she want?" Ryan demanded.

"She needs our help. Got a kid gone missing and with the fresh snowfall, they can't get any tracks."

"Man..." Ethan said.

"You have to go," Holly said softly. "I mean, you have to find the child."

Adam nodded.

"You go on. I'll be fine," she said, hugging her arms around her.

"One of us should stay," Adam said, looking to his brothers for confirmation. "Holly shouldn't be alone." He didn't want to alarm her, but there was no way they'd leave her unprotected with her husband out there. The incident in Denver was still too fresh in his memory.

"I'll stay," Ryan said. "You and Ethan go on."

Adam nodded. "All right."

He enfolded Holly in his arms. "We'll be back as soon as we can, baby."

She reached up on tiptoe and kissed him. "Bet your ass you will."

He grinned. Then he turned to Ethan. "You ready?"

Ethan brushed his lips across Holly's hair then hurried over to the closet where they kept their gear.

Five minutes later, they walked out the door and got into the Land Rover. As he backed down the drive, heaviness settled in his chest. He couldn't explain the feeling, but worry nagged at him.

Holly turned to Ryan as the door closed and spread her arms out. "Just you and me."

He grinned and sauntered over to her. "I can think of worse things."

Her heart turned over in her chest.

"Oh, the things I'm going to do to you," he said wickedly.

She smiled and shoved him playfully. "Oh no, bad boy, what I'm going to do to *you*."

He raised a brow. "I think I like the sound of that."

She fluttered her eyelashes. "Meet me. Bedroom. Five minutes."

He reached out to grab her, but she darted from his grasp. She ran for the bedroom, shrieking with laughter. "Five minutes!" she called back.

She shut the door behind her and headed for the closet where she'd hidden the sexy lingerie she'd bought in Denver. She pulled the silky, peach camisole top from the tissue where it was wrapped then snagged the matching silk shorts.

Quickly shimmying out of her jeans and shirt, she danced out of the closet on one foot as she thrust the other into the shorts. She tossed her hair with her hand and headed into the bathroom for a quick check.

The smiling, laughing girl in the mirror was a long way from the tattered, scared rabbit who'd run for her life just weeks ago.

She picked up a brush and ran it through her now light brown hair. She only had about one minute before Ryan would break down the door. She dropped the brush and scurried out of the bathroom and headed for the bed.

To her surprise, Ryan was there waiting for her. Naked.

"Oh, you're bad," she scolded. "You were supposed to wait five minutes."

He grinned sheepishly at her. "Telling time has never been my strong point."

She stood there, hand on her hip.

"Come here," he ordered.

"I ought to make you wait," she grumbled as she crawled up the bed.

He curled an arm over her waist and rolled her underneath him in one smooth motion. His lips rested an inch above hers, and he lowered them until they brushed across her mouth.

"You look hot in that outfit," he rasped. "It's a damn shame I'm going to have to take it off so quickly.

She laughed. "A terrible shame."

He pulled at the top until it bared one breast.

"I love your nipples. They're perfect. Pink. So feminine."

He rolled his tongue across the puckered tip. "They taste as sweet as they look."

"You're such a miserable tease," she groaned out.

He tugged at the camisole top until the straps fell down her shoulders. He continued to pull at it until it gathered around her waist.

"I could suck them all night."

He licked and nipped at the stiff points. His tongue circled one, outlining it in a wet trail. Then he sucked it between his teeth and exerted firm pressure with his mouth.

The bite of pain mixed with the nearly unbearable pleasure had her squirming restlessly beneath him.

"I like having you at my mercy," he murmured. "One of these days, I'm going to have to tie you up and have my wicked way with you. I bet Adam and Ethan would love it as well."

Oh Jesus. She didn't think it was possible for her to become any more aroused, but she was so wrong. Images of her bound, subject to their every whim and desire sent threads of desire through her pussy and deep into her pelvis.

"You like that idea, I see," he teased.

Yeah, she liked that idea. Too damn much if her reaction was any clue.

He scooted down her body and pulled at her lacy waistband with his teeth. As more of her skin was bared, he licked and nibbled at the sensitive flesh.

Finally, he pulled her underwear all the way down and threw them over his shoulders. Then he moved back up her body, spreading her legs as he went.

He settled between her legs, his large cock nestled in the hot wetness of her pussy. She quivered in response, every nerve ending on fire.

"Fuck me," she whispered.

She felt him swell even larger between her legs.

"God, I love it when you talk dirty," he muttered.

She grinned and sank her teeth into his shoulder.

"Damn, woman, are you trying to make me come before I ever get inside you?"

"If you'd hurry your ass up, you wouldn't have to worry about that."

"Impatient little minx."

He shifted over her, put a hand between them and guided himself to her entrance.

"Much better," she said with a breathless sigh.

"I ought to make you wait."

She bit him again. "Fuck me."

He surged inside her in one powerful stroke. He gathered her tightly in his arms, held her close as his hips began undulating between her legs.

"Harder," she urged.

"Are you trying to kill me?" he complained.

"Wuss."

He yanked at her hair. "Watch it, wench."

He pushed himself up off her and grasped her legs in his hands. He doubled her knees to her chest and withdrew, arced above her.

He slid forward inch by agonizing inch until she was breathless with wanting. Then he plunged deep, his hard thighs slapping against her butt. She gasped at the depth.

"Don't stop," she gasped when he paused.

He grinned down at her. "Not so cocky now, are we?"

"I'm so going to get you back for this," she gritted out.

He pulled back and stopped. She bucked her hips, trying to seat him fully again.

"Fuck me," she begged.

He groaned and slid into her again. "I love a woman with a potty mouth."

She laughed.

He began to thrust harder, setting a breathtaking pace. She tried to catch up, to breathe, but she was robbed of air.

He let her legs go and they slumped to the side. She wrapped her arms around him, pulling him as close to her as she could. Then she circled his waist with her legs, locking him into place.

They kissed hotly, wetly, their tongues imitating the sliding motion of his cock in and out of her pussy. His hands tangled roughly in her hair as he pulled her mouth to his.

Urgency mounted in her groin. Her orgasm raced upon her with speed she'd never experienced. There was no slow build to the finish. It exploded around her in a violent surge. Every muscle in her body strained painfully and then released like an arrow from a bow.

Ryan thrust powerfully against her, his hips rocking her forward on the bed. "Oh, damn," he strained out.

Yeah, damn. She collapsed beneath him as he surged forward again, his seed rushing into her body. His hips twitched and jerked as he continued to jet his release.

Finally he slumped between her legs, his forehead resting on hers. His breaths came in jerky spurts as he sucked in mouthfuls of air.

"You're going to kill me," he groaned.

"But what a way to go," she said.

He rolled to the side of her and drew her into his arms. "Want me to draw you a bath?"

She smiled. "No, I'd much rather stay right here."

"You wore me out," he complained.

"Whiner."

He tweaked her nipple with his free hand. "Watch your mouth or I'll slide my dick in it to shut you up."

"Promises, promises," she chided.

He chuckled and rested his chin on top of her head. "Go to sleep."

She sighed. "You going to get the lights or shall I?"

He groaned but slid out of bed and padded toward the light switch. Before he reached it, the lights flickered and went out, plunging the room into darkness.

"Ryan?" she called out in a wavery voice.

Icy dread snaked down her spine. She knew he hadn't flipped the switch. He hadn't even touched it yet.

Ryan strode back to the bed. He reached down for his jeans and threw her clothes onto the bed. "Get dressed," he commanded.

She hurried out of bed and pulled the camisole over her head. She reached for the underwear and thrust a leg into them.

"Come with me," Ryan said, reaching for her arm.

He hustled her down the hallway, his arm curled protectively around her.

"Is it the weather?" she asked as they entered the living room.

Ryan bent over the desk and dug out a flashlight. "No, I don't think so."

Fear formed a hard ball in her stomach. "What is it then?"

He turned to her, his face barely outlined in the darkness. "Listen to me. I want you to go into the guest bathroom and lock yourself in. There's no windows. Stay until I come get you."

Terror swept over her. "Ryan, what's going on?"

He bent and kissed her hard, taking her breath. "Go."

She ran. Through the dining room and down the other hallway where all the guestrooms were situated. She felt her way in the darkness, her hands sliding down the walls. She threw open the door to the bathroom and rushed in, slamming it behind her.

She bolted the lock then felt around in the darkness. The counter, the rim of the toilet. She fumbled with the seat and quietly set it down then sat and hunched forward, hugging her knees to her chest.

Hours passed or was it minutes? It felt like an eternity. Where was Ryan? There was no sound, only the suffocating cape of darkness.

Then she heard footsteps. Slow, wary footsteps. Closer they came until they stopped outside the door. She sucked in her breath and battled the panic that threatened to overtake her.

"Holly, it's me. Open the door."

She surged from the toilet and yanked open the door. She threw herself into Ryan's arms. "What's going on?" she whispered.

"I'm not sure. I've checked the house, the grounds. The fuses are fine, no cut wires. Must be trouble in the line."

She sighed in relief. "I was scared."

"I know. I'm sorry. Come on out into the living room. I want you where I can see you. I'll build up the fire."

She followed him down the hallway, her hand tucked securely into his. As they stepped into the living room, a shadow darted into her line of vision. Before she could react, a shot rang out and Ryan jerked. He fell to the floor inches from her feet.

Holly screamed. Oh God, Ryan had been shot! She dropped to the floor, uncaring of the danger to her. "Ryan! Ryan!" she screamed.

She ran her hands across his chest, and they came away warm and sticky. Blood.

Pain exploded in her head as someone yanked her up by her hair. She reacted in fury, kicking and hitting. The dark figure threw her away from him, and she hit the wall. Before she could run, he was on her. He backhanded her across the face, knocking her to the floor.

She lay there stunned, pain flashing in her vision. The attacker yanked her hands behind her and slapped handcuffs on her. She struggled wildly, but he had her pinned beneath his knee. He bent her legs, putting them together then he snapped a pair of cuffs around her ankles.

"Get off me, you bastard!" she shrieked.

He slapped her again then shoved a cloth in her mouth. Then he tied a bandana around her head, securing the gag. With his knee still squarely in her back, he fumbled for a minute then she heard the beeping of a phone. He was calling someone. Who?

"I've got her," he said. "Yeah. Taken care of." He paused for a minute. "I'm taking her to the cabin. It's remote. No one will find her, and I'll make sure all loose ends are tied up."

He clapped the phone shut then grabbed her arms and hauled her up. "You and I are going for a ride, bitch."

He dragged her toward the door, and she stared back at Ryan, straining to see him in the dim light. Tears flooded her eyes. *Ryan.* Oh God. The bastard had killed him.

Sobs welled in her throat, escaping around the gag. A blast of cold air washed over her naked legs as the attacker pulled her outside into the snow. Her skimpy nightwear offered no protection from the biting cold.

As if she were nothing, the man threw her over his shoulder and headed for the road. A few minutes later, he stopped and dumped her into the ditch.

She looked up to see a dark vehicle, an SUV of some type. The man yanked open the back then turned to pull her up. He threw her into the back, and she landed with a thump, all the breath knocked from her.

He slammed the door, and seconds later, she heard the driver's door open and then the engine started.

Grief and rage poured over her, swirling, a storm she couldn't control. She ignored the cold, her injuries, she could only think of Ryan lying lifeless on the floor.

The SUV rounded a corner, jostling her. Something smooth and cool slid into her chin. It took her a moment to realize it was a cell phone. He must have dropped it when he threw her in the back.

Her heart beat furiously as she tried to figure out a way she could use the phone. Her hands were secured behind her back, her legs were handcuffed, and the cloth was stuffed in her mouth.

First the gag had to go. She slid her head repeatedly on the floor, trying to move the bandana down her head. After several agonizing attempts, she felt the bandana slip and loosen. She scrubbed her cheek until finally she worked the bandana down around her neck.

She chewed and worked her tongue, shoving the cloth from her mouth. Finally it fell and she sucked in huge breaths, trying to make the panic subside.

Getting the phone open would be tricky. She rolled and contorted her body, flipping over to her other side. She wiggled her fingers, reaching, straining for the phone. Her fingers slid over the surface, and she dug her fingers into the seam until finally she cracked it open.

She glanced her fingers over the buttons, feeling for which was which. Awkwardly, she pushed one, then another until finally she had the sequence of Adam's cell phone number inputted. Then she felt for the send button, praying she guessed right.

As soon as she pressed the last button, she rolled and squirmed, rotating back over until her mouth and ear were close to the receiver.

Let him answer, she prayed. *Let him answer.*

Chapter Twenty-Three

Bitter cold pierced Adam's heavy coat. They'd finally been able to pick up a faint trail in the snow about a mile outside of town. He and Ethan shined their floodlights over the terrain, moving as quickly through the drifts as possible.

Heavy, wet flakes fell, covering the tracks almost as quickly as they could find them.

"There's a shed just ahead," Adam shouted back to Lacey who was bringing up the rear.

He waded through the last heavy drift and shoved his way to the ramshackle shed a few feet away. He grabbed his gun sling and hauled his rifle over his shoulder until his hand curled around the stock.

Ethan shuffled up behind him, rifle trained on the door.

"Shine the light, I'll go in," Adam directed.

He counted to three then rammed his shoulder into the rickety wooden door. It shattered and Adam stumbled inside. Ethan rushed in behind him, light raised, gun sweeping the area.

"There, in the corner!" Adam exclaimed.

Lacey burst in behind them, her pistol drawn. "Find anything?" she asked breathlessly.

Adam didn't respond. His attention was focused on the small child huddled in the corner of the shed. Dropping to his knees in front of the boy, Adam reached out and touched the child's cold skin.

To his relief, the boy stirred and opened his eyes.

"Thank God," Adam murmured.

Lacey immediately began barking orders into her radio as she relayed their position. She requested EMS and told the dispatcher to inform the parents the child had been found.

"Sam," Adam said gently. "We've come to take you home."

"The bad man said I couldn't go home," Sam stuttered out. "Not until..."

"Not until what?" Lacey demanded.

Sam's brow furrowed in confusion, his lips shook with the cold. "Said I had to serve my purpose. What's that mean?"

Adam looked at the others and shrugged. What sicko had taken the child and left him here in the cold to freeze to death?

He reached down and picked Sam up, cradling him in his arms. "We're going to take you home now, Sam. Your mama's been awfully worried."

"Don't let the bad man hurt her," Sam mumbled against Adam's shirt.

"Don't worry, son. He can't hurt your mama."

Sam raised his head. "Not Mama. The woman. The bad man said he had to take care of a woman."

Icy prickles danced up Adam's spine. He glanced over at the others, tendrils of dread clinging to him like a vine. "Take him for me," he directed Ethan.

After Ethan hefted the boy into his arms, Adam dug for his cell phone. He punched in his home number and waited as it rang. He let it ring twenty times before he closed his cell phone. He swore softly.

"It's the middle of the night," Lacey offered. "They're probably asleep."

"Yeah and my signal sucks," Adam said, trying to dispel the heavy foreboding that swelled in his gut. "I'll try again when we get to town."

"Ready to head out?" Lacey asked as she secured the rope to the rescue sled.

Ethan laid Sam down and arranged blankets around him. Then he and Adam took the rope and began pulling the sled through the snow. It was at least an hour trek back to town, and Adam carried a knot the size of a softball in his stomach.

Forty-five minutes later, out of breath and slogging much slower through the snow, Adam and Ethan stopped a moment to rest.

"It's not much further now," Lacey said.

Adam nodded, too winded to speak. The peal of his cell phone ringing rent the night air. Adam dropped the rope and dug frantically for his phone.

He flipped it open. "This is Adam."

"Adam..." Holly's voice, faint and wavery, filtered through the line.

"Holly?" Relief surged through him.

"Adam, thank God." Her voice got a little stronger. "I don't have much time." He could hear tears, thick in her voice, and his pulse began pounding in his head. "He killed Ryan," she sobbed.

Adam's blood ran cold. "Holly, Holly, baby, where are you? Are you all right?" he shouted.

"I don't know where I am," she said, her voice desperate. "He took me. Please come get me." Her voice broke.

"You bloody bitch, give me that!"

Adam held the phone, paralyzed as he heard the scene play out over the phone. Holly cried out. Adam heard the smack of flesh. Then the phone went dead.

"Sweet Jesus."

Ethan grabbed him by the shoulder. "What the fuck is going on?"

"Holly," Adam said hoarsely. "She said Ryan's *dead*. Someone has her."

Ethan dropped the floodlight he'd been carrying.

"We have to get to the cabin. Ryan. My God." Adam couldn't form another coherent thought.

"You two go on," Lacey said. "I can take Sam from here. You'll go quicker without the sled. I'll radio for backup, get a car out there as fast as I can. My guys are still out on the east end coming off their search."

Adam didn't wait to hear anymore. He and Ethan began running through the snow. Ryan. Dead. The words hummed over and over, running through his mind in a sick litany.

The bastard had lured them out, kidnapped a child, and now he had Holly. His blood ran cold. Colder than the snow that wrapped around his legs. Holly would die if they didn't get to her and get to her fast.

Ahead, the shine of the town lights glistened off the snow. Adam put on a burst of speed, his single-minded focus to get to the Land Rover as fast as possible. Ethan kept pace beside him, neither voicing the fears uppermost in their conscience.

The reached the back of Riley's store and raced around to the parking lot and across the street to where the Land Rover was parked. Several townspeople, including Sam's parents called out to them, but Adam ignored everything but the Land Rover.

He threw himself into the driver's seat, started the engine and threw it into reverse. Ethan barely made it inside before Adam roared down the street.

The drive up the mountain took forever, and every minute, Adam whispered a prayer. *God, don't take them from me.*

He gripped the steering wheel, taking the turns and switchbacks faster than he ever had. *Let him be okay. Don't take Ryan from us.*

They tore into the driveway, and both men bounded for the door. The house was dark. Adam burst in, shouting Ryan's name. Ethan shoved past him, flipping at the light switches.

Ethan swore a blue streak when the lights failed to come on then shouted Ryan's name again.

Adam stopped cold when he heard a low moan. He leaped over the couch toward the hallway leading to the guestrooms.

"Get me a light!" he barked back at Ethan.

"Ryan! Ryan!" Adam threw himself to the floor beside his brother's crumpled form.

Ethan appeared with a flashlight and shined it over Ryan's body. His chest was bathed in blood, but his eyelids fluttered as the light hit his face.

"Ryan, it's me, Adam. Can you hear me?"

"How could I not when you're yelling in my damn ear?" Ryan grumbled.

Adam wilted in relief, his body going slack. "You ornery bastard, you scared ten years off me."

"Holly," Ryan began, his voice cracking. "He got Holly."

"Where are you hit?" Adam demanded, not focusing on Holly for just a moment. He had to take care of them one at a time, and at this minute, he had to make sure Ryan was okay.

"Shoulder," Ryan said, his breath coming in short gasps.

"Can you get up?"

Ryan moved then moaned in pain.

"Adam!" Lacey called from the door. "You in here?"

"Over here," Ethan called, shining a light toward her. "How'd you get here so fast?"

"I dumped the kid in town and got up here as fast as I could. Jesus Christ, what the hell happened?" she demanded as she knelt beside Ryan.

"Help me up, damn it," Ryan said desperately. "He's got Holly."

"Who has her, Ryan?" Adam demanded.

He and Ethan lifted Ryan, and Adam wrapped an arm around him so he wouldn't fall. They guided Ryan to the couch and set him down.

"We've got to get you to the hospital," Ethan said.

"No."

"Ryan, you're in no shape to be anywhere but in the hospital."

"It's a flesh wound," he ground out. "I'm not going anywhere with Holly out there with that bastard." He broke off. "He hurt her. I heard him hit her."

Adam clenched his fingers into tight fists. He'd also heard the asshole strike Holly.

"What else did you hear, Ryan? Did he say anything? We have to find her."

"He made a phone call. He said something about a remote cabin and tying up loose ends."

"Christ." Remote cabin. Like there weren't enough of those spread out across the Rockies.

"He acted like it was close," Ryan said as he put a hand over his shoulder. Bright red blood smeared across his fingers.

"You've got to get to the hospital. Lacey, can you make sure he gets there?" Adam asked.

"I'm not going," Ryan bit out.

"You'll only slow us down," Adam said. "We can't afford to waste a minute. He'll kill her."

Ryan looked bleakly at Adam. "I failed her."

"She thinks you're dead," Adam said. "The best thing you can do is get your ass to the hospital so what she thinks doesn't come to pass."

Ryan surged to his feet. "How do you know what she thinks?"

Adam quickly explained the phone call then he made arrangements for Lacey to get Ryan to the hospital. His mind worked furiously, trying to come up with a plan of action.

"Let's go, Ethan."

He stopped long enough to collect more ammunition for their rifles then he raced out of the house to the Land Rover. Ethan jumped in beside him.

"Close, remote cabin. You think he could be taking her to Blythe Meadow?" Ethan asked as Adam roared down the drive.

"Good call," Adam said. "It certainly fits. If not there, maybe the old miner's cabin. We'll hit both."

Ethan stared out the window in silence. Then he turned agonized eyes to Adam. "What if we're too late?"

Adam shook his head and pressed his foot into the accelerator. "We can't be too late, Ethan. We just can't."

Chapter Twenty-Four

Holly slowly opened her eyes, surprised at the effort it took. The air was frigid around her, and her jaw ached. She didn't recognize her surroundings. She was in a one-room cabin, lying on the floor. She tested her arms and found they were free from the handcuffs she'd worn earlier.

Pale shades of light beamed through the one window. Dawn. So she'd been here at least two hours.

Tears leaked from her eyelids. Ryan. She'd never even told him she loved him. And now she'd never get that chance.

A sound startled her then pain assaulted her hip as her captor kicked her.

"I see you're awake. Good. Now get up."

She gazed warily up at him. It was the first good look she'd gotten of him. She'd expected a mean brute of a man, but she stared at what appeared to be a mild-mannered man of average height and size.

He smirked as if reading her thoughts.

"Don't let my appearance fool you, my dear. Now you can get up of your own accord or I'll get you up, and I assure you, it won't be a pleasant experience."

Terror washed through her system. She wanted to vomit. She put her hand out to prop herself up and shoved herself from the floor. As soon as she stood, the man grabbed her arm and jerked her toward a chair.

"Have a seat."

She sank down in the chair situated by an old desk. The chair heaved and groaned as she settled her slight weight on it, and for a moment, she feared it would collapse.

She put out her hand to the desk to balance herself. She was cold. Colder than she'd ever been in her life. There was no heat in the cabin. No protection from the biting cold. Her limbs felt like blocks of ice. She shivered uncontrollably. Once she started, she couldn't stop.

The man lit a cigarette and lazily blew smoke. He leaned against the small sink and watched her with cold eyes.

"I won't beat around the bush. I'm going to kill you."

Panic flooded her. Her throat tightened, and for a moment she couldn't breathe. She didn't want to die.

"But I'm going to be civil about it."

He looked amused at his proclamation. He even emitted a dry chuckle.

"I'll offer you a choice. A very quick, painless death, or," he paused for effect, "it can be a very messy, very prolonged, very painful death. Your choice."

Her mouth went dry.

"All you have to do is tell me who all knows what happened on your wedding night. Very simple. Mr. Bardwell is very keen to protect his interests. Which would be difficult in a jail cell, as I'm sure you can imagine."

He took out a large, sharp-looking knife as he spoke. He caressed the sleek metal with his fingertips, running them over the edge to the point.

Holly's mind raced. He was a talkative bastard. He was clearly enjoying the situation. Obviously if she talked, it would be over with in a matter of minutes. She eyed the knife, abject terror raging through her body.

She closed her eyes and tried to summon her courage. She pictured Ryan and bit the inside of her cheek to keep from weeping. She couldn't allow this bastard to get away with what he'd done.

"So what will it be, Mrs. Bardwell? Shall we enjoy a brief conversation before your untimely demise?"

Her hand splayed out over the desk and she stood to her feet. "Go to hell," she spat.

His eyes hardened. He crossed the space between them and without warning, grabbed her arm and yanked it behind her back. He whirled her around until she faced the desk. She cried out in pain as he continued to exert enormous pressure on her arm.

Higher he pushed. She screamed in agony and then she felt a pop. He'd broken her arm!

He let go and her arm fell, dangling at her side. Spots dotted her vision, growing larger until she feared she'd black out from the pain. Her hand scraped the desk trying to hold herself upright. Her fingertips brushed across a pencil and she curled her hand around it.

Rage taking control, adrenaline pumping through her veins, she whirled around, pencil in hand and plunged it into his face. It sank into his cheek, and he stumbled back howling in pain.

She wasted no time. Ignoring the horrific pain in her left arm, she flew at him, ramming her knee into his groin. Once, twice and a third time until he fell to the floor.

She didn't hesitate even for a moment. She ran.

She threw open the door to the cabin and plunged into the snow. Icy wetness met her hips as she scrambled to gain her footing.

Her heart sank. She'd never make it out alive. The snow was too high. Too deep. She'd freeze to death in her scanty clothing long before she could make it to safety.

She set her jaw until it ached. She wasn't going to die at the bastard's hands. If she died, it wouldn't be without a fight.

Ignoring the pain, the cold and the horrible numbness affecting her limbs, she struggled on, determined to put as much distance between her and her abductor as she could.

She headed for the trees, hoping to lose herself in the wooded area. A hysterical laugh bubbled from her throat. How could she lose anyone in three feet of snow?

Her head popped back. She was yanked backwards, a hand wrapped tightly in her hair. She turned on him, fighting tooth and nail. Her survival was at hand.

Metal glistened in the early morning sun. Then tearing agony exploded in her chest. She fell back into the snow, dimly aware of the man holding a knife above her. Her uninjured arm sank into the snow. Her hand grasped for purchase and knocked against a rock. She gripped it tightly, prepared to make her last stand.

With a cry of rage, she hauled her arm forward and bashed the man's head with the rock as he plunged downward with the knife again. This time the knife glanced off her shoulder, cutting a long gash down her arm.

He fell face first into the snow, and she gave him no time to recover. She rolled, raising the rock high again and hitting him as hard as she could. He went still, and she dropped the rock.

She rolled and scooted away, trying desperately to regain her footing. The world tilted and swayed around her, her mind swimming in sheer agony. He'd stabbed her in the chest. She could feel hot blood running over her skin. Her left arm dangled uselessly beside her. Somehow she had to find a way home.

She stumbled down the hill, away from the cover of the trees. She needed to be in plain sight now. Her only hope was rescue.

She closed her eyes. She'd never told them she loved them. Hot tears fell, mixing with the blood that ran freely down her body. If only she'd told them.

Adam drove the Land Rover to its limits. For two hours, they'd searched every nook and cranny of the mountain. There was only one possibility left, and despite his best effort, he was fast losing hope.

"Around the next bend, take the path off the road," Ethan directed, his voice grim. "We have to hope the snowfall hasn't made the trail impassable."

Adam tore around the corner and braked as the turnoff rushed to greet them.

"Adam look!" Ethan cried out.

Adam wasted no time. A fresh trail down the path. One made recently. By a vehicle. He sped up the bumpy incline, slipping and rocking in the snow. The four-wheel drive made quick work of the path, and soon they rounded the bend to the old mining cabin.

A black SUV glinted in the sunlight. Adam roared to a stop, grabbed his rifle and piled out of the Rover. Ethan followed quickly behind, his gun up and ready.

Adam frowned when he saw the door wide open. He ducked under the window and peered inside through the entryway. It was empty.

He and Ethan rushed inside.

"Someone's been here," Ethan muttered. "Very recently."

Ethan picked up a still lit cigarette lying on the floor and flicked it away.

Adam's heart sank as he looked around. There were visible signs of a scuffle. Blood on the floor. He whirled around and ran out the door, his eyes searching the snow for fresh signs.

Deep trenches in the snow led away from the cabin and into the trees in the distance. He and Ethan leapt off the porch and began charging after the tracks.

A few seconds later, Ethan put a hand out to halt Adam.

"Look!"

Ethan pointed to a body in the distance. They ran over to find a man slumped in the snow. Blood seeped from a wound in the back of his head.

Adam rolled him over. He was unconscious. Hope beat a steady rhythm in his heart. Had Holly been able to escape him?

Then his eyes came to rest on the dark red blood that stained the snow. Blood that did not come from the man. His eyes followed the splatters across the snow where it continued down the hill.

"Let's go!" he shouted.

They powered down the hill. Adam prayed the whole way. God let them find her. Let her be okay.

"Adam, there she is!"

Adam looked ahead in time to see Holly wobble and slump into the snow. He ran the remaining thirty yards, his heart screaming the entire way.

When he got to her, he reached down and pulled her up to his chest.

"Oh God," he moaned.

There was so much blood. It bathed her entire front. Her left arm lay at an odd angle, swollen and discolored.

"Holly! Holly, baby," he cried.

Ethan sank down beside him and helped Adam lift her from the snow.

Her eyes fluttered weakly. Disorientation clouded their depths. She pushed and shoved, trying to stand.

She was running on adrenaline, and she was fast running out. She began to shake violently.

"She's going into shock," Adam said. "We have to get her out of here now. Radio in. Tell them to have the chopper waiting. We'll have to get her as far down the mountain as we can.

"Ryan," she cried out. "Oh God, Ryan." She struggled weakly against Adam, tears slipping down her cheeks.

"Shhh, baby. Ryan's okay. I swear it."

She didn't seem to hear him.

"I never told...I never told them I loved them," she whispered.

Adam held her tighter against him. He buried his lips in her hair and blinked back tears. "God, I love you too, baby. I love you too."

He stood up, holding her carefully in his arms. He had no idea the extent of her injuries, but he had to get her down the mountain fast.

Ethan rushed ahead, clearing a path in the snow for Adam. They struggled up the hill, each step excruciatingly slow. Finally the Land Rover was in sight. Ethan surged forward, redoubling his efforts.

"Get me the first aid kit," Adam barked. "I'll sit in the backseat and lay her down. I need to try and stop the bleeding."

Ethan threw open the back and hauled out the first aid kit, several blankets and a wad of bandages.

As soon as Adam got into the back with Holly, Ethan cranked the engine and roared back down the trail toward the main road.

"How is she, Adam? I need to know something," Ethan said, desperation creeping into his voice.

"The bastard broke her arm. Looks like he stabbed her in the chest. Christ, there's so much blood!"

Helplessness had him in a firm grip. He kept a finger to her neck, feeling for her pulse. It was weak and erratic, but it still beat against his skin.

He wadded the bandages in his hand and pressed them to the wound on her chest. He needed to slow the flow of blood.

"Ryan..."

Holly was only half-conscious and completely unaware of Adam and Ethan. Adam smoothed his free hand over her cheek.

"Ryan's okay, baby. Do you hear me?"

She tossed her head, soft moans rasping from her throat.

"Cold...so cold."

"Turn up the damn heat," Adam barked at Ethan.

He gathered the blankets tighter around her, trying to infuse warmth into her body.

The squawk of the radio interrupted him, and he heard Ethan respond, but Adam's focus was on Holly and the blood-soaked bandages in his hand.

"The chopper's almost here," Ethan called back. "They're landing in Duffy's pasture. We'll be there in about two minutes."

Adam sucked in a breath of relief. They were nearly there, and the sooner Holly got to a hospital, the better her chances of survival.

"Any word on Ryan?" Adam asked.

"Lacey said they life flighted him to Denver. Same hospital they'll take Holly to. They were worried at the amount of blood he lost."

Ethan's voice carried an undercurrent of concern, one that jarred Adam's nerves all the more.

"But he was okay, right?"

"Said he lost consciousness right before they took off. Don't know any more than that."

"Fuck!"

He closed his eyes and wanted to howl in fury and frustration. Tears stung his lids, and he shut his eyes even harder to prevent them from leaking out. He'd never felt so damn helpless in his life.

The two most important people in his life aside from Ethan could be taken from him.

He grabbed at the seat to steady himself when the Land Rover came to an abrupt stop. The door flew open, and a flight medic peered in.

The medic yelled back instructions, and two responders ran over with a backboard and jump bag. Adam backed out of the Rover and let them take over.

A hand slipped over Adam's shoulder and he turned to see Lacey standing there.

"I just want you to know how sorry I am this happened, Adam."

"I know you are, Lacey."

"Is there anything I can do?"

He turned to look at her. "We left the man up at the old mining cabin. He's probably dead by now. You might want to have a deputy go up and get him."

Lacey gave him a sharp look. "You didn't kill him, did you, Adam?"

"No, but I wish I had," he returned softly.

The medics pulled Holly out of the Land Rover and laid her on the backboard. Adam and Ethan ran over but were warded back by the paramedic.

"This is a load and go situation, sir. I'm sorry, but we don't have any time to waste."

Adam's mouth opened, wanting to ask the question, but it stuck. He wouldn't allow himself to voice it. Instead, he watched as they hustled the backboard onto the chopper. The flight medic jumped in and signaled the pilot to take off. Seconds later, the bird lifted into the air and flew toward Denver.

"Let's go, Adam," Ethan said in a strained voice. One that sounded very much like he was holding back tears as well. "It's a few hours' drive to Denver."

Adam followed numbly behind Ethan and they climbed into the Rover. He was afraid. Afraid of what they'd discover when they arrived at the hospital.

Chapter Twenty-Five

Adam managed to piss off no less than six people before he discovered where Ryan and Holly were. He'd torn through the busy ER until he'd been threatened with arrest if he didn't settle down.

Holly had been taken to surgery, but Ryan was still in the ER where he was receiving a blood transfusion. At first, Adam and Ethan had been told they couldn't see Ryan yet, but after Adam swore he'd take down the waiting room piece by piece, the nurse had relented and allowed them back.

Adam shoved into the door, anxious to see his younger brother. Ryan's appearance shocked him. Beside him, Ethan sucked in his breath as well.

Pale, haggard, weary lines etched around his eyes, Ryan looked like hell, plain and simple. His shoulder was heavily bandaged, and he had enough wires and lines running from him to keep a small city supplied in electricity.

Ryan's eyes fluttered open when the two brothers walked in. His head surged up, pain creasing his brow.

"Where is she? Did you find her?" he demanded.

Adam stopped by the bed, his knees weak with relief. There was nothing wrong with Ryan a few days in the hospital wouldn't fix.

"We found her," Adam said quietly.

"Where is she?" Ryan gritted from behind clenched teeth.

Adam ran a hand through his hair, trying desperately to maintain his composure.

"She's here. In the hospital," Ethan spoke up.

Ryan's eyes blazed. "How is she?"

"We don't know," Adam said.

Ryan jerked his head back toward Adam. He swallowed heavily then opened his mouth. "What happened?"

Adam closed his eyes. "He stabbed her in the chest. Broke her arm. She's in surgery. They airlifted her here. We don't know much."

Ryan sank back against his pillows, his face white. Tears streaked down his cheeks. Adam felt a painful twinge in his chest. He hadn't seen Ryan cry since they were kids.

"Will she...will she be okay?" he rasped.

Adam exchanged looks with Ethan. He didn't want to lie to Ryan, but Ryan was in no shape for this kind of burden.

"I think she'll be fine," Adam said, hoping he *hadn't* just lied.

"I let her down. I failed her," Ryan said bleakly.

"I let you both down," Adam said. "I should have never left either of you. But we can't think of that right now."

Ethan put a hand on Ryan's uninjured shoulder. "How are you feeling?"

"I'm pissed," Ryan said angrily. "I let that bastard get the drop on me."

"What did the doc say about your shoulder?" Adam said, pushing the subject firmly back to Ryan.

Ryan closed his eyes again and sank further into the pillow. "Says I'll be fine. Gave me two pints of blood, patched up the wound. Wants me to stay a day or two, but overall, he said I was one lucky bastard."

He cracked one eye to stare at Adam. "How did you find her? What happened? You haven't told me anything."

"We can talk about it later," Adam said. He was sure he didn't need to rile Ryan up any more than he already was.

"Don't coddle me," Ryan said fiercely. "Tell me what the fuck happened out there."

"If you don't calm down, you're going to get us kicked out of here," Ethan said.

They were interrupted when the door eased open, and a nurse stuck her head in. "Mr. Colter? Mrs. Bardwell is out of surgery. I thought you'd want to know. She's in recovery, but the doctor will be down in a few minutes to talk to you."

"When can we see her?" Adam demanded.

"You'll have to ask the doctor. He knows you're here. He won't be long."

Adam sighed in frustration. "Do you at least know how she's doing?"

The nurse smiled kindly. "She made it through surgery fine."

His stomach dropped, and for a moment, he thought he might be sick. Relief poured over him so heavy, he had to find a place to sit down quick or he was going to fall.

He sank into the chair situated by Ryan's bed and dropped his head into his hands.

"Thank God," he heard Ethan whisper.

Adam hadn't realized just how frightened he was. Not until now. His breath came in sporadic fits as he struggled to calm his raging emotions. He clenched his fingers into fists then curled them outward again.

Several minutes passed and the brothers sat in silence. Then the door opened and an older man wearing green scrubs walked in. He glanced between the brothers and adjusted his glasses.

"You're here for Mrs. Bardwell?"

"Don't call her that," Ryan growled. "Her name is Holly."

The doctor blinked in surprise. "I take that as a yes."

Adam surged to his feet and stuck out his hand. "Adam Colter. And yes, we're here for Holly. How is she?"

The physician shook Adam's hand. "Dr. Phillips. I performed surgery on Mrs...Holly," he corrected.

"Is she okay?" Ethan asked anxiously.

"She's doing well considering the condition she arrived in. She lost quite a large amount of blood. She suffered a compound fracture of her left radius. She also suffered a six-inch laceration to her left shoulder as well as a severe knife wound to her chest. I repaired some of the damaged tissue and stitched the cut. Luckily the blade missed all her major organs. Two centimeters more to the right and it would have sliced her lung."

Adam sat back down heavily. "When can we see her?"

"She's in recovery. We'll be moving her to a step down unit, kind of a level below ICU and a step above the floor. I want to monitor her progress for a few days. I don't see any reason you can't step in to see her when she's moved from recovery."

"You'll let us know when she goes?" Ethan spoke up.

"I'll have the nurse come get you," Dr. Phillips said.

"Thank you," Adam said. "We appreciate it."

The doctor nodded and walked back out the door, shutting it behind him.

Adam turned to Ryan. "When are they moving you to a room?"

"Hell if I know," Ryan grumbled. "They poked and prodded on me for damn ever."

Adam saw the pain in Ryan's eyes. He glanced over to Ethan to see if he noticed as well. Ethan's lips set into a fine line.

"Have you had anything for pain, buddy?" Adam asked.

Ryan shot him a dirty look. "Fuck no. I wanted to be awake and aware until I knew Holly was safe."

"Well you know she's fine now, so I'm going to call the nurse so she can give you something."

"I don't need it," Ryan said through his teeth.

"Ryan, you were shot. It can't feel that great," Ethan spoke up. "Quit being so goddamn stubborn and take the medicine."

"You can take it willingly or I swear to God I'll hold you down while the nurse sticks a needle in your ass," Adam said.

"Fuck off," Ryan snarled.

But Ryan slumped down into his bed, his eyes weary and pain-filled. Adam reached for the call button and pressed. A few minutes later, a nurse bustled in, syringe in hand.

"It's about time you let me give you something, young man," she said with a reprimanding stare in Ryan's direction.

She bent over and swabbed the IV port at Ryan's wrist and swiftly injected the pain medication. She patted Ryan on the arm. "Try and get some rest now."

Adam pulled the chair up so he faced Ryan and sat back down. Ethan snared the only remaining chair and positioned it at the foot of the bed.

"Tell Holly...tell her I love her," Ryan slurred out.

"I will," Adam said quietly. "Now get some rest so you can tell her yourself."

Ryan's head slumped and his eyes closed.

Adam leaned back in his chair and laced his hands behind his head. He stared at the ceiling, the tiles swimming in his vision. He was so tired. He'd aged a decade overnight. Had it only been last night that he'd sat in the living room reflecting on how good life was?

Things had changed in an instant.

He and Ethan sat in silence as the minutes ticked by. Ethan looked every bit as tired as Adam felt. But neither would rest until they saw Holly.

He must have dozed momentarily because the opening door startled him.

"Are you Adam and Ethan?" a nurse asked.

Adam scrambled up. "Yes, ma'am, that's us."

She motioned for them to follow her outside.

Once in the hall, she turned concerned eyes on them. "We've moved Mrs. Bardwell from recovery, but she's quite distraught. She's asking for you. We don't want to have to sedate her so soon after coming off the anesthesia. Maybe your presence will calm her."

"Let's go," Adam demanded.

They followed the nurse and Adam had to check his stride in order not to pass her. His impatience nearly boiled over as he allowed her to lead them down the twisting halls to the elevator.

A lifetime later, the nurse entered a large room that housed several smaller cubicles. In the center stood the nurses station where two other nurses walked briskly to and from the cubicles.

"Mrs. Bardwell is at the end," the nurse said.

She walked down and shoved aside the curtain and gestured Adam and Ethan in. Adam shoved past her. He sucked in his breath as he saw Holly lying in the bed, a multitude of tubes and wires coming from everywhere.

Quiet sobs emanated from her, and tears spilled down her cheeks. She faced away from him, and he surged forward.

"Holly. Holly, baby, I'm here," he said as he approached the bed.

Ethan followed closely, going to Holly's other side.

She closed her eyes and turned further away from Adam.

Ethan slipped a hand to her hair and bent to kiss her.

"You're breaking my heart," Ethan said in a hoarse voice.

"Ryan," she whispered. "Oh God, Ryan."

Adam bit the inside of his cheek to keep from breaking down. He leaned forward, needing to touch her, reassure himself she was alive. "Baby, Ryan's okay, I swear it. He's down in the ER waiting for a room."

She shook her head and moaned, the agony spilling from her throat.

"Doll, listen to us," Ethan pleaded. "It's not good for you to be so upset."

Adam watched her, panic rising fast within him. The nurse hovered in the doorway, concern etched in her face.

Holly wasn't cognizant of her surroundings. She was too caught up in her grief. She thought Ryan was dead.

Adam turned to the nurse as Ethan continued to comfort Holly. "Our brother, Ryan Colter is down in ER waiting for a room. Have them bring his bed up here."

The nurse's brow crinkled. "Absolutely not. We aren't set up for a double room here. This is a step down unit. We have to be able to closely monitor our patients."

"And I'm telling you the only way you're going to calm her down is to bring him up here," Adam gritted out. "I don't care what you have to do to make it happen. Just do it."

"I don't have that kind of authority," the nurse protested. "I'll have to call the doctor in and risk sedating her."

"And I'll turn this damned hospital upside down if I have to," Adam snarled. "Don't fuck with me. Not over this. He needs a room. He needs the care. He can come here. There's room for another bed. Hell, you could put him next door and take down the curtain. I don't care how you get it done, just *do* it!"

"I can't authorize something like that," the nurse said. "Only the attending physician can."

"Then call him up here," Adam demanded. "I want to talk to him. Do it now. We're wasting time."

The nurse retreated, and a few seconds later, Dr. Phillips stuck his head in the door.

"Mr. Colter, what's going on in here?"

Adam quickly explained his request. As he spoke, the doctor hustled to Holly's bedside and took in her quiet sobs. He glanced around the room as if considering Adam's request. Then he sighed.

"I don't take well to bullying, Mr. Colter. What you're asking is highly irregular. However, I tend to agree that perhaps the best thing for this young lady is to see your brother. Maybe it will calm her. I'll have to call the ER physician and arrange it with him, but I don't see why we can't make an exception this once. Much will depend on how stable your brother's condition is. I understand he suffered a gunshot wound."

Relief flood through Adam. "Thank you, Doctor."

Adam resumed his position next to Holly's bed, his hand curling around her uninjured one. Her left arm was surrounded by a cast and her entire chest and left shoulder were swathed in heavy bandages.

He'd never seen her looking so vulnerable. Tears continued to seep from her closed eyes, and his chest tightened in response. He leaned forward and kissed her temple.

"I love you, baby," he whispered. "I'm so sorry I never told you."

As he and Ethan kept watch over Holly, she finally drifted off to sleep. Her breathing became more even, and the flow of tears finally stopped. Her head lay limply against the pillow, her face pale with red blotches from the crying.

A few minutes later, the same nurse Adam had gone up against came bustling in. She eyed him with a look of annoyance.

"I've been instructed to open up the cubicle next to Mrs. Bardwell's. Since I don't imagine you'll agree to go home, I'm having a chair and a small sofa brought in as well."

Adam eased his scowl. "Thank you," he said sincerely. "This means the world to us."

The nurse's expression softened. "I know you're worried about her. But we're doing our best to take excellent care of her." Then she grinned a little mischievously. "Besides, chances are your brother would have ended up here anyway. The hospital's pretty full, and he needs care beyond the floor, but he's not a candidate for ICU. And from what I hear, he's not exactly cooperative."

Adam's lips quirked into a smile. "Yep, that's Ryan. But he'll straighten up when he's able to see Holly. He's been pretty worried about her."

Within the hour, the curtain between the two rooms had been pulled, and two orderlies hauled in a chair and a sofa and set them between the two beds.

Thirty minutes afterward, a nurse rounded the corner, pushing Ryan in a wheelchair. She looked less than happy with her charge, and Ryan didn't look like he gave a fuck.

She rolled him toward the other bed, but he put his free hand down to jam the wheels. The nurse's lips pressed together, and she shook her head.

"Into bed with you, Mr. Colter. You got your way. I took you up in a wheelchair when you shouldn't be out of bed, but you'll go now, or I'll haul you back to the ER."

Ryan ignored her, his haunted eyes stroking over Holly.

"Help me up," he said hoarsely, his gaze going to Adam.

"Ryan, you should be in bed," Adam began.

"I have to see her," Ryan said.

Adam looked at the nurse who shrugged in defeat.

"Do whatever it is that will get him into bed the fastest," she said.

"Give me a hand, Ethan," Adam directed. "Let's make this quick."

Adam bent over Ryan, and Ryan curled his good arm around Adam's neck and pulled himself upwards. Sweat broke out on Ryan's forehead, and he trembled against Adam. Ryan's face had gone pasty white, and Adam knew it had cost him dearly to expend so much energy.

He and Ethan helped Ryan to the bed where Holly lay. Tears filled Ryan's eyes as he gazed down at her. He reached his hand out to touch her cheek then pulled it back to scrub the moisture from his own face.

"I'm so sorry," he choked out.

She stirred in her sleep.

"Ryan," she murmured. Then tears slid from beneath her lids once more.

Ryan finally lost the battle to stay upright. He sagged and Adam and Ethan scrambled to catch him. They hauled him over to the bed and with the help of the nurse settled him in. She then proceeded to lug in the IV poles and reattach the lines.

She fussed over him for a good hour before finally leaving them alone.

"Promise me, you'll wake me when she does," Ryan said as he stared at Adam in exhaustion.

"I will," Adam replied. "Now get some rest. You aren't any good to her in your present condition."

Ryan nodded and closed his eyes. He was asleep before his head fully reclined against the pillow.

Adam turned and sank down onto the sofa while Ethan took the chair next to it.

"We came close to losing them," he said quietly.

Ethan nodded. "Too close."

"Something has to be done about the bastard."

Again Ethan nodded.

Adam curled his fingers into fists then flexed them outward again. He repeated the action over and over. "I'll kill the son of a bitch myself before I let him close to my family again."

Chapter Twenty-Six

Holly slowly opened her eyes and blinked a few times to clear the cobwebs. For a moment, she had no recollection of where she was or why she was in such an unfamiliar place. And when she did remember, pain the like she'd never felt crawled through her system.

Ryan.

She closed her eyes and tried to remember all that had transpired, but all she could conjure was the memory of Ryan falling, of her hand coming away from his chest covered in blood.

Hot tears filled her eyes and escaped from her lids. She felt the slow trickle as they trekked down her cheeks. A warm hand cupped her face and gently wiped at the moisture.

She opened her eyes to see Adam standing over her, a concerned look on his face. She blinked again to bring him into focus. She slowly became aware of the rest of her surroundings. She was in a hospital room. Her gaze darted to her other side where she saw Ethan slumped in a chair asleep.

Just the fact that Ryan was so conspicuously absent sent another slow crawl of agony through her heart. A sob welled in her throat—one that she tried to call back—it threatened to choke her with its intensity. She was finally forced to let it out.

It sounded harsh and ugly, even to her own ears. And once released, more surged forth until every breath brought another cry.

"Holly, listen to me, baby. You have to listen to me. Ryan is okay. He's not dead. He's here."

Adam cupped her chin, forcing her to look at him, piercing her with his green eyes.

"Do you understand what I'm saying?" he demanded.

Then she heard someone in the background.

"Let me up, damn it!"

"Ryan?" she whispered. It couldn't be. She'd seen him fall. She'd heard the shot. Felt his blood.

She struggled to sit up and nearly blacked out as pain lanced through her chest. Adam swore above her and held her down with his hand.

"Easy, baby. Don't hurt yourself."

Behind Adam, Ryan came into view, his face haggard, eyes bloodshot, his upper half wrapped in bandages. He blurred before her as her eyes swam with tears. She'd never seen such a beautiful sight in her life.

"Christ, Ryan, you shouldn't be up," Adam protested.

Ryan pushed Adam aside, and in the next moment, Holly felt herself enveloped by Ryan's body. She pressed her cheek into his chest, the bulk of bandages shoving into her face. She didn't care. Didn't care how much it hurt for her to be in such an awkward position.

He pressed his lips to her forehead. "Thank God you're all right," he whispered.

He pulled away and Holly grabbed at his hand with hers. "Don't go."

"I hate to break this up," Adam began. "But both of you are in a lot of pain and neither of you should be doing anything but resting. Which means get your ass back in bed, Ryan. I want you both well so we can go home."

Holly heard the worry in his voice. She also saw the pain in Ryan's eyes. Her own pain was fast taking over all else. But she had to say it first.

She reached out her hand to touch Ryan's face. "I love you. I should have told you before."

Ryan caught her hand and pressed his lips into her palm. "I love you, too."

Adam wrapped an arm around Ryan and pulled him away. Ryan slumped against his brother. Holly looked up to where Ethan now stood beside her.

"Is he okay?" she asked in a low voice.

"He's doing better than you are," Ethan said dryly. He paused for a moment before touching her hair with his hand. "You scared us, doll."

She didn't respond. How could she say that they couldn't have been any more scared than she was? She'd never been so terrified in her entire life. She hadn't wanted to die with so much regret. Things had become so clear in those horrible minutes in the snow when she was sure she would never see Adam, Ethan or Ryan again.

"I love you," she said, allowing all the emotion to escape her in those three little words.

Ethan bent to press his forehead to hers. "I love you, too, doll. So much. I never want to come that close to losing you again."

She closed her eyes as he kissed her softly on the lips.

"I hurt," she said in a low voice.

Ethan immediately stood upright. "I'll call the nurse."

She smiled, wincing at the effort it took. She felt Adam's hand smooth up her arm and over her shoulder. He tenderly pushed back the tendrils of her hair over her ear.

"Get some rest, baby. We're all right here. We aren't going anywhere."

Holly heard the nurse come in, felt her fiddle with the IV, and seconds later, Holly felt welcome oblivion seep into her system.

"L-love you," she slurred, as Adam's face weaved back and forth in her shaky vision.

"I love you, too, baby. Rest now."

Over the next several days, Holly slept the majority of the time. Ryan became crankier and crankier until finally the nurses gave up trying to keep him in his bed. On the fourth day, they officially discharged him.

The same day, Holly was moved from the step down unit to a regular room. Adam finally relaxed. Both Ryan and Holly were out of the woods. Soon he'd have his family back home where they belonged.

He sat in a chair next to Holly's bed while she slept and flexed his neck. He rubbed tired eyes and wondered if he'd ever sleep another night until he knew for certain the threat of Holly's husband was removed.

Across the room, Ryan sat propped on the couch, several cushions around him. His younger brother hadn't rested nearly enough after his injury, Adam knew, but short of tying him to a bed, Adam didn't know how to make Ryan settle down.

Ethan sat in a chair next to Ryan, fatigue ringing his eyes. They were all so damned tired. They all wanted the same thing. To go home.

Adam's cell phone rang, and he hastily scooped it up so it wouldn't wake Holly.

He stood and walked toward the door, away from Holly's bed. "Adam here."

"Adam, it's Lacey. Is this a bad time?"

"No, what's up?"

Lacey hesitated for a moment. "How are Ryan and Holly?"

"Better. They discharged Ryan today and moved Holly to the floor. Both need a lot of rest, but they'll be okay."

"Hey, that's great, Adam. Look, I called because I thought you ought to know we found the guy who shot Ryan and tried to kill Holly. He's dead."

"Fuck."

"Yeah, tell me about it. I wanted the bastard alive. Adam, you know this makes it hard to pin anything on Mason Bardwell."

"Yeah, I know," Adam growled.

"What do you want me to do?"

Adam sighed and ran a hand through his hair. "Don't do anything yet. I need to talk to Cal as well as Ryan and Ethan. We can't take Holly back there if it isn't safe."

"I'll let you know if my investigation uncovers anything else," Lacey promised.

"Thanks," Adam said as he closed the phone.

He turned around to see Holly studying him.

"Hey," he said as he walked toward the bed. He bent and kissed her forehead then smoothed her hair from her cheek with his hand. "How are you feeling?"

Her cinnamon eyes stared apprehensively at him. "Who was that on the phone?"

He didn't want to upset her, but he wasn't going to lie to her either. "That was Lacey. The man who hurt you...he's dead."

Something savage flashed across her face.

"Good. He nearly killed Ryan," she bit out.

"He nearly killed *you*, baby."

"How is Ryan?" she asked.

Adam blinked at the abrupt change in topic. But then Holly's sole concentration when she was awake was Ryan's well-being. He knew she was still dealing with the fright of nearly losing him. It was a feeling he was intimately familiar with.

He glanced over to where both Ethan and Ryan were slumped over asleep.

"He's resting."

Holly closed her eyes for a moment then opened them and nodded her approval. "He shouldn't be out of bed."

Adam leaned in to kiss her again. He couldn't touch her enough. He kissed her, held her every chance he had.

"I want to go home," she whispered.

"I know you do, baby. Soon. I promise."

He stroked her hair and settled on the edge of her bed, careful not to jar her too much.

She seemed to withdraw within herself. Something he'd witnessed with more frequency as she spent more time awake. It worried him. He had no idea what she was thinking.

He started to ask her, but her eyes fluttered, and she slowly closed them. He sat with her until he heard her soft, even breathing then he eased from the bed and sank down into his chair. He could use a few winks himself.

Chapter Twenty-Seven

Holly stared at the ceiling, her thoughts in chaos. Adam, Ethan and Ryan were all asleep. They looked uncomfortable as hell, but she didn't want to do anything to wake them.

Guilt weighed a ton in her chest. Every time she closed her eyes, she saw Ryan falling again. Her worst fear had been the danger she was bringing to the brothers' doorstep. A fear that had now been realized.

It was time for her to make sure nothing more happened to Adam, Ethan or Ryan. Especially Ryan. She loved them all so much. The idea of losing any of them created an unbearable ache in her heart.

She glanced over at Adam just a few feet away. His cell phone lay on the small table next to her bed. She stared at it for a long moment then slowly reached for it.

She knew Lacey had been the last to call so her number should be stored. Holly quietly flipped the phone open and punched the series of buttons to pull up the last received call. Then she hit send.

A few seconds later, Lacey's voice filtered over the line.

"Lacey? This is...this is Holly Bardwell," she said in a stronger voice.

There was a long pause. "What can I do for you, Mrs. Bardwell?"

Holly took a deep breath and checked to make sure she hadn't already wakened the men.

"I need you to contact the district attorney for San Francisco County," she said in a voice just above a whisper.

Another long pause. "Does Adam know you're calling me?" Lacey asked.

"No, and I want to keep it that way," Holly said firmly. "Look, Lacey. I know you don't like me, but I do know you like Adam. Do you want what happened to Ryan to happen to him? I have to do what I can to keep him safe. Keep them all safe."

"What do you want me to say to the D.A.?"

"Tell him I have some information on Mason Bardwell he would be very interested in. Tell him where to find me. I won't talk over the phone. It has to be in person."

"Are you sure that's wise?" Lacey asked.

If Holly didn't know better, she'd swear there was actual concern in the other woman's voice.

"It's my only option. I can't let them be killed because of me."

Silence descended between the two women. Finally Lacey spoke.

"All right, I'll make the call."

"Thank you," Holly said softly.

She closed the phone and carefully replaced it. Then she sank into her pillows, exhausted from the energy she'd expended.

Two days later, the D.A. arrived, two Colorado state patrol officers flanking him. They walked into Holly's room, eliciting immediate reactions from the brothers.

Dread tightened Holly's chest, squeezing her until she struggled for breath. She knew who he was and why he was here.

"What the fuck is going on?" Adam demanded as he stood to his full height.

Ethan and Ryan also stood. Heavy tension clouded the room, so thick you could stir it with a spoon.

"Easy, son. My name is David Masterson. I'm the district attorney for San Francisco County."

Adam crossed his arms and stood, legs apart, staring defiantly at the D.A. "That doesn't explain why you're here."

"I asked him to come," Holly said quietly.

All eyes turned to her. Ryan moved closer to her bed, hovering protectively over her. Which was laughable at best. He still looked like a half-dressed mummy with the bandages wrapped around his chest and shoulder.

"Perhaps I could have a moment alone with Mrs. Bardwell," the D.A. spoke up.

"Like hell you will," Ryan snarled.

Holly put up her free hand to rest on Ryan's arm. "I'll be fine, Ryan."

Adam stared at her, his gaze never leaving her face. "What have you done, Holly?"

"Please understand, Adam. I can't allow any of you to come to harm because of me."

Adam swore long and hard. She winced at the ferocity.

David Masterson gestured at the two policemen. "If you don't mind, escort the gentlemen out so Mrs. Bardwell and I can talk privately."

"The hell you say!" Ethan burst out.

"Ethan, please," Holly pleaded. "Let me do this my way. I'm asking you to leave. For me."

Looks of hurt mixed with anger were thrown her way, but the three finally turned and stalked out the door.

The D.A. turned and gave her a speculative look.

"Mind if I sit down?" he asked.

She shook her head and watched as he settled into the chair Adam had vacated.

"My office has been looking for you for some time, Mrs. Bardwell. Any particular reason you disappeared?"

She stared hard at him. He wouldn't get the upper hand over her. This meeting would be on her terms and her terms alone.

"I asked you here, Mr. Masterson. I'll ask the questions."

He lifted one brow. "Very well. What can I do for you?"

"You wouldn't have come all this way if you weren't keenly interested in Mason Bardwell," she began.

He nodded. "That's true."

"I saw him murder a man on our wedding night," she said baldly.

The D.A. sat forward, urgency lighting his eyes. "You saw him? Unmistakably?"

She shuddered and closed her eyes momentarily. "There was no mistaking what I saw, Mr. Masterson. He shot a man."

"Were there any other witnesses? Think hard about this, Mrs. Bardwell. It's very important."

"Please. Don't call me Mrs. Bardwell," she said quietly. "My name is Holly. And yes, there was one other person present. His business partner Thomas Goins."

David sat back, a gleam of triumph in his eyes. "Are you willing to testify to what you saw?"

"It's why I asked you here," she said. "But I have conditions."

Again he quirked his eyebrow at her. "What sort of conditions are we talking about?"

"I want protection. He's why I'm in the hospital. He's why Ryan Colter nearly died. He won't hesitate to kill me or them."

"Of course, we'd take all the necessary precautions," he said quickly.

"I want Adam, Ethan and Ryan protected as well. They won't like it. They won't want it. But I won't set foot in a courthouse unless you guarantee that someone will be looking out for their best interests until this is all over with."

"Holly, if you help me put away Mason Bardwell, I'll personally baby-sit them. We've been after him for years. He's up to his neck in organized crime in the San Francisco Bay area. Until now, we've never been able to pin anything on him. When Sheriff McMillan called me and said you wanted to see me, I took the first flight out here, hoping you'd tell me what you have."

Holly blanched. "Organized crime?"

David nodded. He studied her for a moment. "This probably isn't the best time to tell you, but then I can't imagine there ever being a good time, but we strongly suspect he had a hand in your parents' death."

She opened her mouth in shock. "But they died in an accident! It was ruled an accident."

"So it was. A rather suspicious accident. He was involved in several investments with them. Investments that went very bad. A week before their accident, they came to my office with claims they had evidence he was involved in fraud."

Holly dropped her head onto her pillow. Tears stung her eyes and she wiped angrily at them. "And you never did anything about it?"

His voice dropped to a softer tone. "We didn't have enough evidence to pursue an indictment. Believe me if we did, I would have done everything in my power to convict him."

"What do I have to do?" she asked. "I want the bastard in jail for what he did."

"Well, I'll take your statement. Then I'll put together an arrest warrant and have the police pick Mr. Bardwell up. We'll move you to an undisclosed location where you'll remain until the trial. I'll arrange for police protection for the Colters as well."

"How long will this take?" she asked softly.

"That I don't know. I won't lie to you. It could drag on for some time, but I'll do the best I can to make sure we get a rapid trial date."

She swallowed the knot in her throat. How long would she be separated from Adam, Ethan and Ryan, and would they even want her back by the time it was all over with? As much as she hated the idea of being separated from them, she knew what she had to do. For her parents, for the men she loved, and most importantly, for herself.

"Let's do it," she whispered. "Make the arrangements."

He leaned forward and folded her hand in his. "Thank you, Holly. You're doing a very brave thing."

Brave? Or stupid? She wasn't sure which. She knew she'd have three very angry men. Men she loved more than anything else in her life. And here she was doing the one thing she wanted to do the least. Leaving.

Chapter Twenty-Eight

Adam sat in brooding silence, his feet perched on the windowsill of the hospital room. After the district attorney had come out of Holly's room, she'd fallen asleep, clearly exhausted by the encounter.

The floor had gone into a flurry of activity, directed by the two Colorado state troopers. Even now, a police guard had been posted at the door, and no one but hospital staff and the Colter brothers were allowed in.

Adam could feel the clock ticking, and he didn't like it a damn bit. He glanced over at Holly's pale face. She was too damn weak, not nearly recovered enough to take on her bastard husband. She needed rest, to recuperate.

"What do you think's going on?" Ethan muttered as he sat down beside Adam.

"Don't be talking in low voices, thinking I won't hear," Ryan said sourly. "If there's something to be said, I want to hear it."

"We're trying not to wake Holly up," Adam said pointedly. He turned back to Ethan. "I wish the fuck I knew what was going on in her head. She blames herself for what happened to Ryan, and she's acted on that."

Ryan swore a streak that would have their mother washing his mouth out with soap.

"So what do we do?" Ethan asked.

Adam shook his head. He felt so damn helpless. "I don't know. It has to be her decision. We can't make it for her."

"I don't want to lose her," Ryan said in a tight voice.

"Do you think we do?" Ethan asked. Anger and frustration simmered in his eyes.

Adam rubbed his face tiredly. They were all on pins and needles. Tired. Frustrated beyond belief. And scared to death of losing the one woman who meant everything to them.

"How can we just let her walk away?" Ryan demanded. "Who's going to make sure that bastard husband of hers isn't going to hurt her again?"

Adam turned his head to the bed when he heard Holly shift and sigh softly. Her eyes fluttered open, and he leaned forward in his seat.

"How're you feeling, baby?"

"Tired," she whispered.

He felt guilty for what he was about to do, but he wasn't going to let go without a fight. She didn't need to be pushed, but that was exactly what he was going to do.

"What's going on, baby? Why did you call the D.A.? I don't like what that implies."

She stared at him with her beautiful eyes. Eyes that were awash in sadness. And fear. Almost as if she was afraid of how he'd react when she answered his questions.

His gut tightened uncomfortably.

"It had to be done," she said.

"No, it didn't," Ryan refuted.

Tears welled in her eyes. "You almost died, Ryan. Because of me. Do you have any idea what that did to me? How badly it hurt? I can't stand the thought of any of you gone. I love you too much."

Adam glanced over at Ryan. His brother looked to be near losing all control. Rage and grief festered like a gangrenous sore.

"I'm the one who let you down," Ryan said in a near shout. "Don't you get it? I let that bastard into our home. I let him take you away from us. I let him nearly kill you. I let you down just like I let those prisoners down in Iraq."

Tears streamed down Holly's face. "Ryan…"

"I won't let you do this, Holly. I won't let you sacrifice yourself for us," Ryan said fiercely.

She struggled to sit up, and Adam leaned further into her, wrapping an arm around her shoulders to help.

"I made a bargain with the district attorney," she said. "A bargain I won't back out of. It's something I have to do. For all of us."

Nausea welled in Adam's stomach, and he and Ethan exchanged panicked looks.

"What kind of bargain?" Ethan asked dully.

"I'm going to testify against Mason."

Adam shook his head. "No. No, no, no! It's too dangerous. He'll go after you with everything he has."

"I'm going away," Holly added softly. "Until the trial. I'll be in protective custody."

Adam surged to his feet. He clenched his fingers into tight balls. God, he wanted to hit something. Put his fist through the wall.

"Why? Why are you doing this?" he demanded. He no longer cared that he sounded so angry. He couldn't bring himself to treat her so gently when she was tearing him apart on the inside.

"I'm doing it for you."

The statement was firm. Accentuated by a sharp lift to her chin. Fire blazed in eyes that had been so fatigued just moments ago.

Adam closed his eyes, drawing a tight rein on his anger. He wanted to fucking howl. Instead, he turned and walked out. He couldn't trust himself to speak when all he wanted to do was shout.

Holly watched as he left and felt her world splinter and break into tiny pieces. He was angrier than she'd ever seen him. At her.

Looks of betrayal loomed in Ethan and Ryan's eyes. Did they all hate her?

"Go after him," she said softly. "He needs you."

"He needs *you*," Ethan pointed out.

"Don't let him do anything stupid," she continued.

"I need some air," Ryan said in a defeated voice she cringed at.

Ethan shook his head and followed Ryan out the door.

Holly clapped her hand to her face as the sobs she'd tried so hard to contain came bubbling out. She tried to suck in steadying breaths, but loud, raspy, harsh sounds kept spilling from her throat.

The nurse came in the door, a concerned expression marring her face. David Masterson followed closely behind.

"Do you need something for pain?" the nurse asked.

For pain? If only a simple drug would take away the agony that clawed at her heart.

Holly shook her head. She wanted her wits about her. She was going to need all she could get in the coming days.

"Mrs. Bardwell...Holly, I've spoken with your doctor, made extensive arrangements to have you transferred to a private facility in another state. If you're agreeable, we'll have you transported within the hour."

Holly's mouth gaped open. "So soon?"

"It's imperative we move you to a safe place as soon as possible. Your husband has already proven he is capable of anything. He hasn't had any trouble finding you. It's only a matter of time before he finds you here."

The brothers. Mason would also find Adam, Ethan and Ryan. Where she was, so were they. If he could find her so easily, what did that do for the Colters?

"I'm ready," she said in a steady voice.

Adam knew something was wrong the minute he stepped off the elevator. The nurse who'd cared for Holly this shift wouldn't meet his gaze. In fact, she scurried off in the opposite direction as fast her legs would take her.

He growled low under his breath. It had taken him the better part of two hours to cool off enough to think rationally. Ethan and Ryan hadn't helped. They'd been as pissed as he was.

The three of them strode down the hall toward Holly's room. Adam noticed the absence of the guard who had been posted earlier. When he opened the door, he was greeted to a freshly made bed. An empty bed. He rushed through the door, slamming it against the wall.

The room was empty. Completely empty. No trace that Holly had ever been there could be found.

He stormed back into the hallway, his brothers close on his heels. He stalked to the nurses' station and slammed his hands down on the counter.

"Where is she?" he demanded.

An older lady, the head nurse, maybe, walked over to him and put out a placating hand.

"She's been transferred to another facility. One that has better security than we do here."

"Where?" Adam bit out.

"She can't tell you that."

Adam whirled around to see David Masterson standing a few feet away. He itched to plant his fist square onto the D.A.'s nose.

"She left this for you," David said, extending a folded note. "Don't worry, Mr. Colter. We'll take excellent care of her."

Adam watched, stunned, as David turned and walked down the hall toward the elevator. He stared down at the paper in his hand, his stomach rolling and tumbling.

With shaking hands, he pulled it open. Three words. So simple.

I love you.

He crumbled the note and sent it flying into the wall. His brothers wore expressions of disbelief. Ryan punched the wall, shoving a hole into the plaster.

"What do we do now?" Ethan asked in a quiet voice.

"We go back to the cabin. And wait for her to come home," Adam said.

Chapter Twenty-Nine

Holly stood at the end of the winding driveway, staring up at the cabin. Summer had come to the mountains. Everywhere she looked, the earth burst with green. She'd only seen the landscape when it was covered with a sheet of white and had thought at the time it couldn't be more beautiful. She'd been wrong. It couldn't possibly look any better than now when she was coming home.

She'd parked down the road, exactly as she had done once before. Somehow she'd wanted to replicate the journey she'd made so many months before.

She smiled as the breeze lifted her long hair and blew it gently around her shoulders. She slid a hand over the bulge of her abdomen, rubbing absently at the gentle swell.

With a deep breath, she started the long walk up the hill to the front door. Butterflies danced in her stomach. In response, the baby kicked and turned over. She stopped and put a hand to her stomach again until the sensation passed.

She smiled and continued on. When she reached the front porch, she hesitated. The door was merely inches away, and yet, she didn't knock. Should she just go in? No. She'd been gone too long.

Would they welcome her back? Would they still love her? Uncertainty nibbled away at her confidence. Adam had been so angry the last time she'd seen him. She closed her eyes to banish the look of betrayal she'd seen in his expression.

Tears swam in her eyes. She'd missed them terribly. She'd lain awake so many nights longing for their touch. She looked down and scrubbed at her eyes. It was over now. She was finally free to live the life she wanted. It was up to her to reach out and take it.

Slowly, she raised her hand and knocked quietly. She waited a moment then mustered her courage and knocked harder.

Her heart lurched when she heard firm footsteps from inside. The door opened and Ryan stood in the doorway, a stunned look on his face.

"Holly?"

She stared at him, praying he didn't turn around and shut the door.

Before she could say anything, she found herself enfolded in his arms. He picked her up and whirled her around, burying his face in her chest.

The baby rolled and kicked between them and he froze. He let her slowly down then backed a space away. He reached out with a shaky hand to cup her swollen belly.

"Is this...is this...?" he broke off his voice hoarse with emotion.

She covered his hand with hers, holding it in place against her stomach. "Yes," she whispered.

He stared at her in stunned silence. Then he hugged her to him again. He buried his face in her hair and stroked her back.

He reached between them to palm her abdomen again as if he couldn't quite believe the evidence in front of him.

"Our baby," he whispered.

He tugged her to the couch and sat down. He reached for her hands and pulled her down until she straddled his lap. Then he placed both hands on her stomach, a look of wonder in his eyes.

He looked back up at her, and his hands traveled over the arm that had been broken then up to where the knife wound had torn her chest.

"Are you all right?"

"I'm fine. Now that I'm here," she added.

He reached up and framed her face in his large hands then pulled her down to kiss him.

"I've missed you so much," he said hoarsely.

Tears slid down her cheeks. "I missed you too."

A noise across the room had her jerking her head in that direction. She tensed as she saw Adam and Ethan standing in the doorway to the living room.

Ethan's face split into a wide smile, but Adam stared in brooding silence. Her heart flipped and her stomach dropped. He hadn't forgiven her for leaving.

She shakily crawled back off Ryan's lap and stood, her fingers wrapped tightly together.

Adam took a step forward. "Promise me." He stared directly at her, his eyes penetrating every layer of her skin. "Promise me you'll never do anything so completely stupid again. Swear to me you'll never leave us again."

She flew to him, throwing herself into his arms. He caught her tightly against him. He held her head against his chest. He kissed the top of her hair, leaving his lips there for a long moment.

When she pulled away, she found herself tugged into Ethan's arms.

"Welcome home, doll."

He kissed her lingeringly then hugged her again.

"Do you have something you want to tell us?" Adam asked, his eyes drifting to her stomach.

She smiled. "You're going to be fathers."

Ethan let out a whoop and twirled her around the living room.

"Put her down, dumbass," Ryan said sourly. "She doesn't need you throwing her around like a sack of grain."

Ethan set her down and molded his hand to her belly.

"Are you hungry? Want me to fix you something to eat?"

"I'm starving," she admitted. "I didn't want to stop even for a moment until I got here."

They herded into the kitchen and Adam sat Holly down at the bar. He settled in beside her, his hand caressing her back.

"What happened?" he asked softly.

She let out her breath in a sigh. "It went faster than we all thought. Mason showed no sign of cooperating even with my damning statement. Then the night before the trial was set to start, he entered into a plea bargain with the district attorney. He pleaded guilty and forewent the trial."

"And he's no longer a threat?" Ryan asked.

She shook her head. "He'll be in jail for a long time."

"You did a brave thing, baby," Adam said. "I'm pissed that you did it, but it took incredible courage on your part."

She gave him a sad smile. "I missed you all so much. I was so lonely without you."

Adam hugged her to him. "You'll never be without us again, baby. That I promise." He glanced down at her belly. "When did you know?"

She looked down, not sure she should answer truthfully. He nudged her chin up until she looked at him once more.

"You knew before you left."

She nodded. "It was such a shock. Amidst all the blood loss, the injuries, when they got routine lab work back, they told me I was pregnant. They fully expected me to miscarry, but I didn't."

She paused before continuing. "I knew...I knew if I told you, that you would never let me go. And I knew I had to do what I did to protect you *and* our baby."

Ethan set a plate in front of her along with a glass of milk. She wrinkled her nose. "Milk?"

"For the baby," he said.

She rolled her eyes. "I hate milk."

"Drink up," he said with a grin. "You need it and so does the little one."

She smiled, allowing her full joy to roll through her. She was home. It was almost as if she'd never left. A single tear slipped down her cheek, and she smiled harder.

Adam reached over and thumbed the wetness away.

"Not a day has passed that we haven't thought about you. Worried about you. Cursed you," he added with a wry grin. "Welcome home, baby," he said in a more serious tone. He bent over and pressed a kiss to her belly. "Welcome home, baby Colter."

"My divorce is final," she whispered.

"And don't think we're going to wait another day to make you ours," Ethan commented as he sat down across the bar from her.

A tingle snaked its way up Holly's spine. "What does that mean exactly?"

"It means we're going down to the clerk's office tomorrow and getting a license. A judge friend of ours will perform the ceremony. He's aware of our situation. While you'll legally be wed to me, he's willing to arrange the ceremony to accommodate your commitment to all of us," Adam spoke up.

Holly stared at them for a long moment then felt her heart swell until she feared it would burst right out of her chest. They still wanted her. Acted as though she'd never left them, hadn't been gone nearly six months.

"I'll really be yours," she said in awe.

Ryan snorted. "You've always been ours. Make no mistake about that."

"Will you marry us?" Adam asked, fingering her hair, wrapping the ends around his hand. "Will you stay with us always? Love us as much as we love you? Be the mother to our children?"

She stood and wrapped herself around Adam as tightly as she could. She hugged his neck to her and held on for dear life.

"I love you so much," she whispered. "Yes. Yes, I'll marry you."

Ethan let out a whoop and Ryan sat back on his chair, folding his arms across his chest in a gesture of supreme satisfaction.

Adam kissed her long and hard, leaving her breathless. For the first time in six months, she allowed herself to relax and revel in the moment.

Tomorrow she'd be legally, emotionally, completely belonging to the three brothers, and more importantly, they would belong to *her.*

Life was full of ironies. Only in running from a past riddled by mistakes, had she found a future so perfect, so bright that she still had trouble believing it was her reality.

"Anyone want to play Monopoly?" she asked.

Only later, as they sat on the porch watching the sun go down over the mountains, did Holly wrap herself in the comfort that she was indeed home. For the first time since her parents' death, she felt a sense of belonging.

Adam reached over to take her hand, his thumb massaging her palm. "I love you, baby."

She smiled. "I love you, too." Her gaze drifted to Ethan and Ryan, both of whom wore relaxed, easy expressions. "I love all of you."

Ethan smiled. "We know, doll. After all, you came back to us."

About the Author

To learn more about Maya Banks please visit www.mayabanks.com Send an email to Maya at maya@mayabanks.com.

Look for these titles

Now Available:

Seducing Simon
Understood

Coming Soon:

Overheard
Undenied

When she breaks free from the bondage of her past, he'll be waiting

Understood
© *2006 Maya Banks*

Jake Turner committed the ultimate mistake of falling in love with his best friend's wife. The distance he puts between them costs both him and Ellie Matthews dearly. Jake will never forgive himself for not seeing what a bastard his friend was. Now that Ellie is free from her nightmare, Jake waits, needing and wanting. He'll be there when Ellie is ready to spread her wings.

Available now in ebook from Samhain Publishing.

Gracie Evans wants a Valentines she won't forget. Luke Forsythe plans to give her exactly what she wants.

Overheard
© *2007 Maya Banks*

Gracie Evans is a woman tired of the men in her life not satisfying her in bed. She's had a string of boyfriends, but none of them have come close to satisfying the vivid fantasies she has. Two weeks before Valentine's Day, she breaks up with her latest boyfriend after a night of lackluster sex.

When her good friend, Luke Forsythe, overhears her talking to their friend Shelly about what she really wants, he's stunned. And very turned on. Gracie thinks there isn't a man alive who can satisfy her in bed. Luke aims to prove her wrong.

Warning, this title contains explicit sex, graphic language, ménage a trois.

Coming in January of 2007 in ebook from Samhain Publishing.

Brianna Wyatt may be a victim of her father's machinations, but one look is all it takes for Cole Masters and Tyler Cannonto offer her their own style of ménage a trois blackmail.

Blackmailed
© *2006 Annmarie McKenna*

Brianna Wyatt's father is blackmailing her into doing what he wants by threatening to send her brother to an institution. She would do anything to keep that from happening, including go along with his demented scheme of her getting pregnant by Cole Masters—a man who's been rumored to share a woman with his best friend, and who leaves Brianna's innocent senses in shambles.

Cole is sure he's about to be blackmailed—why else would a man whore his daughter? But there's something about her that neither Cole nor his best friend, Tyler Cannon, can deny. They want her, and don't hesitate for a second on making their own offer. Her brother's protection for her body.

When danger flirts with Brianna's life, there is nothing they won't do to keep her safe. Including listening to what their hearts are saying.

Available now in ebook and print from Samhain Publishing.

FLY AWAY

Discover the Talons Series

5 STEAMY NEW PARANORMAL ROMANCES
TO HOOK YOU IN

Kiss Me Deadly, by Shannon Stacey
King of Prey, by Mandy M. Roth
Firebird, by Jaycee Clark
Caged Desire, by Sydney Somers
Seize the Hunter, by Michelle M. Pillow

AVAILABLE IN EBOOK—COMING SOON IN PRINT!

WWW.SAMHAINPUBLISHING.COM

GREAT
CHEAP
FUN

Discover eBooks!